The Hand Of Iris

# The Hand Of Iris

**R. Van Brabant**

Copyright © 2024 by R. Van Brabant

All rights reserved. No portion of this book may be reproduced in any form without written permission from the publisher or author, except as permitted by Canadian copyright law. For permission requests, contact R. Van Brabant at contact@rvanbrabant.com.

The story, all names, characters, and incidents portrayed in this production are fictitious. No identification with actual persons (living or deceased), places, buildings, and products are intended or should be inferred.

978-1-7386304-7-9 - Paperback

978-1-7386304-8-6 - Hardcover

978-1-7386304-6-2 - eBook

Book Cover Artist: Cover Kitchen

Developmental Editor: Courtney Zobal

Copy Editor: Hannah Flood

Proofreader: Vicky Skinner

*To my mom, who I hope to scare
and/or gross out the most with this book*

# Meet The Family

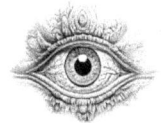

Marcy was warned that her girlfriend's family was a little strange, but she loved Azura more than she feared some local ghost stories. That was why she sat in the passenger seat of Azura's car, watching the cityscape fade into grassy hills and long abandoned farmland. The sky was coated in a deep orange with pink clouds and a sun that hung in the middle of the twilight sea. The car ride was quiet except for the sound of the motor and the tires crushing the pebbles and dirt on the road. Marcy always felt awkward in those quiet moments when her mind was a blank space and her mouth ran dry.

Azura, on the other hand, was solely focused on the road ahead with a cool confidence behind the wheel. Her raven hair was crowned by a ring of braids and the glare of the sun reflected off her glasses, shielding the dark green in her eyes. She had a small, casual grin on her face and Marcy could hear her humming contently to herself.

"Hey, Zu," Marcy said, turning to face her girlfriend.

Azura gave a small nod, glancing briefly at Marcy before focusing back on the road. "Yeah, what's up?"

"Do you think...that your folks are going to like me?" Marcy asked.

Azura's eyes widened in surprise before she quickly replied, "Sure, they're pretty easygoing." Azura lifted a finger. "Just be careful, they're pretty talkative, especially around this time of year."

"I mean, I guess reunions get people pretty chatty, huh?"

"Yeah, we're pretty close. Or we try to be."

Honestly, Marcy was surprised she had been invited in the first place. She wasn't sure if she'd dated Azura long enough to even be considered for an invite to big family events like this. Not that Marcy was complaining. Despite her family having a reputation for being a bit weird, Azura had nothing but good things to say about her family, an energetic and joyful bond Marcy could only wish she had with her own.

"And they don't mind that we're...you know...a thing?" she asked.

"Nope," Azura replied with a shrug. "They're just happy that I found someone that cares about me, loves me for who I am, and all that other young love sort of stuff. Some family members are a bunch of hopeless romantics." Azura slowed the car down to make a sharp turn toward a cast-iron gate guarding a driveway and surrounding an expansive front yard. The gates creaked open, pulling back slowly until they barely avoided kissing the stone pillars hoisting up stone gargoyles.

"Wow. Real old-fashioned," Marcy said, taking in the grounds.

Azura gave a grin and a shrug. "Mom and Dad like their privacy. You can guess how elated they were when working from home became more popular." Azura began to crawl into the driveway, giving Marcy a good look at the house guarded by the iron barrier. It was a sprawling manor with giant towers that scraped the sunset sky with shingles of midnight blue. Stained glass windows with various beasts of legend deep in battle decorated the building, adding a dark splash of colour to contrast with the dark grey brick. Topiary hedges trimmed into a dragon and unicorn poised for a duel sat on opposite ends of the cobblestone pathway that led to the slick black door.

"Whoa," Marcy exclaimed. "Looks like you guys live like royalty." She gave a whistle as Azura parked in the grass next to the dozens of other cars sitting alone on the lawn.

"Wait until you see the inside."

Suddenly, Marcy felt her pocket begin to buzz, and a kooky jingle sounded inside the car. Digging into her pocket and pulling out her cell phone, she sighed, seeing her brother Aiden's goofy mug plastered on her screen. Marcy ignored the call and shoved it back into her pocket.

"Who was that?" Azura asked.

Marcy shook her head and unbuckled her seatbelt. "It's nothing. Just my brother. I can text him back later."

"Alright, sounds like a plan." Azura stepped out of the car, inviting Marcy to follow her to the entrance. She took Marcy's swinging hand and guided her to the door. Despite Azura's grip being soft and warm, Marcy felt chills crawl across her skin, and a bubble formed in her stomach, ready to burst. She could feel the rumbling of footsteps from inside rock the cobblestone sidewalk and heard piercing jeers only barely muffled by the door. Azura enthusiastically knocked on it, oblivious to her girlfriend's building unease. The door quickly opened, revealing a towering man with a slicked-back, auburn mullet, clad in a navy-blue tuxedo. He had a soft smile, and his face was covered in laugh lines that peachy makeup powder failed to cover.

"Ah, Azura Bender-Vee and Miss Marcy. Glad to see you've

arrived safely," the man said with a subtle Australian accent.

"Good to see you too, Leigh," Azura said with a small curtsy.

Marcy gave a nervous nod. "Um…yeah. Thanks."

Leigh took a step to the side and gestured into the house, illuminated by a warm rainbow of lights and fully releasing a cacophony of laughter and idle chatter. He turned his head and grinned at Marcy. "Come on in. We have much to show you, milady."

# The Beast of Hotel Bonner

Travelling through the house, Marcy felt like she had stepped straight into a Jane Austen novel that was edited by Edgar Allan Poe. The great halls were covered in classical wallpaper with floral patterns printed all over. Hanging on the walls were rows of portraits of ghastly, grinning nobles standing in various gardens and windowed rooms, all cast against the dying light of a sunset. The furniture was carved out of dark wood, finely whittled to the smallest detail and ornately set in place. Marcy stared at the vintage space in awe, her body offering no resistance when Azura dragged it into a room with two black sofas that stretched across opposite sides of the room and shelves filled with faded board game boxes. Before she knew it, Marcy found herself bombarded with thunderous laughter and chatter from a hoard of darkly dressed individuals with jubilant smiles on their faces. She couldn't put her finger on who was saying what and turned to Azura with a pleading look. Azura quickly took notice and waved the crowd away.

"Alright, give her some time to breathe. We just got here!" Some faces in the cluster rolled their eyes but all of them stepped back and the thick air became less suffocating. Marcy breathed a sigh of relief and gave her girlfriend a thankful smile. Azura pulled Marcy closer to her and tenderly rubbed her shoulder. Marcy's eyes wandered past the other occupants chatting the day away and focused on the assortment of silver and gold lamps, candelabras, and clocks that lined the dressers and mantle.

"Wow, did you guys descend from royalty or something?" Marcy asked in bewilderment.

Azura laughed. "Maybe hundreds of years ago." She sat the two of them down on the nearest sofa. "The older folk are a bit cagey when it comes to how our family inherited all of this."

Just as Marcy began to settle in her seat, a ginger-haired young woman on the couch across from her sprung up from her bored slouch and gave a smile that reminded Marcy of her cousins getting a sugar rush.

"I heard it could be traced back to the mid-1600s," she excitedly regaled. "A young Irish maid looking for a new life in the brave new world caught the eye of a mysterious gentleman. Swooped her right off her feet!" The blushing woman got up from the sofa and pointed to a grand painting that hung behind the couple.

In the portrait was a gangly man clad in black, cuddling closely to a fair woman with delicate blue eyes and red hair done up in a messy bun. When she looked closer at the painting, Marcy could see that, while the woman's shadow was cast below her, the man's was missing.

"That's them right there! It was said that after she became involved with the gentleman, she never again had a bad day in her life and anything she wanted she needed only to ask of him." The woman sighed dreamily. "That just sounds so romantic."

Azura rolled her eyes. "And conveniently enough, no one knows where he found his fortune or how the two of them died."

An older woman with peachy hair curled up into a beehive-shaped dome leaned over the pair. "Oh, come on, Azura. They say some legends are born in fact," the woman reassured. "Besides, there could've been a reason why not much is known about Fiona and her dear Cary. Times were pretty tumultuous; some records of them could have been destroyed in the chaos."

"Or, and hear me out, Auntie Dara, maybe Great Grandpappy Cary had some things exaggerated about him to make him seem cooler." Azura laughed.

The younger woman placed her chin in her hand dreamily. "Still, I think it makes a cute story." She looked back to Azura. "Hey, do you think Marcy's going to be the one?" Azura's eyes widened and she nearly tumbled out of her seat. Marcy imagined that her face looked pretty similar.

"Uh…what?" Azura asked, her eyes darting back and forth between her girlfriend and her obliviously cheerful relative.

"You know, your soulmate?" The other girl continued, "Someone that's going to stick around for the long term? I mean, the last time you brought someone over, he turned out to only be after the money. Then after the reunion he ended up—"

The older woman, Dara, abruptly cleared her throat and shot a sharp glare at the younger woman. "That's quite enough, Briar."

Marcy turned and saw that Azura's face was beet-red, looking ready to sink into the ground. Marcy offered a soft hand to her girlfriend and patted her shoulder.

The younger woman across from them, Briar, gave an embarrassed frown and scratched the back of her neck. "Sorry, guess I got a little too excited," she humbly said. "But I do kind of wonder what Cary's life was like before he met Fiona. If there was this whole other life he left behind, or maybe he just pulled her into his without much problem."

The red-headed young woman wandered over to the portrait behind Marcy and gazed at the smiling couple trapped in paint. "Love is a weird but still wonderful-sounding thing. It can even save a life." Briar's voice was light and dreamy, her body nearly falling over.

Azura scooted closer to Marcy with a bemused grin, looking at her cousin. "And let me guess, you have a story about just that?"

Marcy's eyebrows furrowed. "What?"

Briar's eyes widened and she clapped excitedly. "Oh, did Azura not tell you? We love to tell stories around here! And this one is one of my favourites." Briar waltzed to the center of the room and stood up straight and proud. In a booming, theatrical voice, Briar announced, "This is a story about finding love in even the darkest of places!"

\*\*\*

He had always been told to stay away from the wrong side of town, but for Osric, that was the only side of town left he had to flee to. Weeks ago, he would've puked at the first whiff of the smoke the vagrants around the corner would huff, but after sleeping in places he shouldn't have slept and wading his way from town to town, the stench of weed and crack seemed to blend in with everything else. He learned to walk inside the shadows and not gaze too long at the people who walked by him. He could never know which was a crook that would shank him for looking at them wrong or, even worse, an undercover cop stuffed in the back pocket of the monster that ran him into the streets in the first place.

Osric would change his look every time he grew wary that he was discovered and leave town. Using strictly cash at the thrift stores or diving into the garbage to look for rags that no one else wanted, he became an urban chameleon, blending in and hopping from joint to joint. He found his list of places to go growing shorter by the week, and he had long ago come to the grim realization he would run out of places to hide But still, he had to try. Anywhere was better than back in that hell hole.

He entered his next stop, Cubare Park, after hitching a ride in the back of a mechanic shop's pickup truck. His greasy, tattered clothes blended in with the beggars that wandered the alleyways, begging for change. Osric lowered the old baseball cap he had looted from the last town's laundromat, until his eyes were almost completely covered. His bones ached and trembled like a newborn calf's, and his stomach rumbled as acid licked and dissolved his insides. His tongue was dry and as rough as sandpaper, scraping at the insides of his cheeks. He needed food, he needed water, he needed comfortable rest, and he needed all of it soon. The pillowcase he carried had only his essential documents; he couldn't afford to burden himself with a heavy load, never knowing when he would next need to skip town. Even with the protection of his cap's visor, Osric could still feel the searing neon lights of the buildings burning onto his skin. His eye caught sight of the bright purple sign for "Miah's Italian Marvels." Perfect. A mom-and-pop restaurant was sure to have plenty of food wasting away in the dumpster. Better to eat it than just let it rot.

But before Osric could start his usual routine of snaking to the back of the building, his steps froze at the sound of shouting and pleading. He tried to tell himself not to turn around, that whatever was happening was none of his business. Yet, despite his mental battle, his body refused to comply. So, he turned around and saw, in front of a vape shop, a burly man with an unkept beard and a sweat-stained beater tightly grabbing the arm of a raven-haired woman in black shorts and a dark shirt with fishnet sleeves.

"Just let me go! You're too drunk," the woman pleaded, her makeup dripping down her face like inky black tears.

"I'm just fine, woman! Quit being so goddamn sensitive," the man growled, his face growing redder by the second.

Osric's feet felt the need to rush over and get between the two. However, the words in his head kept him frozen in place. *It's not your business. It's not worth getting caught and dragged back there.*

Knuckles turning white from how tightly he gripped his pillowcase, Osric bit down on his tongue to try and plant his feet on the ground. As a metallic tinge filled his taste buds, he saw the man punch the woman to the ground.

Osric saw that he wasn't the only passerby trying to ignore what was going on, as people kept passing the couple on the street. He shut his eyes as one thought broke through the walls of his mind and shouted above all the other voices in his head. *Of course, no one was there to help you. The world is a cruel place and confronting a drunk idiot isn't going to change it.*

Just as the thought slithered through his mind like a sinister snake, the man roared and prepared to stamp his foot onto the cowering woman. But he was stopped when, out of the shadows, peeling back the darkness, came a pair of claws with dark red nails. The claws snatched the man by the back of his shirt and lifted him up like he had pillow down for bones. When the rest of the creature emerged from the pall of the night, the other pedestrians stopped to stare. Some began to back away; others took out their phones, to call the police, Osric assumed; and others took pictures or recorded the scenes unfolding before them.

Lifting the visor of his hat, Osric rubbed his eyes to make sure his fatigue wasn't somehow making him see things. Much to his horror, the creature was real and everyone else could see it, too. The slightly muscular figure had a bovine head with horns pointing to the sky and cloven feet that stomped so hard into the sidewalk that Osric was surprised it didn't cause the cement to crumble. The creature's eyes were a fiery orange, its arms and forehead caked in amber markings.

"What the hell?" the man roared in a mixture of shock and fright. The Beast turned the man around so they were face-to-face, and once the man met the monster's gaze, he fell silent, his eyes like that of a lamb in a butcher shop. The man's mouth was agape and his entire body began to shake. The creature's tail whipped around, showing a rounded tip with a sharp needle protruding from it. The tail pierced the man's chest, causing an explosion of red mist to burst from his chest cavity before the tail flipped back around and drilled itself through his forehead and out the back of his skull. The body twitched in the monster's grip before it ripped its tail out and threw the man to the ground like a bag of garbage. The creature slowly shifted its head to the woman, who quickly scrambled to her feet, her cheeks stained black and grey, before pushing herself through the crowd of onlookers to escape the scene.

The creature jerked his head toward Osric, locking eyes with him. A petrifying chill bored through his bones, forcing him to look away and run down the street. Where he was going, Osric had no idea, just anywhere but his old hell hole or the clutches of whatever that thing was.

The soles of his feet felt like they were set on fire, his lungs like they had shriveled up to the size of golf balls in his chest. Just as black mist began to border his vision, Osric dove behind a building and collapsed beside a dumpster. He didn't even care that he had taken a few green paint chips with him as he slid down the giant metal siding. He looked around the alleyway, spotting a collection of large black garbage bags on the other side of the dumpster. His head was light, and with consciousness quickly fading, Osric dragged himself over to the plastic mounds and slumped behind them. As he rested his head against the amorphous bags, it didn't take long to close his eyes and drift off into a dreamless sleep.

"Hey! You still alive, buddy?"

Osric tossed and turned, jumping at the sudden realization that someone was shaking his shoulder. He reeled his bag back, ready to swing at the intruder like it was a baseball bat. The stranger raised his hands up in defense, his golden rings sparkling in the moonlight.

"Whoa, easy there, tiger." The man laughed. "I'm not going to hurt you. Though I'm surprised you can be comfortable sleeping on that junk."

While Osric tried to slow his anxious heartbeat, his eyes focused on the sharp features of the man's face, his casual smile. Even as Osric felt like a cornered dog, the man's grey eyes managed to seem smoky and bright.

Osric shook his head. "I've gotten used to it. I'm not exactly spoiled for choice of places to stay," he muttered, slowly lowering his pillowcase.

The man's smile faded, and his eyes softened in pity. Osric could hardly bear the sight.

"You mean you're homeless?"

Osric sighed, "Yeah, pretty much."

The man hummed to himself, crossing his arms, and eyeing the building. Then, a smooth and bright smile wormed its way to his face before he offered a hand to Osric. "This hotel's got plenty of rooms for you to stay in," the stranger said. "Trust me, the beds are loads more comfortable to sleep on than a bunch of garbage bags."

Osric hesitated, inching away from the stranger's hand. "I don't have much money on me. Definitely not enough to stay in a hotel."

The man shrugged, "That's fine. I'll pay for your room, for as long as you need to get back on your feet."

Osric looked the man up and down skeptically. Dressed in a plain black jacket and dusty blue jeans, only the stranger's shining black dress shoes and rings would indicate that he was loaded in any way. That wasn't the only thing that bothered Osric.

"I'm just a stranger. What's in it for you?"

The man clicked his tongue and shrugged. "I got money to spare, and, well…let's just say I know all too well how it feels to be left alone in a shithole with no idea of where to go next." As he said this, the man's eyes cast down, lost in a forlorn memory. He quickly recovered with the same cheeky smile as before.

"So, what do you say?"

Osric was silent, lifting himself to his feet and nodding. "Sure, why not?"

The man grinned, placing his hand in his pocket. "Cool. Let's go check you in then."

He walked back out of the alleyway, though Osric hesitated to follow him. Sure, he seemed like a respectable fellow, but respectable fellows passed Osric by every day without even batting an eye. Why would one stop by to help him now? Of course, he'd have to pay the man back; he would be a dumbass not to.

Osric's jaw tightened like a vice, and he forced his feet to follow the stranger. It was either follow or risk having his throat slit in the middle of the night. He preferred the former.

When Osric turned the corner, he was immediately ambushed by the blaring, ruby-red sign hanging on a pole. The letters, reading "Hotel Bonner" were in frou-frou cursive and the sign was shaped like a star with a border made of blush lights. The building itself was made of sunset orange brick and was covered with old window shutters, some with cracked glass.

The stranger leaned against the wall by the black door, poking at the OPEN sign that hung behind the door's half-moon window. "Just right in here." He gave an inviting grin, placing his hand around the door's handle.

Osric swallowed a cigarette-scented gulp of air. "Oh, yeah. Thanks." He shambled to the stranger's side and watched as the door to the dimly lit lobby flung open.

The maroon lobby was covered in dark stains, the room barely illuminated by red and deep orange lights. Sitting at the faded front desk was a woman with frizzled black hair, wide brass glasses, and a cigarette cushioned between her burgundy lipstick-caked lips. She looked up from her magazine and put out the cigarette inside a teal ashtray with a topless mermaid sculpted on the front. "Picking up another straggler, Mr. Midnight?" she asked, her Southern drawl emphasizing the dryness and disinterest in her voice.

The stranger laughed, slapping Osric on the lower side of his back to push him further into the lobby. "You know you can just call me Angelo." The man guided Osric to the desk, giving the homeless man a good look at the receptionist's rolling auburn eyes.

"Yeah, but I'm not going to," the woman said, flipping the pages of her magazine.

Osric looked down and saw on the cover a shirtless man in navy blue briefs that left little to the imagination. He tried not to stare too long at the cover, despite the pinching feeling twisting at his cheeks.

"I'll be buying this guy a room," Angelo said, still smiling, despite the woman showing apparently little interest in his presence.

"Do you have a history of abusing drugs, alcohol, or gambling?" the woman asked, her voice droning and dull.

Osric shook his head. "No."

"Are you now or have ever been a crazy psycho killer?" The woman flipped another page in her magazine, not even looking at Osric.

He could feel his eyes widen at not only the absurdity of the question but at how casually the receptionist asked him. "Wha— No! Hell no!" he exclaimed.

Angelo softly chuckled to himself. "Threw you for a loop there, huh?"

The woman placed her magazine down and opened a thick maroon binder. She took out a pen and began to write something down. "For sixty bucks a night, you can have room forty-three." The woman fished out a key from the binder and handed it to Angelo.

Angelo beamed. "Wow. Lucky you. We managed to secure the best room in this place. The last person to take that room later went on to become an extra on Days Of Our Lives." He said, placing the key in Osric's hand, "Maybe your luck will turn around, too."

"Yeah, lucky you." the woman said, picking up her magazine once again.

Angelo rolled his eyes. "A real beacon of sunshine as always, Robyn."

The woman pursed her lips and flipped him the bird, showing a newly lit cigarette sandwiched between two of her fingers.

Angelo threw his head back and laughed, pushing a befuddled Osric away from the desk.

"Is she always like that?" Osric asked.

Angelo shook his head. "Nah, usually she's smoking a bit of Mary Jane." Both men found themselves walking under a wooden archway lined with topaz Christmas lights and into a bar bathed in bright pink illumination.

The black tables were covered in scratch marks and each of them was adorned with an electric candle in the middle. A few patrons were scattered around these tables, each looking disheveled and half asleep over their drinks. Planted on the left side of the room was a black bar with a glass bar top and shelves filled with dark bottles of various liqueurs, wines, and spirits.

The shelf was split in half by a glass fridge filled with a variety of different beers. Behind the bar, a man with shaggy, dirty blonde hair threw his head back and launched a shot down his throat. The man slammed the shot glass down on the bar top. His eyes widened as soon as he noticed Angelo and Osric walk inside.

"Well, what is up? The Midnight Man get himself a new squeeze?" The man planted his shoulders on the bar top and leaned forward.

Angelo chuckled and shook his head. "Nah, he just looked like he needed a place to stay. Found him sleeping in the garbage out back."

The man behind the bar shook his head and took out a bottle of red liqueur from the back shelf. "Oh my. Thank God you got him out of there. Sleeping on trash bags is murder on your complexion." The blonde man turned around and deftly snatched both a bottle of blood-red liqueur and a tall bottle of vodka in one swift motion. "So, how about it, handsome? Just the usual?"

Angelo took a seat at the bar and grinned. "You know, Mark? You treat me too well."

The man behind the bar rolled his eyes. "Yeah, that's not what you said on Valentine's Day." The two men laughed while

Mark took out a champagne glass and poured the booze inside it. He then turned around and swiped a thick bottle of maple-coloured spirits and an olive-green wine bottle.

Mark looked over at Osric with a curious eye. "What about you, big man? Got any I.D. on you?" he asked, the maple spirits pouring out of the spout like a caramel waterfall.

Osric hesitated; his mouth was as dry as a desert but he hesitated to take out his old driver's license. Who knew what would happen when word got out that he was in town?

Osric shook his head. "Just a water, please," he replied, surprised at how gravely his voice sounded.

Mark sighed, pushing the ruby champagne glass toward Angelo. "Well, I guess it could be worse. Could be one of those college kids asking for something fruity and not giving any other hints as to what the hell they want."

When Osric laid his eyes on Angelo's drink, he watched as the beads of perspiration slipped down the glass and across Angelo's sun-kissed fingers, seeping into the engravings of his rings and down onto the bar top.

Then, the red of the drink became the fiery eyes of the monster from earlier and Osric reeled away. Sweat beads boiled against his face and his heart sunk to the bottom of his stomach. The glass on the bar top became like planes of ice and his hands began to tremble.

Angelo tilted his head, his brows pointed upwards like a tent, and his eyes became wide with concern. "Hey, what's wrong?" He reached out to touch Osric's hand, but on base instinct, Osric wrenched his hand away.

His nose wrinkled in disgust, feeling like a complete idiot for looking so panicked, even if deep down, he knew he was in the right to feel like shitting his pants over coming across such a beast. "Just something fucked up that happened down the street," Osric said curtly.

Mark chuckled, pouring himself a shot of the liquor. "Wow, that's a shocker. In other news, water is wet." The bartender chucked back his head and quickly downed the shot.

Osric shook his head before pressing his hands against his eyes. "No, no. It was like some bull or some guy in a demon costume. I don't fucking know. Tore some guy apart in front of a whole bunch of people."

When Osric peeled his hands down, he saw Mark freeze in place just as he was putting the liquor bottles back on the shelf.

Angelo's fingers nervously tapped against his glass. "You saw the Cubare Beast?"

Mark timidly passed Osric the glass of water, quickly turning away to keep himself busy organizing the shelves.

"That thing's got a name?" Osric asked, his eyes filled to the brim with bewilderment.

Angelo nodded. "Uh huh. Been around here for years now." He took a shallow sip of his drink before another patron called out from behind them, "Police was called after the bodies started dropping."

"That bastard was said to soak up bullets like a sponge sucks up water!" another patron with a Jersey accent added.

"Oh please. If anything, it's doing this dump a favour," a blonde woman with wild hair hummed. "Seems to be pretty picky on who it kills. Saves the savagery for the real rat bastards."

"Yeah, there was this brute that beat Blooming Becky," another woman at the same table said as she swirled the ice cubes in her glass. "Such a sweet girl, and yet he beat her so bad, she nearly lost an eye. Come the next week, that man was found hanging on a streetlamp by his intestines. The coppers had no idea how he got up there, but some of his drinking buddies said they thought they saw a creature with a bull's head scampering down the highway just before the man disappeared."

"What about that Paris Hilton wannabe?" a man in a fedora shouted, holding up a lit cigarette. "Spent all of her mama's money on drugs and clothes she never even wore. Then word got out that as thanks for her mama's generosity, that girly beat her black and blue and refused to let her out of the house anymore. Not even two days later, the Beast came stampeding down the road with that little diva's head in its mouth like the world's fugliest football."

"Ugh, can't you tell those stories *after* I'm done eating?" a grey-bearded man in one of the vinyl booths bellowed, his mouth full of half-chewed chicken.

"Finish what's in your mouth and you got a deal!" the fedora man shouted back.

Osric shifted his glass around on the bar top before returning his attention to Angelo. "So, that thing's got quite a reputation around here," he muttered.

Angelo nodded grimly. "Oh yeah."

Mark tried to put a smile on his face and started cleaning the glasses under the bar. "I've found that just staying indoors when night falls does the residents of this place a lot of good. Night seems to be the time the Beast likes to do its thing the most. There haven't been a lot of Beast sightings in broad daylight."

Osric took a quick sip of water and asked, "Why at night?"

Mark shrugged. "I don't know; maybe it's allergic to sunlight? Would fit right in with everyone else in this city. A bunch of cracked-up night owls."

"Not me!" the blonde woman shouted, raising an empty shot glass in the air.

Mark scoffed. "Girl, I didn't say you were." The entire room soon burst at the seams with laughter.

Osric looked over at the crowd in awe, the patrons so quickly flipped their attitudes around, as if the conversation on the Beast had never happened. Osric raised a cautious finger. "Wait, does anyone know where the Beast—"

"Uh uh uh!" Mark quickly shoved a finger across Osric's lips. "Let them have this moment. It's the best we can really do, given the circumstances."

Osric shot the bartender an incredulous look. His body became chilled at how casual the man was at dismissing any more talk about such a vicious beast.

Angelo nodded. "Who knows? Maybe it'll buzz off and find another place to raise hell."

Mark smirked. "Of course."

Osric nodded in return, though his mind was still on high alert. Not only did he have to worry about someone knowing who he was, but now some crazed animal was running around the streets at night tearing people apart. Osric turned his head to look through the crowd and began to drink his water.

No particular face stood out, though he couldn't help but feel like a sunglasses-adorned man sitting in one of the booths was trying to study him. Suddenly, Angelo slammed his hand down on Osric's, snapping the ragged man out of his stupefied staring.

"Starting to look a little pale there," the sharply dressed man consoled. "Maybe you should get yourself settled in your room. Get some rest."

Osric looked over to his empty glass and nodded dumbly. "Yeah. Yeah, that'll be good." Osric let himself be hoisted out of his seat by Angelo, letting himself get lost in his soft but strong arms, smelling the sweet breath of liqueur from his lips.

*What am I doing? What's wrong with me?* Osric looked back up and saw Angelo waving towards Mark.

"Try not to get everyone too wasted there, alright?" he

called to the bartender.

Mark waved back with a large, cheerful grin. "Hey, whatever gets them tipping, right?" The bartender laughed. As was guided out of the room, Osric saw Mark line up a row of shot glasses and cup his hands around his mouth before shouting, "Who wants a shot of Lady Bourbon?"

The sounds of boisterous roaring from the crowd died down once Angelo and Osric made their way to the stairs. Robyn was still occupied with her magazine, looking as bored as ever.

"Whatever mess is made is Mark's problem, not mine," she muttered. Angelo gave a brief thumbs up to the receptionist before gently pushing Osric up the black and red-carpeted stairs. It was almost a relief for Osric when the sharp stench of booze grew further away. He was worried it would bring back memories of the old hellhole.

Four floors worth of stairs later, the two men found themselves walking towards a black door with a brass forty-three posted below the peephole. Angelo gestured toward the door, looking down at the hand Osric used to hold the room key. "Alright, this is the place."

Osric hesitated, struggling not to stare too long into Angelo's eyes. The ragged man cleared his throat. "Right. Yeah, cool." He stuck the key inside the cold black lock with cast iron floral designs that seemed much too intricate and classical looking for the seedy establishment it belonged to. Osric twisted the key inside the keyhole, unlocking the door after hearing a heavy *click*.

The door creaked open, showing off a small room with dark mustard wallpaper, a dresser with a dust-caked, beige lamp on top of it, and a bed with a plain olive bedsheet and gothic wooden bedposts that nearly scraped against the crumbling grey ceiling. Osric took a cautious step inside before plopping his pillowcase onto the bed. He began to reach out toward the bed, only to wrench his arm back as a chill tickled at his spine.

"What's wrong? You think there's some bed bugs hiding in there or something?" Angelo chuckled.

Osric looked back to Angelo and cleared his throat. "Uh, no. No, of course not. Just a bit…" He struggled to string his sentence together. "…different."

Angelo laughed. "Yeah, that's probably the nicest thing you could say about this place. And I guess this city, in general. But we just try to make it work as best we can, you know?"

Osric nodded. "Yeah, I get that. Well, at least you and Mark seem to stay in high spirits, despite everything." He sat down on the bed and watched as Angelo leaned against the doorway. It was strange, though the city was musky and covered in such gloomy shadows, Angelo and Mark seemed to be two beacons of light that kept him from drowning in the same sadness everyone else was infected with. A strong impression for two men he had met less than two hours ago.

*Or maybe you're just jumping to conclusions,* Osric thought grimly. *You should know better than anyone how appearances are deceiving.*

Angelo tilted his head curiously. "Are you okay?" the bright-eyed man asked. "Looks like you've got something on your mind." Osric contemplated for a moment everything he kept locked up in his memory like a rabid animal clawing at a cage. He shut his eyes.

*No. Even if he isn't in her pocket, I don't need him to borrow any of my drama. I mean, we just met.*

Osric shook his head and looked back up at Angelo. "It's nothing, just something stupid," he replied, his voice faltering from the lack of conviction in his answer. Angelo raised a skeptical eyebrow and pushed himself from the doorway.

"I mean, alright. But just to let you know, I can keep a secret, so if you ever change your mind, then remember I've got an open ear."

Osric nodded glumly. "I'll keep that in mind."

Just before closing the door behind him, Angelo gave a small wave. "Sleep well," he called right before the door clicked shut.

Osric pushed out a large puff of air, finally letting himself settle into the room. He kicked off his shoes and crawled under the covers, going out like a candle in a storm the moment his head hit the pillow. Before his mind completely fell into dreams, Osric's insides twisted at the thought of letting his guard down so quickly. Yet there was a small remnant that held onto hope that this would be the time that he'd finally get to stop running.

Though his dreams consisted of nothing more than him wandering through shadows, as usual, Osric felt himself toss and turn and tangle himself in his blankets. The curtain of shadows was split apart with the image of the monster tearing the man apart and glaring at Osric with his hellish red eyes. Suddenly, he catapulted himself back into the waking world and sat up covered in a blanket of sweat. The sky was just a bit brighter than pitch black, though he wasn't sure if it was because of the lights from the buildings or the crack of daybreak that was about to emerge. He slipped out of bed and stared out the window. Could the creature think to scale the building up to his floor? He inched closer to the window, reaching his hand out to the shutter.

"Hey!" he suddenly heard a familiar voice shout from behind the door, "what do you think you're doing?"

Osric looked away from the window and crept closer to the door.

"Oh, I just thought that, well… I know the guy who lives here. His name's Osric and—" another voice stuttered.

Osric's heart sank. He didn't remember giving anyone in the establishment his name. How long had he been watched?

"Get out of here, you creep!" It was with that final shout that Osric recognized the first voice belonged to Mark the bartender. A pair of heavy footsteps scampered away in a panic; Osric could hear whoever had been driven off thump down the stairs before the thundering footfalls faded back into faint echoes. A few seconds later, there was a knock at the door.

Osric stumbled to the door and barely avoided slamming his head against the wood as he went to peer through the peephole. Standing alone in the hallway was Mark, now with a face as red as marinara sauce and his lips tightened in an irritated scowl.

Osric unlatched the door and slowly opened it to let Mark see his face. "What? What is it?" Osric asked, his voice as rough and bumpy as a gravel country road.

Mark leaned forward, his eyes darting from side to side. "Listen, I don't want you to get all panicked or anything," the bartender whispered, "but some douchebag who thinks wearing shades in the middle of the night is supposed to make him look all hot and mysterious was trying to force your door open. Like, he was trying to dig through that thing like the world's clumsiest and ugliest badger."

Osric felt like throwing up what little was left in his stomach. He knew that he was being watched, and yet he still wasn't being careful enough.

His eyes dropped, and he leaned his head against the door. "I can't believe this is happening."

Mark gave Osric's shoulder a light smack and a small, reassuring smile. "Hey, don't you worry about it. One of the few good things about this block is that there's always someone with an eye open. If anyone tries to bust through your door, I guarantee someone is going to give him a proper Cubare Park hello."

Osric tried to smile but his cheeks forced the corners of his mouth to stay down. If someone was already trying to break into his room, then he knew he didn't have long to stay. Word would spread and someone would be dragging him back to the one he had tried so hard to run from.

Mark lifted Osric's chin. "At least we finally got a name for you. I was going to get a bit tired of Angelo just calling you Baseball Cap Guy."

Osric's eyes widened and his heart oddly skipped a beat. "He was talking about me?" he asked. Mark raised his eyebrows and he let out a cackle.

"I knew it! I saw you giving him that look," the blonde man exclaimed.

Osric's breath was caught in his throat. "What look?"

Mark gave a playful smirk. "Oh, you know. That kind of look where you're just like, 'I've been famished for a long time and this guy looks like a delicious snack.'"

Osric's insides twisted around, and he frantically shook his head. "What? I don't know what you're talking about." Osric struggled to look Mark in the eye. He contemplated bolting back inside the room and barricading the door so he wouldn't be able to leave it again.

"Uh-huh." Mark rolled his eyes and crossed his arms. "Okay, maybe my gaydar needs an oil change or something. But—and this is a big but, so pay attention." Osric forced himself to look back up and meet Mark's sharp, determined eyes. "If I'm right, which I'm sure I am, I wouldn't recommend asking him out right away. It's better to take it a little slow, just to let everything simmer, and then you can figure out if you want to shoot your shot."

Osric thought back to the strange feelings that Angelo seemed to stir in him. Despite not knowing him for long, Osric felt safer when he was closer to Angelo and he seemed like an easy man to talk to, not something Osric saw in a lot of people. These were only seedlings of these feelings, a small crush, and Osric knew it. Though it would have been nice to have those blossom again. It had been years since…

Osric pulled the brakes on his train of thought, lest he risk the train going out of control and derailing.

"He's often seen hanging out around this place." Mark added, "Though he also likes to go watch a few movies at the theatre down the street on the weekends. The one that plays old movies from like the '70s or '80s or something in that zone. That's how I met him, after all."

Osric placed his hand against the doorframe. "Do you guys have a history or something?"

Mark laughed. "Oh yeah. But admittedly, I kind of jumped the gun on the whole thing. After a while, we kind of agreed that we make way better friends than partners. So, no harm, no foul. He's all yours, if you want to go for him."

Osric's face contorted, struggling to process all the information running through his head. He nodded dumbly. "Cool. Thanks."

Mark backed away from the door and placed his hands on his hips. "You know, you seem a bit jumpy." The bartender then looked down the hall. His smile briefly dropped before quickly re-forming back on his face. "The three of us should go out for drinks sometime. Not here of course, but maybe a little bit of the spirits can help you relax and settle in."

Osric again nodded dumbly. "Sure, yeah. Thanks for the tips."

Mark then began to walk away, raising his hand in the air. "No problem. Catch you later, Oz. Lock your door. Sleep well."

Osric raised a hand in return, watching Mark sink down the stairs. His heart finally began to slow down and pace itself. Osric slowly closed the door, quietly latching it shut and walking back to his bed. He began to ponder what Mark had said, wondering if maybe the budding feelings he was developing could be worth exploring.

He knew Mark was right that he shouldn't jump into a relationship right away, but at the same time, if the would-be intruder was anything to go by, then he didn't have much time to spare lingering in the town.

As he lay in bed, his mind came to a somewhat firm conclusion. He had wandered alone, moving from place to place for too long. Maybe it would do him good to at least find a friend. While he doubted Angelo could completely change his situation, Osric hoped he could at least keep him away from that hellhole.

The next day, Osric washed his face and hair in his room's bathroom sink. Whatever the water was pumped with, it helped to rejuvenate him with electrifying energy that added a bounce to his step.

After getting himself together, he took his wallet and walked downstairs to find Robyn in her usual spot at her desk, smoking a cigarette and reading a magazine. Sitting on the desk was a silvery bottle of vodka and a mug filled with steaming coffee. Osric stopped in front of the desk and asked, "Hey, do you know how to get to the theatre? The one that plays old movies."

Robyn sighed, before pointing to her left. "Down the block, take a left and keep following the road until you see the building with the billboard and sign shaped like a film reel."

Osric nodded. "Right, thank you."

"Yeah yeah," Robyn muttered.

Before he pushed himself out the door, Osric remembered the near encounter with the intruder the night before and lowered his baseball cap low enough to cover his face. Though his nerves were still working overtime at the thought of being spotted again, he refused to let them confine him to his room.

This time, he would try to enjoy himself during his stay in town.

The city block was quieter than it had been the night before, with only a few pedestrians populating the sidewalks and a few cars blitzing down the road ten or so kilometres over the speed limit. Osric looked up and saw the lights of Hotel Bonner's sign flicker on and off, the glow of the bulbs blending in with the film of fog and newborn daylight.

Osric followed Robyn's directions, taking the right turns and travelling down the right roads before stopping at his destination.

A small building with a marquis upfront reading "Now Playing: A Bucket Of Blood – The Corman Classic Considered Too Explicit For Its Time" against faint amber light. The building itself had a film reel sculpture planted on top of the roof. The entrance was crowded with old movie posters that stopped just before the dark violet doors.

It looked the part of an old theatre and yet there was no one around. The place also seemed abandoned, or maybe it was because of the rest of the bustling city settling down during the day. He felt a hand tap his shoulder, causing him to jump two feet into the air.

"What are you doing?"

Osric howled and turned around with a fist raised, ready to fight. It sunk in him a few seconds too late that the voice belonged to Angelo, now in a casual crimson sweatshirt.

Osric breathed a sigh of relief and sheepishly shoved his fist behind his back. "Angelo. Hey, um…how long have you been standing there?"

The other man shrugged. "I actually just got here," Angelo replied. "A little birdie mentioned you may be paying this place a visit."

Osric sighed and shook his head. "Let me guess, the bartender?"

"How'd you know?"

The two chuckled, somewhat easing the tension forming in his nerves. Out of habit, Osric swivelled his head to glance over his shoulders and check for people watching too intently to the exchange.

Angelo raised an eyebrow. "Are you expecting anyone?" he asked.

Osric snapped his attention back to Angelo and shook his head. "Um, no. It's just, um…" Osric stopped himself.

*Oh, it's nothing. Just on the run after finally having enough of subjecting myself to a crappy situation and then having the source of said situation spread rumours that I was this evil monster.*

"Just what?" Angelo asked softly, tilting his head.

Osric sighed. "It's nothing; it's dumb." Angelo nodded but he kept a skeptical twinkle in his eye. Osric glanced toward the doors and pointed at the building behind him. "So, do you know any good movies playing right now?" he asked, trying his best to hide the anxiety building in his voice.

Angelo shrugged. "Like the billboard says, they just got Bucket of Blood. I also found Tenebrae pretty good. Fun fact: it was put on the UK's list of video nasties." Angelo raised his eyebrows as he spoke. "The movies that were considered too violent for innocent eyes." He began to laugh just as he finished his sentence, with Osric finding himself laughing along. The sensation seemed so much more natural and infectious than usual.

"Well, hopefully, the tickets are cheap," Osric said.

Angelo shook his head and reassuringly patted Osric on the shoulder. "No no no, it's alright. I'll pay for it." He pulled out a black wallet with a silver buckle, decorated with a black snake engraving.

"Oh no, you don't have to do that," Osric stuttered, shoving his hands in front of him.

Angelo grinned, cheerfully pushing Osric toward by his shoulders. "Aw, come on. It's only money," Angelo quipped. "And it's not like I can take it with me when it's my time to go."

Getting closer to the entrance, Osric couldn't help but feel a lighter feeling take some weight off his chest. Such a free-spirited nature, the likes of which he hadn't seen in a long while. He could only hope that he would be able to repay his new friend for all his generosity.

Those hours spent at the old theatre would be the first in a month-long string of excursions the two men would spend together. The pair would traverse the city square, exploring the many sights, sounds, and smells. Osric began to look over his shoulder less and less every day. He had even nearly forgotten his experience with the Cubare Beast.

On the latest of these nights, Angelo and Osric had returned to Hotel Bonner after spending hours at a bowling alley said to be older than the town itself. Though the muscles in his arms begged for mercy, Osric didn't feel the least bit tired. If anything, the fire in his veins was encouraging him to beg for another round. He could only guess by Angelo's constant laughter that he didn't want it to end either. If only the bowling alley hadn't closed at eleven.

The pair had nearly missed the hotel as the lights in the Hotel Bonner's sign had shorted out. Angelo sighed, pulling Osric back by the shirt collar before he could obliviously stumble past the building.

"Looks like Robyn's going to need to call in the electrician again," Angelo muttered.

Osric leaned on his pal's shoulder, wearing a dumb smile on his face. "Maybe we'll slip a note into that magazine of hers." He laughed, causing a bemused Angelo to roll his eyes.

"I mean, sure it's the best way to get her attention, but do you really want to risk losing those fingers?"

Osric chuckled. "Okay, probably not," he concurred. As he and Angelo opened the doors to Hotel Bonner, he figured nothing could yank him down from Cloud Nine.

That was, until he saw who was at the front desk. A woman with wild blonde hair covered in gold highlights leaned over the desk, the heels of her red boots hovering above the carpet as she did so.

"Listen, I'm telling you that Osric Cabrera is a dangerous man." The stinging familiarity of her voice froze Osric in his place and his lungs felt like they were completely deflated of air.

*Laurel.*

Angelo was quick to catch Osric's look and stopped alongside him.

"Him and most of the other men that live here. What's your point, lady?" Robyn asked, her voice dripping with apathy and disinterest. Osric could see Laurel stir angrily, slamming her hand against the desk.

"The point is, I need to make sure he isn't making life a living Hell for another girl just like he did with me," she screeched.

Robyn's eyes darted to Angelo and Osric, and though her irritated expression remained unchanged, she did give the two a slight nod. "Ma'am, if he *is* causing trouble then we have dozens of patrons that can beat him into paste," Robyn droned. "Besides, it's against policy for me to give out personal information about our guests without their consent, unless it's with law enforcement."

"Can't you just make an exception?" Laurel begged. Angelo slowly guided Osric in the direction of the bar, placing himself in front, much to Osric's relief. He held his breath, hoping his footsteps wouldn't cause the floor to creak and expose him to the same woman who had driven him to the streets.

"No, ma'am," Robyn replied, her tone becoming increasingly annoyed.

From his new angle, Osric could make out his former paramour's face contorting with frustration and her eyes becoming two fiery daggers.

"This is ridiculous!" she shouted. "You're defending a convicted felon, and you don't even care."

Robyn's lips became pinched together and she stood up out of her chair. "Listen here, lady. I may not be fond of this job, but I still appreciate the paycheck it gives me. So, unless you got yourself a search warrant or a police escort, I'm not just going to go waving that information around for you all willy-nilly."

Osric grabbed for the corner of the bar's wall and tried to slip into the nearest booth. Angelo stood in the entryway and began to preen his hair. Osric swung his legs around and started to try and slither under the table. However, before he could completely sink toward the ground, he banged his head against the edge. The corners of his mouth pulled back when he heard the salt and pepper shakers ringing against the table before toppling over.

From underneath, he saw Laurel snap her head toward the bar area. She stomped over to Angelo, causing Osric to scramble to squeeze himself into the furthest, darkest corner he could find.

"Excuse me, sir, have you seen a man that goes by the name of Osric Cabrera? He's got black hair, is about five-foot-nine, and has a big scar next to his nose."

Of course, and he now had a partial view of the woman that had given him said scar. Osric saw Angelo shrug, carefully shuffling to position himself in front of the table.

"Nope, haven't seen him," Angelo casually fibbed. "Why?

Does he owe you money or something?"

"No, but even if he did, I would've let him keep it," Laurel cried. "No amount of money is worth letting him run free, knowing what he's capable of."

Osric always found it remarkable how she could switch from showing the fury of a thousand demons to sobbing and pleading like a lost child.

"Capable of what?" a cowboy-sounding patron from the other side of the room asked. Laurel began to make sobbing noises, reaching up to cover her face.

"He used to beat me. He beat me so bad he almost killed me." She began to choke out sounds that imitated weeping.

Osric huddled further into his corner at the sound of shuffling utensils and chairs scraping against the floor.

"He did what?"

"That's unbelievable."

"That poor woman."

Many other murmurs of shock crowded the room, dragging Osric's heart to the bottom of his stomach. It was happening again, only he had nowhere to run to. He was quite literally backed into a corner, with no feasible way to escape. He covered his mouth, even somewhat pinching his nose to try and keep any noises from escaping his hideout.

Angelo leaned against the table. "Sheesh. Sounds serious. But if he's out of your life, why not just leave it to the police? You're putting yourself in a lot of danger trying to go after him by yourself." Angelo's voice was soft and gentle, as if he was talking to an injured animal.

Laurel nodded. "When I tried to have him arrested, the police said there wasn't enough evidence to make an arrest. When he fled, I knew I had to do something before he killed someone."

Osric remembered that day all too well. It seemed like his

worst nightmare, having the police show up at the front door of his house with handcuffs at the ready.

The black eyes, the cuts, and the bruises could've easily been written off as her inflicting those wounds out of self-defence, and he knew it. Osric remembered sitting in the bathroom, becoming dizzy and nearly fainting from the panic of his life being upended for good. The panic that he would be dragged out and brought to trial. Watch her sit on the stand to make the performance of a lifetime, painting a picture of the abuse that he had supposedly inflicted on her. The same abuse that she had inflicted on him once the doors were closed.

All those hours locking himself in the bathroom whenever she was in a foul mood, having to duck out of the way of flying dishes as if they were bullets in a war zone, being told day after day how worthless he was and that no one would believe him if he sought out help or left.

All that turmoil being turned around to make him look like the monster, rotting in jail for the rest of his life and being the perfect punching bag for inmates because he was a "wife beater."

He was lucky some neighbours hadn't been able verify her story and that the officers hadn't been able find any evidence of domestic abuse-related injuries on her. But even after they had left, Osric had known that didn't guarantee the end of the torment. One of these days, she was going to kill him. He had had to leave the hellhole before it swallowed him up. For months, he had tried to stay a step ahead of her and yet, she always found him.

Including at the Hotel Bonner.

"Well, we'll be sure to keep an eye out," Angelo said, placing a consoling hand on Laurel's shoulder. "If we catch him, we'll be sure to call the police before he lays a hand on another woman. Alright?"

"Alright." She nodded, wiping away her invisible tears. Angelo then began to carefully guide her back to the entrance. He heard other patrons get out of their chairs and follow Angelo and Laurell out of the bar.

"Yeah, we'll find him."

"Rip his head straight off of his spine."

"His days are numbered, we can promise you that, lady." Watching the bar empty, Osric struggled to breathe, puddles of sweat soaking into his clothes and his heart beating so fast he thought it would explode. His eyes darted around the area. He couldn't hide under the table forever and he knew it. He had to track out an escape route, one that would allow him to slip away before anyone in the forming mob squad could find him.

That was when he caught sight of a pale grey door with a glowing red EXIT sign at the back of the room. The door had a bar that could push it wide open. Thankfully, that meant less time to fidget with the doorknob. Hopefully, it would lead to the alleyway he had wandered to when he had first arrived at Hotel Bonner. Just hop from shadow to shadow, and he'd be out of town in no time.

Osric shifted into a crouch before pouncing out from under the table. He shoved the chairs and tables that were in his path out of the way and turned his body around so that his shoulder faced the door.

Mark, still behind the bar, nearly dropped the glass he was cleaning as he jumped away from the runner. "Whoa, hey! That's the emergency—"

Too late to hear the warning, Osric blasted the door open, tumbling out into the cold, musty alleyway. Suddenly, the building erupted into a cacophony of sharp beeps and chirps. Osric cursed under his breath, slamming his fist into the freezing concrete ground. He struggled to pull himself up as he heard the rumbling of footsteps behind him. Osric sprinted down the path, ducking behind the familiar green dumpster to catch his breath.

"Hey, the bastard ran out here!" he heard one of the patrons shout. Not leaving himself enough time to map out another escape route, Osric jumped up and grabbed onto the edge of the garbage bin. He gritted his teeth and pulled himself inside, landing roughly on his shoulder in a mound of garbage bags. He tossed away the bags, creating a hole for him to stuff himself into in case anyone had the bright idea to look in the dumpster.

Sinking into the plastic black sea, Osric covered his mouth and nose to keep himself from gagging at the stinging odour of rotting food. He pushed himself to sink further, hearing the footsteps against the concrete clap louder and heavier.

"He went this way!"

"Bastard's not getting away that easily!"

"Stomp his head in until he's nothing but another stain on the sidewalk!"

Hiding in the pits of food scraps and plastic bags holding who knew what, he remembered hearing those same voices happily chatting the night away with him when he made a stop at the bar after his excursions with Angelo.

Then again, Laurel always seemed to have that special gift to make people believe her and have them follow her like a pied piper. Back when things were stable, the two of them would joke that she could sell ice to penguins. Still, he felt the only reason his lungs didn't pop like cheap balloons was that he didn't hear Angelo as a member of the mob. But still, Osric wondered, could he really count on Angelo to take his side against an angry, drunken mob?

A few minutes later, the echoes of the mob's footsteps became faint echoes that disappeared into the center of town. Still,

Osric stayed in his self-imposed plastic coffin. Maybe someone stayed behind to keep watch, or maybe someone was still lingering in the bar and would sound the alarm if he crawled out.

Carefully, Osric tried to plant his foot on top of a bag, but he struggled to balance himself, as he felt like he was trying to step on a large mould of stale Jell-o. His fingernails scraped against the chipped paint as he squirmed to get a solid foothold. He prayed that no one would hear him struggling and yank him out to throttle him like a stick shift. He gasped when he finally grabbed a hold of the edge. He slowly pulled himself up until he could just barely see the alleyway and the doorway of the emergency exit.

Luckily for him, the alleyway was as empty as a ghost town, and the only sound he could make out was the crinkling of the plastic bags holding him up. The cold wind bit at his face, turning his beads of sweat into pellets of ice. Osric took a breath. If he wanted to make a break for it, he knew that this was his moment.

He sighed, even if his experience with this city ended the same way as all the others had, Osric was still glad to have spent what little time he did have with Angelo. That man had given him something he hadn't experienced for a long time, a chance to live like a free man. It pained him to know he would never get the chance to repay him for that gift.

Osric clumsily tossed himself out of the dumpster, eating clumps of gravel and nearly knocking out a few teeth as he made his landing. He pressed his hand against his forehead to try and force out the ringing banging against the sides of his skull.

"Alright, that was pretty stupid," he muttered to himself. Osric hocked a lump of spit into the gravel before slowly pulling himself onto his feet. He pressed his hand against the wall, digging his hand into the gaps between the bricks. Just had to stick to the shadows and he'd slip right back out.

But before he could turn the corner, he felt his head slam against the wall with a thick *thud*. His eardrums rumbled like they were in the middle of an earthquake and his body's limbs flailed around uselessly. After his head was slammed into the wall a second time, Osric used what was left of his strength to turn his head around to face his attacker.

Laurel's eyes were fiery balls of overtly righteous fury, and her teeth were bared like a wild bear's. Osric collapsed into a heap, his vision turning into a gyroscope stained with red. He hugged his legs to his chest just as she reeled her foot back. She smashed her foot into Osric's arms, and he felt his blood catch on fire as the heel of her boot stabbed into his wrists. She then dug her toes into his guts, causing Osric to nearly cough out a lung. Digging her heel into his eyes, Osric screamed as his eye felt like it was being torn apart and some sort of liquid oozed out from under his eyelids and spurted down his face. He struggled to grab at her ankle to pull her heel out of his eye, his arms strained as his muscles cried out for mercy.

His eye tugged out as he pushed her foot back. *I've survived this long. Take my eye all you want. I'm not dying in some gutter. Especially not by your hand.*

Osric let out a feral roar and forced himself up. He headbutted her in the gut and forced her to the ground. Osric saw globs of dark red liquid drip down his face and land with a plop onto the concrete. He raised his hand up to his face and covered his wounded eye, or what was left of it to salvage. His world spun around him, and his ribs felt like they were stabbing into his lungs and heart. The woman in front of him clutched at her stomach and rolled around on the ground.

Laurel turned over onto her knees and growled at Osric, "I'm not going to let you ruin anyone else's life like you ruined mine." Osric's bleeding eye stung like it had been attacked by a hundred bees, but still, he bit his tongue and tried to turn the corner. As far as he knew, she was alone, so it would be easier to retreat. He began to shamble down the alleyway when a figure stepped out of the shadows and imposed himself in front of him.

"Angelo?" Osric asked, his chalky voice shaking as he spoke before he was forced to cough up a small puddle of blood. The heavy clacking of heels was heard behind him, now with the intensity of a jackhammer to the side of his head. Osric turned and saw Laurel staggering out of the darkness. Her face was covered in scratches, and she was holding her arm. Her eyes turned up toward Angelo's and they suddenly became as wide and watery as a doe's.

"Oh, thank God!" she cried. "You were right. I shouldn't have gone out alone. He found me. I had no choice, I had to—" Her eyes darted back and forth before she collapsed onto her knees and covered her face. Laurel's shoulders shook and she started howling out sobbing noises. Angelo brushed past Osric, nearly sending Osric tumbling to the ground. As Angelo walked closer to the woman, Osric saw the last spark of hope he had grow dimmer. He knew she would have no problem convincing Angelo about the authenticity of her narrative. She had a way with words and now all Osric had was a ruined eye.

Angelo kneeled and pulled the woman back onto her feet. He wrapped her into a delicate embrace and slowly began to stroke her back.

"I know, I know. It must have been so difficult for you to go through this," Angelo whispered.

Laurel nodded, smothering her face into his shoulder and neck. "Yes, it's been so exhausting and so awful. I just want it to end."

Osric turned to face the city strip, catching a small ray of reignited light from the sign of the Hotel Bonner. Maybe while

Angelo and the woman were distracted, he could try to make a break for it. Sure, his eye injury would make him easier to spot in a crowd, but maybe the diversion could buy him just a little more time.

He slowly began to step away before Angelo said in a hushed voice, "Don't you worry, Laurel. It'll all be over soon."

A cold wind fell upon Osric, stopping him in his tracks. He saw that his ex-lover must have come to the same conclusion as her eyes quickly widened and she shoved Angelo away from her. Angelo's head slammed against the wall behind him, and he covered his face, reeling in pain.

"How do you know my name?" She slowly began to back away, her voice filled with panic.

Angelo's shoulders began to shake as he stumbled forward. The ringing in Osric's ears faded, allowing him to hear that Angelo was chuckling. This chuckle, however, wasn't the easy-going, jovial laugh Osric was so accustomed to. Instead, his friend let out a baleful cackle before finally removing his hand from his face. Osric's bones became locked in place and his blood ran cold as his eyes landed on Angelo's. They were two small balls of orange fire, and his teeth were now glistening fangs.

"Oh, I know all about you and your little situation with Ozzy here." Angelo's voice became deep and gravelly. Blood-red talons tore their way out of his fingers and the top of his head peeled apart, giving way to a pair of horns.

As Angelo began to saunter toward her, Laurel gasped and tried to make a break back to where she came from. However, a tail tore through Angelo's pants and whipped around to drill into the wall, blocking Laurel's path. Laurel shook her head, and her entire body began to shake.

"What the hell? What are you?" For the first time that night, Osric heard genuine fear coat her voice. Her knees began to shake, and she grabbed onto the wall behind her for dear life.

Angelo gave a wicked smirk, "Oh, you know, just your average extra-planar tourist. From a place that's been waiting for you to visit for a long, *long* time." Suddenly, Angelo seized Laurel by the throat and pinned her against the wall.

Osric was left paralyzed, watching Laurel be lifted off the ground and struggle to pry Angelo's claws from her neck. She dug her nails into his unmoving hand, only to instantly peel away Angelo's human skin and reveal pulsating, infernal flesh covered in amber markings. Angelo looked over at the patch curiously before giving a casual shrug.

"Guess there's no need to keep that on anyway," he said. The skin around the patch began to peel back like old tree bark, revealing the rest of the amber-marked skin underneath. Angelo's head stretched, the skin pulled apart like taffy, and his jaw became elongated with a visceral roar. The skin on his face was torn to shreds, revealing a bovine head.

In an instant, Osric once again found himself staring at the Cubare Beast. Laurel's legs kicked furiously against the wall, and she frantically clawed at his arms.

"No! Please! Don't do this! Someone! Anyone! Help!" Laurel shrieked. The Beast slowly reeled his free arm back before suddenly driving it through Laurel's chest. Her cries slowly died with a faint whistle, and blood began to pool from her chest and down both her legs and the Beast's arm. The Beast reached his arm back, ripping Laurel's heart out of her chest, taking a few veins and fleshy tubes with it. The Beast threw Laurel's body on the ground, leaving her in a dark pool of blood.

Osric tried to look away, only to be met with the sight of the Beast prying his jaws wide open and dropping Laurel's heart into his mouth. The Beast snapped his head toward Osric and began to march forward.

Osric's veins began to push his blood flow into overdrive, prompting him to run. However, in his rush, he stumbled over his own feet and collapsed onto the ground. Osric rolled over and stared at the Beast glowering down at him. "Angelo?" he gasped. "You… you're the Cubare Beast?"

The Beast stopped in his tracks and gave a slow, stilted nod.

"Always have been," Osric heard Angelo say, even though the Beast's jaws stayed still. "I'm sorry you had to find out like this." The harsh tone of the Beast was softer as he spoke, and he bowed his head.

Osric tried to settle his rapidly beating heart to no avail. He sat there shocked in disbelief that the same man he had become so close to was also the Beast that had butchered two people with ease.

"Then again, my time here was running short anyway," Angelo continued. "My boss said I'm to be assigned to a new post, somewhere in Detroit or something. So, I guess in a weird way, your timing worked out in my favour. A fiasco like this is the perfect cover for me to take my leave."

A fiery portal opened behind Angelo, and a torrent of boiling hot wind roared around him, enveloping Osric.

Angelo turned his head and sighed. "Speak of the Devil. And quite literally, I might add." He chuckled solemnly. "Though, before I go, I got to say thank you for the good times."

Osric's eyes widened. "Wait, what? You knew?"

Angelo laughed. "Well, sensing feelings of romance and lust is kind of my thing. But even then, you weren't exactly subtle about it. You kind of wear your heart on your sleeve, Oz."

Osric felt like his cheeks were being pinched. Judging by Angelo's continuous laughter, he could only assume that meant he was blushing. Angelo then walked toward Osric and gently caressed the side of his face. After Angelo removed his cold hand from his face, Osric found the blood near his eye was gone and that the side of his vision was no longer blanketed in red.

"Hope you don't mind a little parting gift." Angelo then got up and turned to walk toward the whirlpool of flames. Just before the Beast could enter, Osric sprung to his feet and grabbed Angelo's arm.

"Wait!" Osric waited for Angelo to turn back to him before continuing, "Do you think…your boss would mind if I joined you?"

Angelo tilted his head curiously. "Well, he's not one to say 'no' to such an offer. But are you sure? My line of work isn't exactly the life of luxury." His rough voice had a tint of cautious optimism. Osric shrugged,

"I mean, I like to think I've gotten used to roughing it. Besides, it'll give me plenty of time to pay you back for all that you've done for me."

Angelo appeared to think for a moment. He looked to the portal and back to Osric.

"And I don't exactly have much of a life to go back to here," Osric added. "May as well use what time I have left to give you a hand with whatever you need."

Angelo pondered for only a moment more, then he reached his hand out toward Osric. Even with the beastly face Angelo wore, Osric swore he could see a faint smile cross his friend. Osric tenderly took Angelo's hand and, side-by-side, the two dove through the fire. What would happen next, he didn't know, but for the first time in his life, the feeling left Osric at peace.

# The Imposter's Torment

"So, in the end, the true beauty was within the beast." Briar clapped her hands with delight. "So, what did you think?"

Marcy sat, stunned, on the couch, trying not to let her mouth go agape. Here was this cheerful and upbeat young woman telling such a tale with a blithe smile on her face. Next to her, Azura sat unfazed and simply nodded along with the rest of the tale.

Finally, Marcy forced herself to speak. "It was…very interesting. Where did you hear that story?" she asked.

Briar, seemingly oblivious to her gobsmacked audience, gave a casual shrug. "My Dad used to tell me that story all the time when I was a kid."

"As a kid?" Marcy didn't mean to blurt those words out, but it was as if they had built up so much in her head and so quickly that they tumbled out of her brain and out through her mouth.

Briar laughed. "Yeah? I used to ask him to tell me that story over and over again before going to bed." She raised an eyebrow and smirked. "Is there something wrong with that?"

Marcy was stunned into silence, desperately trying to grasp at words to say like a drowning victim would gasp for air. Suddenly, it felt like all eyes were plastered onto her and she begged for the cushion she was sitting on to let her sink inside.

Luckily, Azura swooped in. "Oh no, it's just a bit different from what she's used to is all," she quickly reassured.

Briar gave a bright smile with empty eyes and clasped her hands together. "Oh, well I'm glad I could be the one to introduce our family tradition to her then." The rosy woman tilted her head toward the doorway. "Anyway, I think I'm going to go get something to drink. That story left me parched." With that, Briar skipped off down the hall, leaving the couple to themselves.

Azura moved her hand from Marcy's shoulder to inside one of her own and squeezed. "Hey, are you good?" Azura asked.

Marcy sighed and shook her head. "Yeah, I'm fine. I just didn't expect a story like that, you know?"

Azura nodded. "Fair enough but just try to grin and bear it. My family is really proud of their stories. It's kind of a tradition of ours, and some of them are pretty weird." Azura then lifted Marcy's hand and gave it a quick kiss. "If they see you liking their stories then that's pretty much half the battle of winning them over."

Marcy laughed. "That easy, huh?" As Azura laughed along, Marcy felt her phone buzz in her back pocket, letting any warmth accompanying her melt away. No doubt Aiden was getting antsy, and he wouldn't appreciate being kept waiting. Swallowing her accumulating anxiety, Marcy stood up and glanced at the hallway.

"Hey Zu, where is your bathroom?" she asked.

Azura pointed toward the hall. "Oh, second hall to the left and then the third door to the right."

"Thanks," Marcy said with a nod. She forced her legs to slow down to keep from rushing down the halls and giving away the building pressure threatening to burst her heart that had been festering ever since Azura picked her up.

The relatives chatting were blurs that grazed past the sides of her vision before she stopped to catch her breath alone in a hallway. When she looked back up, she saw the walls were covered in framed newspaper clippings, faded with age into a shade of dark yellow.

Marcy's eyes became fixated on the clipping that read in bold, black letters, "God Of Death Claims Another Victim. Identity Still Unknown."

Her finger traced the indents of the frame's corner, barely avoiding adding streaks to the glass. The picture in the bottom left corner was a thick black blob shaped in the vague image of a body sprawled on the ground. As she squinted her eyes to read the text, a cold wind caused a prickly field of thorns to sprout on the back of her neck.

"Interesting reading material, isn't it?"

Marcy whipped around with a gasp, nearly falling onto her rear from the shock.

The first thing she noticed about the man standing in front of her was his dark, smoky eyes, sunken into his pale face and surrounded by heavy, violet bags. A close second was the reptilian smirk that stretched across his face, dripping with venomous smugness. He gave a dark chuckle, bobbing his moppy hair along with his shoulders.

"What the heck is wrong with you? You can't just sneak up on people like that!" Marcy asked, failing to catch the words before they came out of her mouth. The man chuckled in response, causing every hair on Marcy to turn into a frosty spike.

"Is there anything wrong with welcoming my dear cousin's

partner to the festivities?" his raspy voice hissed.

Despite the minefield of goosebumps popping across her skin, Marcy swallowed her fear and crossed her arms. "I mean, no, but did you have to sneak up on me like that?"

The man gave a casual shrug, his slimy smile not shifting an inch. He took a step forward, tightening the cold air around her neck. The man pressed his fingers into his chin. "And here I almost believed Azura when she kept gushing about how attentive you were." He chuckled. The man gazed into Marcy's eyes and curiously tilted his head. "What's the matter? Is something else burdening your mind?" His faux-sickly voice slithered into Marcy's ear and turned her stomach inside out.

She shook her head. "No."

At her retort, the man hummed to himself and crossed his arms. "You don't have much of a silver tongue, do you?" His eyes glanced at the phone in Marcy's hand. "No matter. The truth has a way of worming its way out eventually. And when it does, well…you'll see that we don't have much patience for liars."

He slithered around to the newspaper clipping, gently pushing on the corner of the frame to make it straight. "Take the so-called God Of Death in this paper for example. They likely thought they would never be caught, hiding behind the mask of normality. But the mask can only remain on the face for so long before it slips and someone gets a peek underneath."

\*\*\*

Good old Vancouver, the city that never slept and never stopped raining. Despite the cold and wet monsoon seasons that tormented the city, the metropolis remained bright, and the people remained in even brighter spirits. All the more reason the God of Death carving a bloody swath through the city shook it to the very core. A ruthless killer that often painted the scene of the crime with the blood of his victims. The bodies would be arranged so that their hands lay on their chests, the bodies under a mural of blood. The mural would consist of a dripping skull and bright, bold letters proclaiming, "Hail the God of Death."

Despite cameras being posted at every corner of the city, no one managed to get more than a blurry shot of the killer's face. All shots taken of the God of Death showed them clad completely in black, minus a few white streaks surrounding his mask's eyeholes. His weapon of choice seemed to be an ordinary knife, though forensics found traces of dirty water inside the penetrative wounds of the corpses. The police said across several news shows that they were keeping a close eye on the streets for any sign of the one who called himself the God of Death.

And no one was paying more attention to his crime spree than Clifford Pickton. The walls of his sardine tin-sized bedroom were covered with newspaper articles covering the gruesome details of the God of Death's crimes. The killer would need to have enough knowledge of how to handle bodies to avoid leaving fingerprints. This would be an especially delicate process when painting his murals.

Clifford brushed his hand against the newsprints, tracing his finger over a picture of the jawless body of a young blonde woman found behind a coffee shop. Clifford wondered what she could have been thinking the moment she drew her last breath. Could she have been worried about the people she was leaving behind? Was she devastated there was so much business left unfinished? Or could there have been a spark of relief that she no longer had to suffer the drudgery of the mortal world?

Clifford's meditations were jolted to a close by the shrieking beeps of his alarm clock. The dishevelled man groaned. Six-thirty a.m., right on the dot.

Perhaps he left himself enough time to continue to study the articles, but then again, Clifford knew how easily he could get lost, plunging himself down the rabbit hole. As much as he wanted the shadows of the hole to embrace him, Clifford had to remind himself there was still much to do in the land of the living.

He dragged himself into the bathroom, nearly blinding himself as he flipped on the lights. He pulled open a drawer, being greeted with shimmering silver bottles. The key to the shine that glistened against his face every time he stepped out of his apartment. He opened his hand and squeezed a dollop of mineral-filled cream into his palm. Not too much. Not only would too much cream make his face all greasy in the present, but it would dry up and chip his skin days later.

Just because he didn't live in the most luxurious district in the province didn't mean he couldn't look like he did. He carefully massaged the cream around his face, taking care to avoid his chestnut eyebrows and his dark hazel eyes. With the cream applied, Clifford left the bathroom and went to the kitchen to fix himself a cup of coffee.

He plucked a metal straw out of a pile of utensils and planted it into a plain black mug. After all, getting crumbs stuck on the cream would ruin the process and likely clog his pores. For ten minutes, he sipped his coffee through the straw before wiping the cream from his face with a small white cloth.

However, when he removed the cloth from his face, he found spots of red had stained the fabric. Clifford gasped, looking up to the mirror. Despite the new bloody stains on the snow-white fabric, Clifford found his face was as pristine and spotless as he intended it to be. He looked back down at the cloth, turning it around in his hands with a puzzled look. "A reaction to the bleach?" Clifford asked himself.

But he had used that cloth multiple times, and this was the first time that it had been ruined by his routine. He sighed, hanging the cloth up on a small rack under the light switch. He couldn't waste his time with such a trivial matter, not when he had to pay the bills. If he could help it, he would ditch his workplace and spend his time analyzing the God of Death murders, contributing to society for a change. Not like the bloodsucking landlords that sat on their butts siphoning away his well-earned money, money he could have used on something more useful than fattening them up. But alas, such was the disease of greed that devolved humanity into the mindset of a rat.

So, Clifford marched to the front door and picked up his tawny briefcase. He snatched up his grey umbrella and opened the door to a downpour of rain washing away the lights of the apartment complex.

"Got to love Vancouver weather," Clifford muttered before popping open the umbrella and marching down the steps to the parking lot. He stepped inside his milky white Jaguar and switched on the radio. He just caught the tail-end of some kitschy pop song before a woman's voice broke through the mechanical jingle.

"And I've just received word that another body attributed to the so-called God of Death was discovered in the truck bed of an abandoned F-150 found off the shoulder of the Burnaby Highway. The windows were painted with the same gruesome message as the other crime scenes: 'Hail to the God of Death.' The body was identified as twenty-seven-year-old Patrick Malone, who had been reported missing a week prior to the discovery."

Clifford rolled his eyes. "Got some lazy do-nothings on the police force. They have to be to take that long to find the body." The sharply suited man slammed the gear into reverse and turned his way out of the parking lot.

"Police are advising citizens to stay in their apartments after dark, lock their doors, and not pick up any hitchhikers in the

Vancouver area until further notice."

"I'm telling you, Vanessa, these are some pretty scary times," a male voice added. "It's like Vancouver's got their very own Jack the Ripper."

"Luckily, forensics has made many advancements since the days of Victorian London. While we have no information on how close the police are to catching the perpetrator, it should only be a matter of time before the killer gets careless and…"

Clifford tried to peer through the puddles forming on his windshield as the report continued to drone on. Even after the trail of bodies, the people remained confident that the killer would be found.

*Or maybe he's just too smart for everyone else to keep up,* Clifford thought with contempt. Pushing through the overflowing roads, Clifford heard the strums of a tense harp fill his car. He looked at his radio and went to switch it off. But when he turned the knob, it remained stuck.

"What the—?" The radio was already off. The discordant melody continued to fill his ears, the soundwaves threatening to crush the sides of his head. Clifford's eyes widened as the melody was interrupted by a car suddenly stopping in front of him. He cursed under his breath and slammed against the horn. "Nice going, pal! You almost got yourself rear-ended, you idiot!"

He figured maybe if he had been going a little faster, he would've crushed the inconsiderate moron like an accordion. Clifford growled. If only it were legal, he would jump out of his car, smash his arm through the jerk's window, and slit his throat with whatever glass he could grab. Probably would've done society a favour. Whoever was in there couldn't be contributing much to society if he didn't even know how to brake properly. The white-hot anger in his mind soothed as the car in front continued forward, prompting Clifford to do the same.

*No, not worth making myself late because of some moron.*

As his car rolled over the potholes in the road, he noticed that the harp music was gone, and all was quiet except for the pattering of rain and the honking of other cars. Twenty dull minutes passed, and Clifford pulled into the parking lot of the great grey tower he called his workplace. He wandered through the halls, passing by those who had accepted their place on the social ladder. Those who were satisfied with leading a life of mediocrity, the ones who didn't see their future past their next paycheck. Clifford knew his current position was just a stop on the way to being remembered by all for years to come.

He eventually arrived at his desk, signed the time he checked in on his hours index card, and booted up his computer. His eyes wandered to the windows next to his desk. The rain was like tears from Heaven staining the glass.

Clifford wondered, if God was real, how often did he weep over the failed state of his pet project? He must have had more patience than Clifford, who figured that if he was in a divine state then he would have swept humanity off the planet as punishment for their complacency. He was tugged out of his ponderings when his computer finally booted up and Clifford opened his graphic design software. His movements with the mouse and keyboard were rigid and mechanical. Typing messages of congratulations and well wishes he would never utter and decorating the files with gaudy pastel colours.

As much as the files made him want to vomit all over his keyboard, that was his job, and he was going to put in as much effort as he could. Even if those efforts were for making greeting cards, the favoured tool for people who couldn't put in the effort to wish their loved ones well in their own words.

Suddenly, his right ear was slammed with a glassy thud. He and the coworkers in his neighbouring cubicles jumped out of their seats. Clifford turned around and saw a large, black bird flying in place outside his window. The avian reared its beak back and slammed against the window, repeating the ugly sound. The bird continued to ram itself into the window, shaking the giant glass pane.

"What is it trying to do?" a co-worker asked. Clifford recognized him as the ugly sounding one who smoked his lungs out every minute he could spare during his break.

"That poor thing…" another said mournfully, the woman who could never shut up about her kids. Suddenly, the window broke apart, inviting a chorus of screams from everyone in the office space. A shower of glass cascaded onto the ground, forming a translucent mosaic on grey linoleum. The black bird slid toward Clifford, its wings sprawled out and its feathers coated with pinprick-sized shards of glass.

"Holy crap!"

"Someone call management!"

"What the hell are *they* going to do?"

"I don't know! Call an exterminator?"

While his brainless co-workers scrambled around the office like headless chickens, Clifford continued to admire the postmortem beauty of the bird. The beak, despite flying through a plane of glass, remained without a scratch and the blood added pristine highlights to the bird's wings.

"Clifford, come on! What are you doing?" A woman with her ginger hair done in a hideously messy bun dragged Clifford away from the macabre display.

The office block residents sat in the hall while a man in a sharp tuxedo stepped in front of the crowd. "Alright, everyone, calm down!" he shouted. "I'll go call maintenance and the police to get everything under control. As for all of you, take the rest of the day off. Just stay safe on your way home."

Clifford nearly bit off his tongue to keep from rolling his eyes. Good old general manager Russell, the one who had to put himself in the center of every situation and make himself seem all high and mighty. Clifford began to wonder just how high and mighty he'd remain if faced with a true life-or-death situation. Inside, Clifford let himself smile. That prick would get what he deserved. It just wouldn't be him delivering the karma. A bit too risky for his taste.

Clifford joined the herd of ants checking out of the office. He could almost laugh at how shaken and panicked everyone looked rushing out of the building. It just seemed ridiculous to get so wound up over one dead bird. He ventured to the parking lot, not bothering to look at any of his co-workers. None of them deserved one second more of his attention than necessary.

Once he stepped inside his car, his frozen heart began to furiously pump adrenaline throughout his body. Sure, he was ridiculously ahead of schedule now, but that just meant more free time when he was done. Clifford pulled away from the drudgery of his day job, trying hard not to pump the gas in anticipation of dabbling in his true passion.

He weaved through the highways and down the hills, avoiding the morons that didn't know how to drive and racing against the monsoon. Eventually, he pulled over to the side of a lonely woodland area. He snapped open his glove compartment and took out a pair of leather gloves and a black mask with white eyeholes.

Clifford reached under his seat and swapped his work clothes for a black sweatshirt, skin-tight jacket, two layers of dark jeans, and a pair of thick hiking boots. He looked around for any signs of cameras, only stepping out from the passenger's side when he was certain no one was watching him. Clifford crept around his car and popped open the trunk. Inside was a bright red cooler. He popped it open and yanked from a pool of ice cubes a large shiv made of thick, sharp ice. He closed the trunk and disappeared into the trees.

A cloud of mist escaped his lips, and the rain stuck his knife to his glove like glue. Clifford peered through the treeline to get a view of the road, which he followed until he returned to the city block. He melted into the brush and watched the ants trudge through the puddles. Many faces passed by, though their eyes darted anxiously around the block. They were on guard; they knew the God of Death could reach out from the darkness and snuff out their lives at any given moment.

Good. A hunt was always more exhilarating when there was a bit of a challenge. It made securing the quarry even more satisfying. His sharp eyes caught a dull blue SUV pull over toward the woodland, further down the dirt road Clifford had come from. Perfect. Someone had pulled away from the protection of the herd. He bolted through the trees, stopping a few feet before the side of the car. The hazard lights flashed to life and a wiry man with thick-rimmed glasses and a dirty blonde rat's nest for hair stepped outside. The man popped open the hood, only to be greeted by a waft of thick smoke. Poor fool, so oblivious to the fact that car troubles would become the least of his problems.

Clifford made his move, using the smoke as a cover, and slammed the hood onto the man. The man wasn't allowed time to scream. His panicked muffling barely audible over the sputtering of the car's engine and the thick metal shield smothering the upper side of his twig-like body.

Clifford laid his entire body onto the hood; a bolt of energy struck his body at the sound of snapping bones and squirting sinew. Dark red liquid began to spill from under the hood. Clifford knew he had to be quick before the cops arrived at the scene.

The police force might have been filled with brain-dead

morons, but they weren't completely ignorant.

Clifford slid off the hood and let it rise back up. He then raised his knife and swung at the blood-covered man's head. The man raised his arms, blocking the icy shiv and snapping the knife in half. Clifford growled before striking the man's face with the blunt side of the block of ice. The man flopped onto the ground like a ragdoll. Clifford's vision was crowded in red, and he drove the ice knife into the man's head like driving a peg into the ground to keep a tent in place.

"Sorry pal, there's always a bigger fish," the killer growled. Clifford saw that the car's door was still open. He dipped his gloved fingers into the spurting pool of blood forming on the man's head and rushed into the car. On the dashboard, Clifford wrote his message, adding a morbidly beautiful mural of a bloody bird rising above a canopy of trees.

"Hail to the God of Death," was displayed in all its glory inside the car.

Clifford sprinted away from the scene, taking a few odd paths in the woods until he returned to his car. He took off his bloodstained clothes and stuffed them into a bundle. He jumped into his car and stuffed them under his seat. Clifford then peeled back onto the road and whipped around to the path that would lead him back to his apartment.

"Woo! That's what I'm talking about!" Clifford shouted. Serotonin added a cool dose of energized fluids into his veins, keeping him at an elevated level of elation. Soon people would crowd around that unlucky fool's car, mourn the loss of another life to the dreaded God of Death.

The addition of the bird would drive people crazy; they would ask themselves what that meant. Just what was this mysterious killer trying to imply?

Only Clifford would know the answer to that question,

just adding a little extra flair that the man clearly lacked in life. He could barely make out the signs as he zoomed by. This might have been his most exquisite work yet. A true work of post-mortem art. However, his joy was quickly drained out of his system when the pattering of rain was joined by the shrill ringing of police sirens.

"Oh, great," Clifford groaned. He slowed his car down and pulled over to the side of the road. A white police car with flashing blue and red lights slowed down behind him. The car door whipped open and out stepped a woman with her pitch-black hair done in a bun stuffed just below her black hat. Her eyes were surrounded by smoky midnight blue eyeshadow, and she wore a black coat with various police patches decorating her chest and sleeves. Before he could roll down the window, he could hear the woman whistle to herself. Strangely, the tune seemed familiar, but Clifford couldn't quite put his finger on where he had heard it before. The woman stopped by his door and laid her arm over the top of the car.

Clifford put on his best boardroom smile and rolled down the window. "Good day, ma'am. How can I help you?"

"No need to get all formal." Her voice was thick with a Southern twang and seemed quite naturally relaxed. The woman flashed him a half-smile before pointing a finger with a sharp nail down the road. "Were you aware that you were going eighty kilometres in a seventy zone?"

Clifford's heart stopped; he knew he had to be careful after leaving one of his displays. And yet, he had been so stupid. He couldn't let himself be caught over a stupid speed limit. "No, ma'am." he replied.

The woman shook her head. "You know, even if it's only ten kilometres over, if someone were to step in front of you, they'd be a goner in an instant," the woman said, her voice deep but still light in tone.

Clifford fought the urge to roll his eyes. If anyone was dumb enough to pull up in front of him, it was their own fault, as far as he was concerned. Of course, she didn't need to know that, lest he talk himself into a reservation in a jail block.

"Oh, I am so sorry, ma'am," Clifford said in his most syrupy sweet voice, "I just wasn't paying attention. I didn't mean any harm. But I guess I still have to pay the piper."

The officer nodded, taking out her notebook. "Everybody does," she muttered, flipping the cover of her notebook, briefly showcasing the galloping pale horse on display. She took out her pen and began to jot down on the paper. "It's kind of sad how many people believe they are above the repercussions of their actions. They either don't understand or they don't care about the fact that every action they make changes the direction of the wheel of fate."

Clifford nodded along with the officer, pretending to soak in what she was preaching. As far as he was concerned, he was living his life just fine and that wasn't going to change just because some little girl with a badge told him to.

The officer raised an eyebrow. "But you're not one of those folks, are you?"

Clifford shook his head with a grin and briefly released his grip on the wheel. "Nope, I just do what I got to do to get by."

The officer nodded, peering at her notebook with disinterest. She then tore the slip of paper out and reached her arm through the window to Clifford with the ticket in hand. Before Clifford could grab the paper, the woman looked down and her nose crinkled like a bag of chips.

"Did you spill something in your car?"

Clifford felt ready to faint; he could hardly breathe. Could she smell his clothes? Did blood really have that strong of a scent and he had just become desensitized to it over time? No matter the reason for her questioning, Clifford tried to maintain a casually calm demeanour.

"Not today. Maybe I spilled some coffee in here a few days ago and forgot to clean it." Clifford's foot was twitching against the gas pedal and his hand was eager to shove the car out of park and into drive. He needed to peel out of the area before this woman started asking more questions. But of course, trying to run from the police was a suicide mission and he knew it. So, Clifford sat still, hoping his answer had satisfied the officer enough to leave him alone.

The officer pursed her lips together and slipped her notebook into her back pocket. She took a step back and placed her hands on her hips. "Sir, I'm going to need you to step out of the car." Her voice was sharp and had lost most of its laid-back gravel.

Clifford's heart felt ready to explode. He was backed into a corner; there was no way he could explain the bloodstained clothes under his seat. Still, Clifford nodded. "Uh, yeah. Yeah, sure. I could do that," he said, tightly gripping the gear shift.

The officer dove her head inside the car and grabbed his arm. "Don't even think about it," the officer growled, her eyes narrowed. "I know you think I'm an idiot, but I wouldn't go about testing that theory."

Clifford's eyes widened and his hand squirmed in the officer's frost-bitten grip. "What are you doing?" he yelled.

The officer casually placed her free hand inside her other back pocket and a small smirk crawled onto her pale face. "I'll bet you thought Ben Joyce was an idiot, too," she said.

Clifford heard the officer scratch against something bumpy and metal with her free hand. He had never caught an episode of *CSI* but he knew she was growing eager about unholstering her gun.

He shook his head at her. "Look, I have no idea who you're talking about."

The officer snickered. "You know Ben. Was studying at Vancouver Community College and graduated high school on the honour roll a few months before his mom died of leukemia. He was getting himself into electrical engineering and apparently was doing pretty well." As the officer stopped her diatribe, the picking at her gun became harder and faster. Her smirk dropped and she narrowed her eyes once again. "Just a shame that he died so young, isn't it?" she asked. "And all he wanted was someone to give his car a little jump."

Clifford's mouth went dry and his arm became numb in the officer's iron grip. "Why are you telling me this?" he asked, hoping the panic in his voice would aid in his act of playing dumb.

The officer chuckled to herself. "I think we both know why I'm regaling you with this life story cut short," she whispered. Her picking stopped and she reeled her free arm back.

Clifford's body took over, crossing his free arm across his body to shove the car back into drive. He slammed his foot down on the gas, causing the woman's grip to be torn away. His car spit out a storm of gravel and mud in its wake. Clifford planted one hand on the wheel and the hand that was previously stuck in the officer's grasp hung uselessly on the gear shifter.

The outlaw wasn't given much time to process his encounter before gunshots started ringing out around him. Holes pierced through his windshield and the fabric surrounding his door. Clifford looked back to see the rear windshield so cracked and distorted it looked more like modern art.

The police cruiser was peeling behind him with lights flashing viciously. The officer leaned out of her window, almost looking relaxed, if not for the tight grip on her pistol.

Clifford looked back to the front windshield and slammed his head against the headrest. "Goddamn, was she a part of Indie 500 before joining the force?"

In front of him was more mud and gravel down a long, winding road sandwiched between two treelines. Three more shots rattled the car, nearly taking out his driver's side mirror and adding more holes in the windshield.

Clifford turned his head to the side of the road and jerked his wheel to the same side.

*This is a stupid idea, but screw it, we're going anyway.*

Clifford gritted his teeth, bumping his head against the ceiling as his car tossed him around inside. The car rocked around as it was pulled across rocks and dunes. The side mirrors were blasted into clouds of glass, plastic, and metal after being smashed against a couple of trees. Suddenly, the hood of the car smashed into the trunk of a bare, thick tree. Clifford found himself flying through the windshield in a shower of glass before his head slammed against something hard. That was the last sensation he felt before his vision went black.

After what seemed like hours swimming in nothing, Clifford woke up to the side of his skull seeming like it was set ablaze, and his hair was soaking wet with a thick, warm liquid. He reached his arms out and dug his hands into the cold, muddy grass. Clifford yanked himself up, disgusted at the muddy rags his nice suit had become. He stumbled down the valley, his head feeling like it was pumped full of hot air and his limbs seemed like they were underwater. A sharp ringing filled his ears, blocking out even the sound of the hard-hitting rain.

"How am I going to explain this?" Clifford muttered. "'Hey, Clifford, why do your clothes look like they've been yanked through a bloody woodchipper?' Oh, you know, nothing major, was just minding my own business when some insane police lady ran me off the road after shooting up my car."

He tried to laugh himself silly, but his cackling instead sounded like the pained cries of an animal. Word wouldn't take long to spread; Clifford knew that even if he managed to get himself home, his life was over. Even if he sold everything he owned, he couldn't buy the lunatic officer's silence. He had no real alibi, and no one was close enough to be willing to act as a character witness.

"Maybe if I get my stuff together, I can make a break for the states," Clifford said, his mind wandering so fast his mouth could hardly keep up. "Yeah, could pay some guy to get me some new I.D. and I could find some under-the-radar place to set up shop. Or at least buy enough time to book it to Mexico. Always hated this weather, anyway. Could use a little Latin sunshine in my life."

As Clifford wrapped his aching arms around his shaking body, he saw a light red shower trickle down from his head to his clothes. He shut his jaw tightly to silence the chattering of his teeth as a cold wind whipped against the back of his neck.

"Hello? Is someone there?" a crackling, weak voice called out.

Clifford turned his head and saw a ragged old woman huddled in the brush. She was using a slab of soggy cardboard as an umbrella and was cloaked with an old, patchy parka.

Clifford tried to march past and ignore the woman, but she persisted.

"Sir, did something happen to you?" she asked, reaching out a soft, wrinkled hand that shivered against the downpour.

Clifford felt his face ignite with righteous fury, marching across the hills toward the woman, nearly losing his shoes in the mud on the way there. "Why yes, something did happen to me," he snapped. "I was out going to work, actually contributing to society, which is more than I can say about you. Then my car was destroyed by someone with so many screws loose I'm surprised her limbs are all still attached. That car cost more than everything you own combined, and she just shot it up until it had more holes than your jacket."

The old woman's eyes widened, and she gave a sympathetic frown. "Oh goodness, that sounds awful. Well, is there anything I can do to help you, sir?" The old woman reached a soft hand out to softly take Clifford's arm.

He jerked his nose up and ripped his arm away from the old lady. "Yeah, you can get yourself a job instead of hustling the people who actually work for their earnings instead of feeling sorry for themselves, you old crone!" Clifford yelled. The woman shrunk back, quivering under the irate man.

Clifford began to march away but the woman called out, "Better an old crone than a needy child that needs to destroy other's lives to get the attention he doesn't deserve!"

Clifford ignored the chill seeping past the gaps in his spine and whipped around. "I'm sorry, what did you say?" After completing his swivel, Clifford was thrown into another tree. The old woman had grabbed him by the throat. Her eyes began to glow a deep white.

"What, are you having trouble hearing me?" the woman whispered. As she began to cackle, the tree and the ground began to rumble around Clifford.

The crone's cold fingers dug into his neck, slowly closing around his esophagus in a vice grip. Clifford struggled to pull up his arm, but once he did, he curled his hand into a fist and struck the hag in the face. The woman dropped Clifford onto the ground and reeled back from the strike.

Clifford grabbed the bark of the tree to pull himself up. He didn't wait for his throat to recover before he started running into the woods.

The old woman's shrill cackling danced through the piercing wind. "You'd make it much easier for yourself if you just gave up!"

Clifford didn't bother to look back as he ran. His heart pumped enough blood to make a regular man's lungs explode but he still kept going. Past the drenched thickets and out of the mudholes forming in the ground. He felt twigs and branches slapping him across the face, leaving burning scratch marks all over his mug. Though the cold sting numbed his face, he still steeled himself and kept running.

After what felt like hours of sprinting through the woods, Clifford felt as if his lungs were being squeezed like a lemon being juiced. He hacked up a glob of spit and flopped behind a thick tree, hugging tightly to the bark. He began to bang his head against the trunk.

"You're just dreaming. None of this is real. Wake up, you idiot!" he hissed to himself.

"What isn't real?"

Clifford raised his head in shock at the sound of the officer's voice. Though she sounded like she was talking directly in his ear, she was nowhere to be seen.

"Is this not real?" After the voice asked the question, a shot rang out, showering Clifford with moist splinters.

He screamed, tumbling back to see a hole burrowed in the tree, just a few inches above where his head was resting. Clifford looked around and saw a thick branch sticking out of a pile of leaves and mud. He yanked the branch out, sending heavy clumps of dirt flying. He swung the branch around like a madman with a baseball bat.

"Where are you, huh? Come out!" Clifford hollered. "If you're really so tough then why don't you put that gun down and face me?" His hair stood on end; he could hear leaves being crushed underfoot behind him. He smirked and whispered to himself, "Gotcha."

Clifford whipped around and swung the branch in the direction of the intruder. However, he didn't strike the head of the officer but that of an unfamiliar man in a yellow raincoat and black rubber boots. The man screamed as he was knocked onto the ground. Clifford felt his equilibrium scramble. He struggled to keep from shifting from side to side as a cold splash of embarrassment washed over him.

"Jesus Christ," the man muttered, cradling the side of his head. "What the hell's wrong with you?"

Clifford couldn't help but throw his head back and laugh. "What's wrong with me? What's wrong with you? You're the Einstein who thought it'd be a great idea to sneak up on someone when there's a crazy lady shooting her gun all over the damn place!"

The man pushed himself up, struggling in vain to keep the blood from trickling down his face. He squinted his eyes at Clifford in confusion. "But I haven't heard any gunshots."

Clifford's eyes widened in mad disbelief. "Wha— huh? You didn't hear the gunshots? How? Are you deaf or something?"

The man narrowed his eyes. "Are *you* drunk or on something? If there was someone shooting up these woods, I'm pretty sure someone in Kelowna would've heard those shots." The man then reached his bloodstained hand out and grabbed onto Clifford's branch. Clifford struggled to maintain his grip. His hand began to slip on the soggy bark and the rainwater.

"Son, put that thing down before anyone else gets hurt," the man chided behind gritted teeth.

Clifford tried to keep his hold on his last weapon, but the weariness in his bones and the fire screaming in his muscles meant his grasp on the branch was precarious. Eventually, the man in the raincoat ripped the branch out of Clifford's hand and tossed it into a ditch.

"Right. We're getting you out of these woods before you drive yourself further down into the looney bin." The man then grabbed Clifford's arm and began to drag him down the muddy path as if he were taking away an unruly child.

"Hey, she shot at a tree I was resting at!" Clifford shouted. "If you don't believe me, why don't you go check out the hole she left?" Despite his protests, Clifford was ignored by the raincoat-clad man and continued to let himself be dragged away. Clifford glanced over his shoulder; his heart sank as he saw in the shadows the figure of the officer. He could barely make out the officer waving him goodbye before the raincoat man dragged him down another hill.

When the pair of men broke through the trees and returned to the road, it was as if Clifford was bathing in new, fresh air. He had managed to escape his coniferous prison and was so close to returning to proper society.

The raincoat man pointed toward a logging truck sitting by the side of the road. "Look, I'm not sure what you're on but like hell am I going to leave someone wandering alone when the so-called God of Death is still on the loose." The man dragged Clifford to the truck and opened the passenger door. He hoisted Clifford up, inviting a waft of old wood and sap to intrude Clifford's olfactory senses.

Still, Clifford figured it would be better than having to walk all the way back to his apartment. He buckled his seatbelt, taking a moment to mourn his now ruined suit. The man in the raincoat pulled himself into the driver's seat. The truck sputtered and rumbled as the raincoat man started the behemoth of a vehicle up.

"Alright, where do you live, son?"

Clifford looked down at his dulled dress shoes and sighed.

"The apartment block on Catrina Road," he replied.

The raincoat man nodded with a slight smile. "Fancy," he said, turning the wheel so the truck would get back on the bumpy gravel road. The driver shook his head, switching on the windshield wipers. "I swear, Mother Nature just has it out for us."

Clifford nodded, though he didn't feel like he was completely attached to Earth at that moment. He felt like he was staring into space or another dimension. All Clifford cared about was getting home and drinking himself into a day-forgetting stupor. For several minutes, the ride remained silent except for the sound of splattering rain.

Then, the driver finally broke the silence. "So, what do you think this killer really wants?" he asked, "Like, why do you think he does what he does?"

Clifford snapped his head toward the driver and a jolt of shocking electricity zapped through his chest. Clifford tried to remain casual and just shrugged. "Who knows? Fame, maybe?"

The driver sighed. "Hell of a way to make a name for yourself." The raincoat man muttered, "There are lots of ways to carve out your legacy without having to ruin other people's lives. We've got stuff like YouTube and other websites to promote yourself. If you want to make a jackass of yourself, don't go dragging others down with you."

Clifford was biting down on his tongue so hard he could taste blood. If that chase in the woods hadn't left him so banged up, Clifford would have been tempted to grab the driver by the throat and squeeze the breath out of him. Then he'd see who the real jackass really was.

"Do you think he'll get caught?" Clifford asked.

The driver nodded. "Oh, yeah. He's going to get his eventually. Or hers. You can only run for so long until karma catches up to you."

Clifford chuckled, causing the driver to chuckle alongside him. The driver must have been laughing because he thought Clifford agreed with him. But Clifford wasn't laughing with him; he was laughing at his sentimentality. The world is a cruel place and the only way to survive is to be both the strongest and smartest in the room. If that meant having to crack a few skulls, so be it.

Finally, the truck pulled up back into the city. But when it stopped at an overcrowded traffic light, Clifford noticed a strange bird perched on top of the poles holding the traffic lights. A rather plump bird with a red face and milk-white beak. Its feathers were black as night with white and grey tips. A pressure formed on top of Clifford's head as he looked into its crimson eyes.

The driver whistled to himself. "Huh, we got ourselves a turkey vulture. Weird. You'd think it would have flown off to someplace warmer than this." While the raincoat man laughed to himself, Clifford felt his stomach twist into knots. The vulture continued to stare at him, even turning around once the truck drove past the traffic light. The driver playfully nudged Clifford. "Don't worry, it won't eat you until after you're dead." He chortled.

Clifford nodded dumbly, not at all assured by his driver's jovial attitude. His nerves remained tense, even when the truck pulled up to his apartment block.

"So, am I supposed to check my ride in somewhere or anything like that?" the raincoat man asked.

Clifford looked down the driveway leading to the other apartments and shook his head. "No, I should be able to find my place on my own."

The driver shrugged. "Welp, in that case, remember what the news has been saying. Lock your doors and don't open them for anyone you don't know."

Clifford nodded and quietly stepped out of the truck. He wrapped his arms around himself and bowed his head. The cold raindrops dug into his skin and red-hot tears began to pour down his face. His body began to shiver, but he wasn't sure if it was from the cold or if the day had just ticked him off that badly.

*Of course, I can't kick my feet off and relax,* Clifford thought in frustration. *People are going to come looking for me. I need to get some bags packed, then I'll figure out what to do about the car situation.*

Clifford trudged up the stairs to his apartment and struggled to pull his keys out of his pocket. When he looked up, he saw a trio of black roses lodged between his door and the doorway. He growled, kicking the flowers until they were clumps of smashed petals on the ground. He managed to pull out his keys and twisted them into the lock. As soon as he heard the metal click, he slammed the door open and threw himself inside.

His heart sank, seeing the walls of his living room decorated with the articles he kept inside his bedroom. Painted on the newspapers was every passage he had written for his victims. Clifford wandered around the room, quickly feeling like a stranger in his own home. He developed a sinking feeling about who may have broken into his apartment.

Clifford bolted for the kitchen area, nearly ripping out the utensil drawer in his quest for a knife. He pulled out a sharp steak knife and crept down the hall toward his bedroom door. Reaching the door, he gently pushed it open with his foot and stepped inside. The walls were decorated with photos of smiling strangers. He stepped forward and brushed his thumb against a picture of a blonde woman.

Only when he pressed his thumb against her jaw did it click for him just who she was; the woman he had been admiring that morning, the one found at the coffee shop. He turned his head and stared at the rest of the walls' photos. These weren't strangers; these were the victims he had turned into macabre works of art.

"Interesting collection you have there."

Clifford jumped, whipping around to see the officer casually lying on his bed. He thrust his knife forward and gave her a sharp glare. "How did you get in here?" he asked.

The officer laughed and sat up. "I have my ways," she said, pulling out her gun and twirling it around on the bed. "Still, I'm surprised that it took you so long to recognize them… God of Death." The woman smirked, freezing Clifford in place.

There was no use denying his secret. She must have been the one to move the articles around and she had found a photo of each of his victims. The officer got off the bed, indulging in the shock that had paralyzed the man in front of her. "Of course, I never forgot about them. After all, I was there when you took their lives and made a mockery of their deaths." The woman tightened her grip on her gun and her voice dropped a few octaves.

Clifford shook his head. "What are you talking about? I never saw you before in my life." Clifford sputtered, swinging his knife around madly, "Are you some sort of stalker?" His rambling was cut short when a gunshot rang out. Clifford felt himself slam into the wall and his shoulder shrieked as the smell of smoke polluted his nose. The officer pointed her gun in his direction with an icy glare.

"Are you really that thick?" she snarled. "The only reason you never saw me is because I saw no need for you to. Until now, anyway." The woman kneeled and stared into Clifford's panicked eyes. She poked at his gunshot wound with the muzzle of her pistol, causing bolts of fire to flow through his body.

"That feeling of helplessness, knowing that no one is coming to save your worthless life. Have you ever felt that before?" she teased. "Of course you haven't, but that's what you inflicted on your victims."

The officer laughed. "You know, I think I'll cross 'strike a god with fear' off my bucket list."

Clifford roared, jamming his knife into the officer's eye.

The woman paused for a moment before shooting him an unimpressed glare and raising her gun back up.

Clifford, with a lump in his throat and his stomach becoming a cold abyss, bolted out of his room and pulled himself into the bathroom. He frantically locked the door and ran to the sink. He shook his head and planted his sweat-covered face in his shaking hands. "Who is that woman? Is she even human? Is this even real?"

"You tell me; you're the God of Death, after all."

Clifford looked up and saw her leaning against the bathroom door, the knife still lodged in her eye. Clifford gasped, tripping over his toilet and collapsing into his bathtub. Pushing himself onto his knees, he saw the woman easily pull out the knife. Her eye was still intact, without even so much as a scratch. Clifford caught something in the mirror in the corner of his eye. Instead of the officer's reflection, he saw a figure clad in a black cloak and arms made of bones.

Goosebumps covered Clifford's entire body and his heart thumped a million kilometres a second. "No," was all Clifford could weakly muster.

The woman laughed, tossing the knife into the sink. "Now it's starting to click, isn't it?" The gun stretched and bent in her hand like it was made of putty. When the morphing and twisting stopped, taking the pistol's place in the woman's hand was a towering scythe with the blade a few inches above her head.

"You know, I like to take pride in my work. Helping to bring souls to where they need to go, when they need to go, it's an honest millennia's work." Her eyes turned a deep red and she looked down at him. "So, you can imagine, I don't much care for people taking my name and dragging it through the mud. Like say, some spoiled child with such little disregard for the beauty of life."

Clifford tried to open his mouth to protest but the part of his mind responsible for his smooth talking was clogged with overwhelming panic and his mouth became locked in place. Before he knew it, a searing pain spread from his stomach to the rest of his body.

Clifford found himself hoisted into the air. His feet kicked against the edges of the tub. He looked down to see that the woman's scythe had been driven through his body. He felt the cold tip of the blade brush against the back of his head. Clifford felt his senseless body slide down the scythe until he was face-to-face with the woman.

A sinister grin crossed her face. "Sorry, pal, there's always a bigger fish." The woman pulled her scythe back, dragging the blade out of Clifford's body.

A sharp pain peeled down Clifford between his shoulder blades and out of his groin. He collapsed onto the ground, unable to scream even as he saw the other half of his body squirting blood onto the tiles of his bathroom floor. He felt himself unable to speak or even squirm as pangs of agony beat against his body. Tears filled his eyes and spilled down his cheeks, stinging his skin like acid as the hours passed.

The pain only ended when the woman kneeled next to him and gingerly placed her hand on his forehead.

# The Augury Doll

Marcy and the man continued to stare into the photo printed on the newspaper, the picture started to clear up and look more like a bathroom. The man grinned, soaking in the morose expression on Marcy's face.

"So, in addition to not caring for being cheated, it would seem Death isn't too fond of having their name dragged in the mud by those far below them." He leaned uncomfortably close to Marcy's face, allowing her to smell the earthy stench of coffee coming from his breath. "Well, little Marcy, if there's anything you need to get off your chest, it'd be best to do so now before it's too late for you."

Marcy's windpipe felt like it was being crushed under the weight of the man's poisonous stare.

Luckily, a woman in a ruby dress with a pattern identical to the one on the man's tie grabbed his shoulder with a sharply manicured hand. "Carmine, that's enough," she chided.

The man, Carmine, narrowed his gaze at the other woman,

a scowl darkening his pale face. He carefully plucked the hand off his shoulder and retained his slimy grin as he turned back to Marcy. He gave a slight bow. "Maybe another time, when my dear sister has no need of me." He then followed the woman out of the hallway, once again leaving Marcy alone.

She finally allowed herself to breathe before rushing into the bathroom and closing the door behind her. "Charming guy," she muttered. Marcy plopped down on the toilet seat and took out her phone. She opened her text messaging history and made her way over to Aiden. She sighed as she read her brother's string of messages.

*Hello? Are you in?*
*Did Azura bring up the family treasure yet?*
*Hello?*
*???*

Marcy sunk her head into the palm of her hand before pushing back the boiling bile bubbling in her stomach. With a dry mouth, she finally typed her response. *Don't know about the treasure yet. Give me some time. Butler at the front door. Don't get caught.*

Marcy waited as three dots appeared at the bottom of her chat, expanding and contracting like her heartbeat. When the dots disappeared, the next message read, *Thanks for the heads-up. But hurry up already.*

Marcy rolled her eyes before stuffing her phone back into her pocket and turning on the sink. She let the water run for a minute before turning it back off and leaving the bathroom. Marcy wandered aimlessly through the hall, not paying attention to the turns she made until she realized she was stuck in a deep red labyrinth with walls lined with old-fashioned photos entrapped in golden frames. She spun herself around as the halls seemed to close in on her.

"Where even is this part of the house?" Marcy asked herself. As she felt her lungs begin to collapse, Marcy jumped out of her skin when a hand grabbed her shoulder. She yelped as she raised a fist and whipped around. A woman with blonde hair bound in a pigtail and an arm covered with beautifully tied bandanas raised her hands in defence, nearly flinging the tablet she held into the ceiling.

Marcy's heartbeat calmed. "So sorry!" she said to the newcomer.

The bandana-clad woman smiled and tapped against her tablet. When she finished tapping away, a robotic voice from the tablet said, "It's all good. I've been told I can be kind of quiet."

Marcy took a breath and glanced around the room. "Man, it's easy to get lost in this place."

The woman soundlessly chuckled before typing in her tablet again. "Yeah, I had my issues when first introduced to the family, too." The woman gently guided Marcy down a winding hall with a confident pace but awkward hand placement on her back.

"Um...my name's Marcy. I'm Azura's girlfriend?" Marcy sheepishly introduced herself.

The mute woman stopped in her tracks, her eyes widening in surprise before turning her head back to her tablet. After the woman finished typing, the tablet replied, "Marigold is my name. I'm one of Azura's millions of cousins." The woman smirked as a baffled expression spread across Marcy's face.

"Wow, that big?" she asked in bemusement.

Marigold laughed, the sounds coming out reminding Marcy of the hissing made by air escaping a balloon. "A bit of an exaggeration but yeah, there's a reason we have to gather at a house this size. No other place could fit all of us." Marigold stopped before a large mirror before tugging at the side and pulling it off the wall, revealing a thin passageway lit by a row of bare bulbs screwed into the walls.

"Whoa! Secret passageways, too?" Marcy followed Marigold down the hall in awe. "I'm surprised people aren't getting as lost as I am right now."

Marigold shrugged. "Well, it's like my mom, Aunt Amber to Azura, always says: 'Keep your eyes peeled and your hopes high, even when it feels like there's no way out.'"

*I feel like this is leading to another story,* Marcy thought.

As if on cue, Marigold added, "Eventually, you'll find your escape. After all, no prison is truly inescapable."

\*\*\*

The Rotenbarry Institution said they helped to educate and treat children with special needs, but Andrea and Linda knew the truth.

The so-called educational center was a house of horrors that made life a living hell for the unfortunate residents trapped inside. When someone entered the building, they would be greeted with bright colours and smiling caretakers parading around their charges, wearing grins forcefully glued onto their faces. But once the doors were locked to visitors, the rainbow halls became a minefield of eggshells the kids fearfully tiptoed around, and the cheerful smiles of the caretakers became omens of horrible things to come if one were to step out of line.

Most nights, the other girls in their room learned to keep quiet, keep their "stimming" under the covers so the workers wouldn't see, and keep their eyes shut when the workers came in. While for them this might have been a period of fear, for Andrea and Linda, these were the hours where they were the freest.

Safely huddled under Andrea's covers, she and Linda flipped through the pages of the books Linda had smuggled from the library. Though they didn't read along with the simplistic stories the workers insisted were just right for their age, they looked at the little puppy that insisted all you needed to do to stop bullies was to kill them with kindness.

"Oh yes, pretty please, can you stop calling me a baby, Ms. Carol?" Linda laughed.

Andrea lifted her pyjama pant leg, revealing the black box bound to her blistered leg. "And take off the shock box?" she added.

The two girls quietly giggled to each other. After the hushed giggle-fest had ended, Linda rolled her eyes and closed the book, nearly knocking the flashlight off the bed with her elbow.

"Why do we keep being given baby books?" Linda muttered before digging her fingers into the braids that Ms. Tabitha insisted that she wear. "I'm almost fifteen. Give me something less boring to read." Finally, her fingers tugged the black elastic bands out of her dirty blonde hair and let it flow freely.

Andrea lifted her glasses a few inches from her nose to let the building fog escape. "What would be… less boring?" Andrea struggled to keep her voice quiet, remembering the times she had gotten the shock for talking too loudly in class or getting caught being awake during sleep time.

Linda shrugged. "I don't know, maybe 'To Kill A Mockingbird' or something? Emmett said in his last letter his class was starting a novel study on it. It seems a lot less boring to read than this." She gestured to the garishly pastel book.

Andrea picked the book up and stuffed it down her shirt. "If you don't… want it—"

"Yeah, you can keep it. Just put it somewhere the teachers won't find it before we get up for breakfast."

Andrea's face crinkled up like a wrapper from a muffin. She knew she was a slow talker but that didn't mean Linda had to interrupt like that. After all, it wasn't Linda's fault the words on her mind took a longer time to reach her mouth than they did for others. Still, she managed to summon a smile. Friends were a good gift to have in a place like this and she wouldn't throw it away over some communication flub.

Linda's eyes suddenly widened. "There's something else I think you'd like." She reached under her bed and pulled out a doll with yellow yarn for hair, blue eyes that matched Linda's own, milky fabric for skin, and a blue dress dotted with sea-green flowers with glittery accents.

Linda held the doll toward Andrea. "My parents gave this to me for my birthday," Linda said. "Too bad for them, I haven't been into dolls since they dropped me into this dump."

Andrea gazed at the doll, lost in its beautiful eyes. Still, before she made a grab, she had to make sure. "Do you... want me... to have it?" Andrea asked her friend.

Linda gave a nod and gently placed the doll in Andrea's hands. Linda twisted her hands around and quietly chuckled, the bruises on her arms adding blots of darkness inside the light of the flashlight. Andrea's blood grew cold as she heard the clicking of heels echoing down the hall.

Linda's eyes grew wide, and she shoved Andrea out of her bed. "Quick, Andy, get back to bed!" Linda hissed.

Andrea stumbled back under the covers on her bed and slammed her head into the pillow. Andrea felt the coils of the mattress dig into her body, she closed her eyes and shivered as she heard the creaking of the residency door.

The raw soreness lingering on the back of her neck was a potent reminder for Andrea of the consequences if she was caught. Beads of sweat spilled as memories of being alone in the Buzz Helmet flooded through her mind. Her heart was pounding so loudly in her ears that she almost missed the sound of the screeching door being slamming shut.

The panic waned as she heard Linda mutter to herself in

the bed beside hers, "Yeah, 'Sorry that we can't handle your disability and dumping you in this hellhole. Will a doll make you feel better?'"

Andrea heard Linda's bedsheet shuffle as her friend tossed and turned in bed. Andrea struggled to drift off into sleep, thinking back to the last words her parents had said before dropping her off: "These people are here to help you in ways we can't. Trust in their methods and they'll help you get better."

The words bounced around Andrea's head as she contemplated the question she wished she had asked her parents before they left: "Better from what? Is something wrong with me?"

Morning rolled around and the grinding screaming of the bell burrowed its way into Andrea's ears. As much as she wanted to bang her head and drown out the noise, Andrea knew if the workers strolled by when she did so then she would just be asking for a treatment from the shock box. The other students shambled out of bed and flooded out the door like a pack of zombies. Before she could join the hoard, Andrea saw she was still clutching Linda's ragdoll. A boiling sensation in her gut stopped her in her tracks. Her eyes wandered back over to her bed before she patted the yarn strands that made up the doll's hair.

*I can't let them find this doll.* Andrea wasn't sure where the thought had come from, but it was enough to guide her to the bed and make her stuff the doll under her mattress. Afterwards, she hurried to join the rest of the students as they lumbered down the hall. The pastels and rainbow colours that plastered the walls and doorframes were as irritable to Andrea's eyes as looking at the sun. However, she couldn't take off her glasses to rub her eyes, not with Ms. Carol looming over her, with her icy blue eyes staring daggers down at the girl. Instead, Andrea tried to push her unease further down and continued following the line of students to the first classroom.

As soon as Andrea stepped inside the garishly bright yellow classroom, she was ambushed by a waft of freezing air. She immediately wrapped her arms around her body and rubbed all over her skin to warm herself up.

She stopped when Ms. Carol dug her manicured fingers into her shoulder. Andrea gazed up at the auburn-haired teacher's soulless smile and empty eyes, pretending to be warm.

"Keep your hands to your sides, young lady."

Andrea wanted to protest that she needed to keep herself warm. However, she knew the consequences of talking back to a teacher, a lesson she had first taken to heart two years ago. So, Andrea reluctantly dropped her hands to her sides.

"That's a good girl." Ms. Carol beamed before gently pushing Andrea toward her desk.

She slid into the plastic blue chair, grimacing as she heard it creak and bend underneath her. The girl looked over at the times table taped to her desk and reached out to pick at one of the corners. Suddenly, her body surged with a sensation like she was being stung by a swarm of bees. Andrea jerked her arm back and turned her head to see Ms. Carol pocketing a black box with a large red button. Andrea turned her head back to the front and sighed.

*Right, no picking,* she thought begrudgingly. Andrea sat still and fought the urge to continue picking at the tape, biting down on her tongue to focus more on the pain than the temptation. The nagging thoughts didn't quiet down, even when Ms. Tabitha walked inside and made her way to her desk at the front of the classroom.

A cold smile formed on the teacher's face as she caressed her doctor's certificate, displayed proudly in a gold frame on the wall. She then clasped her hands together as she tried to fake enthusiasm for her students. "Good morning, class!" she announced, her dusty brown hairdo nearly knocking out one of the hanging lights.

"Good morning, Ms. Tabitha!" the class replied in monotonous unison.

Before the teacher could continue her morning spiel, her head cranked toward the right side of the class. Her eyes narrowed and contrasting her empty smile, Andrea found a spark of emotion in her glare. And that emotion was rage.

"Linda, please take off your coat."

Andrea's heart sank as she turned to look over at her friend, clad in a bright red jacket.

Linda looked up from her desk and shook her head. "No, it's too cold," she retorted.

Ms. Tabitha loomed closer, slithering through the rows of desks. The other students watched the teacher with weary eyes and a curtain of dread fell upon the room. "It's a simple request, Ms. Aswald." Ms. Tabitha's words were forced out with the velocity of shotgun shells.

Linda remained undaunted and leaned forward in her seat with fiery eyes. "No, it's freaking cold in here," the girl retorted. "I'm freezing!"

Ms. Tabitha stopped before Linda's desk and slammed her wrinkled hands onto the table. "You will do as you're told, young lady," the teacher growled.

Linda shook her head. "No, it's fucking cold in here!"

Ms. Tabitha took out a black box and jabbed her thumb into the red button. A loud buzz erupted, and Linda was sent flying onto the ground. Her screams filled the room, so loud Andrea thought she would shatter the windows. Andrea sat with her jaw dropped as Linda flailed about on the ground.

"Stop screaming," Ms. Tabitha spat before pressing the button again.

Andrea watched Linda panic and flail on the ground like a fish struggling for air while screaming bloody murder.

"Knock it off," Ms. Tabitha snarled.

Andrea looked up at the teacher. The older woman's gaze was ice-cold. Ms. Carol ran over to the scene and pressed her knees into Linda's back. The auburn-haired teacher grabbed the student's wrists and shoved them onto the ground.

"Get off me!" Linda turned to look at Andrea's side of the classroom. Her face was covered in tears, and blood smudged the underneath of her nose and her mouth.

The sight was too much for Andrea to bear and she pushed herself out of her seat.

Ms. Carol scowled at Andrea, freezing the girl in her tracks. "Stay back!" the teacher's aide barked; her orders barely audible over Linda's screams.

"You're hurting her!" Andrea protested. Before she could take another step, she was brought to the ground as an electrical surge coursed through her body, rendering her bones useless and her body numb. She could barely move her head; her eyes were fixated on the scene of her panicked friend.

She saw Ms. Tabitha's hand grab the back of Linda's head, forcing the girl's face into the ground. Her muffled screams continued as she struggled against the grip of her teachers. Andrea heard the door swing into the wall before she felt herself being picked up and carried out of the classroom. The last thing she saw before her vision went dark was Linda continuing to struggle under the weight of her teachers.

When Andrea opened her eyes, they were immediately assaulted by a blinding white light. She rolled over to her side and immediately shut her eyes. Her rest was short-lived as she felt her shoulder being shaken.

"Wake up, Andrea," Ms. Carol's voice cooed. Andrea felt

her body being jostled about across the polished floor, to the point that her glasses were flung off her face and she heard them clatter against the ground. Her eyes peeked open, and streams of water poured down her face as the glare of white pierced her retinas or corneas or whatever Linda had said they were called.

Andrea rolled over to her side and saw Ms. Carol with a bright white lab coat, white slacks, and white dress shoes. The young girl felt her insides recoil at her teacher's empty grin, but still, Andrea strained her eyes to stare at Ms. Carol.

"Now Andrea, we're going to need you to stay here for a little bit while we calm things down outside, alright?" Ms. Carol slid a white bowl of plain rice toward Andrea, not breaking eye contact.

Andrea felt her chest tighten as she thought back to her last memory before ending up in the blinding white room. "Wh-where's… Linda?" she asked.

The sides of Ms. Carol's mouth twitched, as if threatening to break from the weight of her forced smile. The teacher shook her head and forced a laugh. "She's quite fine. Linda will just need some time alone before we can find more…appropriate conditions for her."

Andrea's insides felt like they were boiling, the images of Linda's face shoved into the ground imprinting further onto her mind. And Ms. Carol's smile, disingenuous as ever, only intensified with building bile within Andrea. "Why? Where are you—"

"Don't worry yourself about that. You'll only work yourself up, and besides, Linda wouldn't want you to worry about her so much." Ms. Carol reached out to pat Andrea's head, but Andrea immediately scooted herself away.

Ms. Carol's hand rustled in her pocket before she turned around and walked out of the room, a crack of colour briefly giving Andrea relief from the snow blindness.

Much time passed; minutes, hours, or even days, Andrea didn't know. She picked at the grains of rice, squeezing them between her fingers until they turned to cold mush. Trapped in a world of white, Andrea felt tears well up in her eyes as a grim thought breached her mind. *Linda's not just gone from the facility. She's gone for good.*

Andrea felt her way through the room until her hands contacted a wall. She gritted her teeth and reared her head back, ready to strike against the wall. Anything to block out the memories and the piercing white. Suddenly, cold air forced itself down upon Andrea and she froze at the sound of another voice.

"Hold up, Andy!"

Andrea slowly turned around. A soothing periwinkle light flooded the room, casting shadows that gave the room dark blue corners and allowed Andrea's eyes to relax and stop straining themselves. At the back of the room was Linda's doll, standing on its own two feet and surrounded by dancing blue sparks. Andrea rubbed her eyes in disbelief. *Have I spent so long in here that I've gone crazy enough to hallucinate?*

Andrea hesitantly walked towards the doll before she found herself kneeling before it. The doll waved and tilted its head. "Hi!" the new voice greeted, though the doll's lips didn't move.

"Have I… gone crazy?" Andrea asked, though she wasn't sure to whom.

The doll covered its stitched mouth with its hand and giggled. "Oh no, I'm very real," the doll replied. "I just didn't see the need to act until now." The doll leaned toward Andrea and appeared to cup its mouth. "So, you want to get out of here, right?"

Andrea nodded. "But not just me." She thought back to how Linda, strong and tough, had been so easily made helpless and how quickly her life had been snuffed out on the floor. If the teachers could take *her* life so easily, how quickly would the rest of the kids in the building follow?

"Ah, you think big, don't you?" the doll said with amazement. "Well, if you want to get everyone out of here, then now is the time to act."

Hours passed as Andrea wandered around the white room restlessly. After much time had passed, the doll crawled up the wall and stuck itself above the door. The doll put its hand to its mouth in a *shush*. Andrea nodded and pretended to zip her smiling lips shut.

A few minutes later, the door swung open, and Ms. Carol walked inside with dull eyes and an even duller grin. "Are we all calmed down, now?" the teacher asked.

Andrea's eyes briefly darted up to the doll before looking back to Ms. Carol and nodding. In another second, the doll had launched off the wall and clamped itself onto the back of Ms. Carol's head.

The teacher screamed as she was thrown all over the room, bouncing off the walls like a ping-pong ball and splattering the walls with bursts of red. Andrea sidestepped out of the flailing teacher's trajectory, her screams grating on the girl's ears like nails on a blackboard. With one last bounce off the wall, Ms. Carol collapsed onto the floor into a sticky, red puddle. The doll rolled across the room and left a crimson trail as it tumbled into a wall.

Andrea backed into the door, nearly collapsing into the hall as it swung out. Ms. Carol slowly turned herself over with a low groan, her hair stained black, with strands sticking to the floor. She struggled to strain her head up, showing a newly formed dent caving in at the top of her forehead. Her eyes were swollen and purple, the gaps in her teeth a deep scarlet. The teacher reached an arm out toward her student. "An-Andrea," Ms. Carol croaked.

The ragdoll sprang back to life and pounced onto Ms. Carol's face, slamming the teacher's head into the ground over and over. Ms. Carol's hands violently shook as the doll's body muffled her screams.

"Andrea, there's a keycard in her pocket," the doll cheerfully instructed. "That key will let you into security, and then you can let everyone out."

As Ms. Carol continued to flail and kick, Andrea carefully scuttled across the bloody floor, her legs quaking as she tried not to slip. When she came to her teacher's side, Andrea leaned down and was quickly greeted by a sickly-sweet odour that reminded her of pennies.

She stuck her hand into Ms. Carol's boiling pocket and riffled through the contents. Andrea's hands clutched a thick box and yanked it out of her teacher's pocket. Her heart sank as she guessed what it was that she was grabbing. She gazed at the shock box that Ms. Carol had used to terrorize so many over the years.

"She won't need this anymore," Andrea muttered. Her thumb twitched and pressed itself into the box's button. Andrea's heart skipped a beat as she awaited the wave of electricity that would stab into her leg. But to her surprise, nothing happened. She looked down at the box, dumbfounded, before turning to the slowly struggling figure of Ms. Carol.

"The shock box can't hurt you anymore," the doll reassured. "Now you can focus on getting everyone out."

Andrea, not wanting to dwell on the whys for long, tossed the box aside and continued to search Ms. Carol's pockets. Finally, the girl yanked out a thin, white card made of plastic. She flipped the card over and saw Ms. Carol's soulless smile trapped in a small square in the bottom-right corner.

On the opposite corner was a small barcode while the top left corner read in large, sky-blue letters, "SECURITY."

Andrea smiled and looked down at the doll. Ms. Carol's movements were more sluggish, and the teacher could barely lift her arms. "Now, go get to the security room. I'll be right behind you," the doll said, its voice not losing its cheer, even as Ms. Carol's breathing became shallower and more gurgled.

Andrea nodded and ran out into the hallway, crimson footprints following her. Her eyes relaxed as the rainbows of the hallway broke the eyesore of white that surrounded her for so long. Andrea weaved through the halls, eventually stopping at a thick metal door with a glowing red sign above it that read, "SECURITY." The cold steel stuck out from the rainbows of the rest of the hallway like a puddle of red paint on a white tablecloth.

Andrea eyed the side of the door, seeing a black scanner with a small red light in the middle. She lifted the card and placed its barcode in front of the light, her heart skipping a beat as the light turned green and she heard a quick metal click from the direction of the doorknob.

After a deep breath, Andrea turned the knob and gingerly walked inside. The cold blue room had rows of large computers, each sitting at a black checkerboarded desk and showing a different angle of the building. A flurry of lights dashed across the console, bouncing from the sides as fast as a mosquito. Unfortunately for Andrea, the computers weren't unmanned.

One by one, each lab coat-clad worker looked up from their computer and stared at Andrea with wide, horror-filled eyes and mouths dropping down onto their desks.

Andrea steeled herself and stepped into the room, her hands curled into fists. She felt heat pinching all sides of her face.

She held out Ms. Carol's card to the others. "How do… you… open… the doors?" Andrea asked.

The workers sat in stunned silence, giving Andrea the push to keep walking into the room. She approached the front desk and looked at a man with curly black hair, gobsmacked behind his computer.

"Open… the doors!" Andrea repeated, her voice lowering to a growl. The man didn't move. His hands began to shake, and he continued to stare at the young intruder. Suddenly, Andrea became aware of the sound of clicking echoing from the back row. Standing above the rest with her finger frustratingly stabbing the button of her shock box with her thumb over and over was Ms. Tabitha.

Her eyes were ice-cold daggers that tried to pierce into Andrea's heart and the teacher's lips were tightly sewn into a scowl. She looked down at the box in frustrated confusion before tossing it onto her desk with a sigh. "I believe it's long past your bedtime, young lady." Ms. Tabitha's voice was dripping with venomous contempt.

Andrea marched across the room and slammed her free hand on Ms. Tabitha's desk, sending a few pencils, papers, and paperclips into the air for a moment. The girl pointed at her teacher's monitor, pressing her finger into Linda's old bed. "Let everyone out!" Andrea shouted.

Ms. Tabitha sighed and brushed a dirty blonde curl behind her ear. The teacher reached out to place her hand on her student's shoulder, but Andrea quickly yanked herself away. Ms. Tabitha shook her head and knelt before Andrea to meet her at eye level.

"I understand that you're in distress right now. What happened to Linda was a terrible thing. But you need to understand that she wouldn't have been put in that position if she had just chosen to listen."

Andrea let out a roar as she took a swing at Ms. Tabitha, who just as quickly shifted her head to the side and avoided the blow. The young girl was ready to throw another punch when she found herself pulled from behind onto the ground. Bells rang in her ears as her head was slammed into the ground and her brain felt like it was launched into the back of her skull.

The other workers pressed themselves onto Andrea and squeezed her wrists and ankles until she had no feeling left in them. Andrea bucked and tried to pull herself up, but the grips of the other workers proved too tight.

Ms. Tabitha loomed over Andrea like a vulture and stared down at her prone student. "You need to realize that this is the best avenue for you to receive the care you need," the teacher coldly scolded. "If we were to let everyone go then you and many others would end up hurting yourselves again. That or be taken advantage of by those who don't have your best interests at heart." Ms. Tabitha leaned closely to Andrea's face, making the young girl's skin crawl. "Now, are you going to be a good girl and go back to bed?"

Andrea scowled and reared her head back. She sucked her cheeks in before letting a ball of spit slingshot out of her mouth and strike Ms. Tabitha in the face.

The teacher reeled back and wiped her face with a growl. She looked down at the workers and pointed at Andrea's shock box. "Someone replace her GED; this one seems to be defective," Ms. Tabitha hissed.

A worker by Andrea's leg gave a curt nod and pulled up the young girl's pant leg. Just as the man began to undo the Velcro strapping the box to Andrea's leg, a sharp buzz erupted from the leg, and the man was blasted back by a bright blue light. He crashed through a desk, smashing it into a cloud of papers and splinters.

The other workers looked on in shock, some covering their mouths while others cried, "Oh my God!"

All Andrea needed was for the workers to lift off her a splinter-sized space. The shock, both literal and figurative, gave the girl that opening. Andrea swept her legs to the side, knocking the workers down before springing back onto her feet. She reached for the first object within range, a black keyboard, and smacked it across the faces of the two workers closest to her.

Keys were sent flying, along with streams of blood and broken teeth. Andrea gave herself only seconds to register the movement in the corner of her eye before whipping around and striking a man in the back of the head. Even when he flopped down like a fish, Andrea continued to repeatedly slam the keyboard down until it snapped in half. He stopped moving, but some low gurgles still bubbled from the body.

Andrea's lungs felt like they were being roasted over a bonfire, and her heart beat faster than a hummingbird's wings. She looked down at the sticky keyboard and saw her hands coated in red. Her skin became cold, and she felt the rice she had eaten earlier begin to build up in her throat.

"What am I doing?" she asked in a hoarse voice. Andrea felt a shadow loom over her before her mind registered the dark blanket dimming her vision. She was snapped out of her stupor by the sharp yelp of Ms. Tabitha before two thuds hit the floor, one thick and one lighter, slightly metallic.

Andrea turned around and saw Ms. Tabitha sprawled on the floor and the doll standing in the middle of the slick floor with the teacher's certificate in hand. The glass of the frame was covered in a field of cracks that reminded Andrea of a spiderweb.

"Well, that was quite a workout. We should do this again sometime." the doll laughed. Andrea looked down at the groaning figure of the teacher.

"What do we do… with Ms.… Tabitha?" Andrea asked. She jumped back as she saw Ms. Tabitha twitch. The doll lifted its other hand toward one of the backroom's desks. Andrea's eyes widened when it finally registered that she was staring down at the source of the second thud. A discarded pistol lying by the wall. She turned back to the doll and frantically shook her head. "I can't… do that."

The doll shrugged before pointing to Andrea's ankle. "How about a taste of her own medicine?"

Andrea pondered for a bit before she unstrapped the shock box from her leg and crawled over to Ms. Tabitha. She lifted her teacher's pant leg and wrapped it around her pale, wrinkled ankle. "She says…it's supposed to help us." Andrea smirked. "Maybe it can…help her too?"

The doll laughed before pilfering Ms. Tabitha's button from her pocket. "Maybe, but right now we have some other stuff to sort out first." The doll strolled to the desk closest to Andrea and then spun the chair around to invite her to sit.

Andrea plopped into the seat and turned toward the monitor. She bit her lip and tapped a finger on the keyboard. "How do I open the doors?" she muttered.

The doll tossed the shock box button onto the desk. "Press the key with the window on it and the R key at the same time. Then type 'unlock all' in the black box that pops up."

Andrea nodded and pressed the first two keys as instructed. A small black box popped up on the screen in the top left corner of the monitor. A series of white words Andrea couldn't be bothered reading scrolled across the small black box before ending with a small white square that blinked in and out of the dark background.

Before Andrea could type in the final command, Ms. Tabitha launched off the ground with a guttural roar and lunged forward.

Remembering the shock box, Andrea swiped the box's button and slammed the red button with her thumb. The teacher's barbaric wail was stifled by the waves of electricity that flowed up her body. Her limbs became stiff as a scarecrow and smoke began to rise from the bottom of the leg with the shock box. Crimson tears flowed from her reddening eyes and her hair began to turn into silvery static.

Andrea watched in horrified awe before feeling her leg being softly batted against.

"Come on, open the doors!" the doll shouted. Andrea shook her head and returned her focus to the computer, trying to ignore the smell of burning flesh beside her. She typed in, "Unlock All" and slammed the enter key. Before her, each room shown on the monitor's doors swung open and a blaring alarm coerced the other students to herd out of their rooms.

Andrea reached down to grab the doll's hand, but when she looked down, the doll was gone, and she was just grasping at air. She looked up and saw Ms. Tabitha become engulfed in flames before collapsing onto the ground.

Andrea screamed, tumbling out of her chair in panic before scrambling to sprint out of the room. During her race against the smoke, she tripped a few times, running through the halls. Though every bone in her body cried out in pain, Andrea pushed forward before she found herself at the building's entrance. She looked back and saw the flames slither around the corner and lick the ceiling. With the increasing heat of the inferno building a sticky sweat on her body, Andrea rammed the doors open and found herself tumbling into soft and chilling ground.

She looked up and saw before her a field of snow, covered in small footprints. Other students were scattered across the pasture, partaking in a chorus of squeals and cries.

Whether the sounds were of fear or joy, Andrea had no idea. She picked herself up and turned to watch as the building's flame tried to turn night into day. Past the draperies of smoke, Andrea saw a figure floating above the crumbling rooftop of the institute. The figure turned, and Andrea was greeted by Linda's smiling face.

Linda revealed from behind her back the rag doll that guided Andrea in her escape. Andrea grinned and waved at her old friend. Linda waved back before ascending into the sky in a puff of white smoke.

When Andrea looked further up, she saw another star flicker to life in the night sky.

# The Assault in the Polar Night

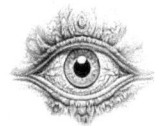

"Holy smokes, how long does this hall go?" Marcy asked. Her knees were burning as she continued to trudge through the halls. She trailed behind Marigold, who never lost her pace even when typing her story into her tablet.

Marigold smirked and replied, "Depends on where the closest trick mirror is." The bandana-clad woman stopped before a long mirror and her eyes brightened. Marigold pulled the mirror open and let it gently swing out, revealing a doorway leading to a dimly lit room with a pool table on the other side. Crowded around the pool table was a trio of partygoers, each with a pool cue in one hand and a plastic red cup in the other.

"With all these passageways, you'd think the family was hiding something that could blow the world up," Marcy mused.

She ducked her head as she stepped out of the passageway and into the next room.

Marigold followed behind her and typed in her tablet, "Not much to hide other than maybe our family heirloom."

"Oi, Mari!" one of the pool sharks called. "You're not blabbing to the new girl about the Hand of Iris, are you?" The young man's shoulder-length ponytail swayed as he took a large gulp out of his cup. Red liquid spilled down his chin and left pinpoint-sized stains of crimson on his mustard suit.

Marigold shook her head. "Not any more than she needs to know."

The second partier, another young man, threw his head back and laughed, nearly sending his canary-coloured fedora flying off his head. "Well, guess that makes one less mess we need to clean up."

The suited man slapped the side of the hatted man's head with a scowl. "Shut up, Boyd! You make it sound like we're the mafia or something."

The second man readjusted his hat and continued to give a mocking grin to the first. "Please. If we were, you would have gotten the cement shoes a whole long while ago!"

The men began a shoving match that splashed crimson drink all over the brown carpet and the pool table.

At that point, the third partygoer, a woman with a top hat made of midnight blue felt, slammed her drink down on the pool table and shoved the two apart from each other. "Alright, boys, you can measure each other's dicks later."

"Whoa, watch the language. Never know when Granny's going to pop out and read you the riot act," the hatted man chortled. A myriad of questions ran through Marcy's head, but before any of them could formulate into spoken word, Marigold stepped forward and gestured towards the bickering trio.

"Marcy, these are my siblings, Boyd, Oriol, and Saffron."

"But everyone calls us the Disaster Triplets!" Boyd proclaimed proudly, gallantly lifting his hat off and waving it around in the air. His gesturing was stopped when Oriol shoved the hat back on his brother's head.

"Only *you* call us that, dipshit."

Suddenly Saffron perked up and waved toward the doorway behind the boys. "Oh hi, Grandma!" she called.

Oriol's face turned pale, and he sheepishly turned toward the hall. His face changed to beet red when he saw there was no one there and looked over to his cheekily grinning sister. "You shithead," the suited man playfully snarled.

Just as Saffron collapsed into a heap of laughter, Marcy cautiously raised a hand. "Hey, what's the Hand of Iris?"

The triplets stopped their roughhousing and turned to Marcy. The three of them dusted themselves off and Oriol cleared his throat. "Supposed to be this ancient relic that existed even before our family got its name. It is said to be the responsibility of the eldest of the family to look after it."

"Not sure why the old bats were considered the best to guard it," Boyd muttered, "especially if a burglar were to bust in here."

"Maybe because they know the best places in the house to hide the thing," Saffron suggested, her body swaying like a dinghy in the ocean. Oriol tapped Saffron's shoulder and pointed to Marcy. "Hey, aren't we supposed to be telling a story or something?"

His brother scratched his head with furrowed brows. "I don't know, I'm pretty sure we're supposed to tie it to one of the guests or something in the house."

The triplets paused for a moment before they once again tripped over each other in laughter.

Marcy looked on in confusion while Marigold simply rolled

her eyes in amusement.

Saffron raised her arms before letting them slap down on her sides. "Fuck it, let's just tell a vampire story."

\*\*\*

Selene thought the dealer of life had given her a bad hand when she had learned she was practically allergic to the sun. Xeroderma Pigmentosum. Not only that, but her hearing had become fainter as the years had gone by. When she was twelve, all sounds disappeared, and she struggled to relearn to talk with her hands, spending countless hours reading up on sign language and falling further behind in her studies than she already was.

Forever doomed to be cooped up in the darkness like a rat, to not even live to see her fortieth birthday. Selene counted it as a miracle that she even managed to graduate high school. Online, of course.

Her parents had thought her fortune would change when they moved further up north to Nunavut, the greatest and whitest of the Great White North. Shorter days, longer nights, and a higher paying job for Mom. It seemed like the perfect place for Selene to finally live her life.

Turned out a flock of vampires had the same idea.

On that night, Selene was curled up in a tattered brown armchair with a book illuminated by a simple lamp. The television was left unnoticed and stuck on a news channel. Selene flipped through the pages, trying to absorb herself into a world of dashing knights, slippery dragons, and devious sorcerers. Her eyes grew weary, and her bones felt as brittle as crackers. Still, she kept herself awake, determined to see how deep in the book she could get in one night. She was already past the halfway point in just two nights. If she could just get a few more chapters done, then she'd be well on her way to breaking her record.

Her eyes wandered to a dull, rose-gold picture frame sitting under the lamp. Entrapped in the frame was a photo of the world's most handsome man with his arm draped over her shoulder.

Titus was his name; one he had chosen for himself after graduating high school. They were sitting together with identical smiles plastered on their faces, and the bar was lit up in purple, green, and orange neon lights. His long black hair was done up in a ponytail and his uniform was a sleeveless tuxedo covered in beer stains.

Selene picked up the picture frame and placed her thumb next to his round, tan face. She grinned. *That employee policy of yours really had me looking underdressed, Titus,* she thought, gazing at her visage.

Her blonde hair blanketed her shoulders, and her eyes were more sunken in, almost looking like dark, empty sockets. If she had only known back then how much light he would bring back into her life.

Selene gently placed the frame back down on the dresser. As far as Titus knew, she was just a very dedicated night owl who had also become an expert at lip reading, albeit out of necessity for lack of hearing. Selene had mulled over how she would tell Titus about her strange condition, but she could never pinpoint the best place to start. Suddenly, she caught the title displayed on the latest news report from behind the black box of subtitles. *Undead Terror Invades Nunavut's Polar Night.*

Selene sat up and slammed her book down on the couch. Of course, she knew about the upcoming Polar Night. She had a whole list of things she'd like to do the next day to kick off her months of freedom from her matchbox of a house. However, what she hadn't expected was the sight she saw when she looked out the window.

The moon was blotted out of the sky by a black swarm that

tore through the dancing Northern Lights like strips of paper. The cloud descended onto a set of houses on a snowy hill that sat across from Selene's house. The cloud broke down into smaller pieces, each speck piercing through the houses and taking with them into the skies new specks before disappearing behind the glacial mountain peaks. What remained of the swarm grew larger as it gathered closer to the town square.

Selene began to feel the glass plane rumble under her hands before she quickly backed away from the window. The ground underneath her began to shake, as if she was caught in a minor earthquake. Shadowy blurs zipped across the curtains as cold sweat trickled down her face. As if her body was put on autopilot, Selene ran across the room and pried open the door leading down to the basement.

Before she descended the steps, she looked at a white panel on the wall and pressed her finger against the screen, letting the lights roar to life. Selene punched the code into the digital keypad that appeared, allowing the home security system option to pop up before her eyes. She quickly pressed her finger on the button leaving the security system mode on 'Occupants Home' to 'Occupants Away.' She felt her heartbeat drum against her ears as she saw the countdown to the system arming begin before she rushed down the stairs, letting the magnets on the frame close the door behind her.

The frosty cold of the stone floor stabbed through her socks to get to her feet, and the smell of dirty lake water gently rose to her nose. The basement was covered in clutter that included a yellowed mattress, a partially opened bag of birdseed that Selene's mother had left leaning against an antique China cupboard, a pile of dusty picture frames, and old plastic buckets that sandwiched an old stone fireplace between them.

She yanked open the China cupboard door and pulled out

an ornate silver mirror with a pointed handle. Selene rushed to tuck herself inside the fireplace, accidentally kicking over a bag of birdfeed. She squeezed into the sides until she was sure the stone walls completely hid her figure.

Cramped in the corner, Selene waited with cold, bated breath, alone in the freezing darkness. Her thoughts wandered to her parents; the last time she had seen them they had been heading out the door to buy groceries.

Her worries shifted to Titus and her stomach twisted into knots. Just a few days ago he had been complaining about his bar suffering from break-ins due to most of the security team being let go a few weeks back. There was no chance the place would be equipped to deal with the situation; she just hoped he and her parents would've gotten to a safe place in time before being attacked.

Suddenly, she saw the hole in the fireplace let in a flurry of flashing white lights, illuminating the discarded seeds on the ground. A hot lump of coal built up inside Selene's throat and she covered her mouth, feeling the tears pour across her fingers.

Inside, she begged that her parents had somehow found somewhere safe to go. Her heart jumped as a bony, pale hand with dull, dark blue talons reached out and dragged one of the seeds out of sight. Soon, the hand dragged another seed away, and another, and yet another.

Selene tightened her grip on the handle of the mirror, her skin feeling like it was being poked all over the place with dozens of needles. Every inch of her was screaming to drive the pointed end of the mirror handle down into that hand and then go to town on the intruder. But still, Selene stayed where she was. Who knew how many others were inside? One thing that caught Selene's eye was that, unlike the seeds, the hand didn't cast a shadow.

*What the hell is in my house?*

When Selene next looked down, all the seeds were gone and the pale hand inched closer to her foot. Before could stop herself, Selene threw herself down and plunged her makeshift shiv through the decrepit hand. The fingers spread out so quickly that they almost blew away from the palm, and thick black liquid that reminded Selene of tar oozed out of the wound. She scampered out of her hole like a manic panther and stood over the owner of the hand.

The bald, gaunt figure's sickly pale skin shone against the flashing lights of her alarm and its black, marble-like eyes widened in shock. It opened its fanged mouth to scream but Selene was quick to tackle it down into the ground and plunged the mirror handle in a flurry of frantic stabs. The storm of black blood waned once the intruder stopped flailing about.

Selene's clothes were stained black, and her arms were covered with scratches. She took a breath and looked around the room, squinting her eyes to avoid being blinded by white lights. When Selene found she was still alone in the room, she got back up to her feet and grabbed a handful of birdseed out of the bag. The nutty aroma was almost soothing to her erratic nerves, though the idea of more intruders prowling inside her home was still fresh in Selene's head.

She crept up the stairs, trying to keep her steps slow and keep her heart from exploding. The door to the rest of the house was wide open and there appeared to be no other signs of life past the doorway. But still, after remembering the creature from before casting no shadow, Selene stopped just before the doorway and tossed the handful of seeds into the hall. She ducked back down the steps and waited. Her eyes darted all over, her hands began to shake, and her heart beat furiously.

Just as she was ready to climb back up, Selene was met with

the sight of another pale, gangly being slithering into the hall. Its pointed ears were like a demon's horns in the flashing white lights, and it leaned down to slowly count the seeds. Selene crawled up the stairs and when her eyes laid across the creature's back, she gritted her teeth and plunged the mirror handle into the creature's back. She continued to stab after the creature reared its head back and she had it sprawled in a black puddle on the floor. Selene only stopped attacking when the intruder stopped moving. After she stood back up, Selene made her patrol around the rest of the house until she was sure it was empty of undead trespassers.

Once her surveillance was complete, she made her way back to the security panel, entered the code, and stopped the alarm. She turned her head to the window but suppressed the urge to look outside. She didn't want to bear witness to the chaos her parents and Titus would have to face on their own. Instead, Selene ran back downstairs and huddled herself beside the bottom of the steps for the rest of the night, until she collapsed into a deep sleep.

This would be her first encounter with the Nosferatu.

After that day, Selene established a new routine. From what she had gathered watching the undead townsfolk shamble around town, they tried to keep a usual routine. For a long time, she worried they would turn their attention to her house.

Instead, they kept to their own devices, occasionally gnawing on a human limb or small animal carcass as they walked. Once she ventured out herself, people would rarely pay her much mind, except for a polite nod or wave. Selene would then march into the woods and set up a field of snares. If she was lucky, she would find a few rabbits to keep her hunger at bay for a while. After storing them in her house to be skinned and prepped, Selene would go to the back of her house to check on the Tupperware containers she had hanging under the roof like wind chimes, prime for catching fresh snowfall to melt into fresh water. Selene kept to herself, immediately snuffing out the fireplace in the basement after cooking her rabbit. It was a nice, calm routine that allowed Selene some semblance of peace.

But she still got very few winks of sleep. Whenever she laid down to rest, her mind wandered to her parents and dear Titus. She imagined them either laying in red snow in a ditch or would have nightmares about them forcing her to the ground and ripping the veins out of her neck. And each time, she would sit back up and try to tell herself she needed to let go of the hope that even one of the three would walk through the door unchanged. And then her heart would fall like a bag of stones, and she would stuff a pillow in her face to smother the crying.

For three months, Selene's routine was quiet, predictable, and without any major hiccups. Until she went to check on the snow traps. She sighed after inspecting the containers, seeing nothing but a thin coat of frost covering the plastic. She peered into the house through the open door and gazed at the pile of empty plastic bottles on the kitchen counter. Her eyes wandered to the town surrounding the house and she thought back to Titus' bar.

She shook her head. Probably only serving blood cocktails. She joylessly chuckled at the thought of the bartenders making a Bloody Mary joke. Selene closed the door behind her and went over to the sink. She turned on the faucet and sighed as thick, crimson sludge poured into the sink and a sharp metallic odour nearly caused her to gag. She turned off the sink and looked over to the front door. She shook her head.

*Well, it's either risk getting caught by the vamps or die of dehydration.*

With her mind made up, Selene grabbed a garbage bag and tossed every empty bottle she had inside. She tossed the bag over her head and rested it on her shoulder before waltzing out the front door. Selene tried to maintain a casual stride down the empty, slush-filled road despite the threat of her heart being on the brink of exploding.

A fresh chill crawled up the side of her body as she passed by each walking corpse on her trek. Their eyes were downcast, despite their fang-filled grins being almost too wide to be contained in the confines of their faces. Unlike the Nosferatu Selene had encountered months before, the infected vampires were nearly indistinguishable from their warm-blooded prey, except for the razor-sharp teeth and ravenous appetite for blood, of course.

Selene also noticed the strong stench of rotting meat that followed these ghouls wherever they went, a nice signal that they were approaching, but not so great a smell to sniff when trying to feast on a rabbit.

At the second four-way stop, she nearly passed the beige building, only stopping when she noticed "Carmilla's" in large violet letters nailed to the front.

Before the invasion, the letters would shine as bright as a lighthouse, acting as a guiding light telling Selene where to go when she had gotten lost in her first weeks in town. A pit formed in her stomach as she gazed at the extinguished beacon, her wistful tears of times gone being covered by the shadows that hid the rest of the town away from the world.

Selene sighed and wandered over to the back of the bar, laying her eyes on the overstuffed dumpsters. A twister of flies danced over the giant containers and the sharp stench of rotted meat attacked Selene's nostrils, threatening to fish her last meal out of her stomach. Selene quickly covered her mouth and nose with her hand and continued marching to the back door. Only when she placed her hand on the rusting knob did she realize that she didn't have a plan for how to fill up her bottles without getting caught by whoever else was inside the building.

Selene paused, shaking her head. *Screw planning. I just need to walk in like I'm supposed to be here, just like when walking the street.*

Selene tried to force a confident smile onto her face before turning the knob and letting herself inside. The ceiling was caked in darkness like an umbral canopy, the only lights being weak oil lamps placed on many different tables and small white Christmas lights that lined the walls.

She turned a corner and stopped before the kitchen area. A pale woman with dark hair and magenta highlights waltzed out of the walk-in cooler. Before the woman closed the door, Selene saw through the crack in the door a row of rattling cages, but the door was sealed before she could see what was inside the small pens.

The woman licked the blood from her hands before turning around and walking into the women's bathroom.

Selene quickly hopped into the kitchen and dashed for the sink. She grabbed onto the taps and turned them. After putting some extra force into twisting, Selene grinned at the sight before her.

A stream of clear and clean water flowed freely from the faucet. She knew she had little time to celebrate, so she scrambled to yank her bottles out of her garbage bag. With each bottle, she watched as the water filled the plastic to the rim before quickly twisting the caps back on and dropping them back inside the bag.

Just as she was twisting the lid of the last bottle back on, Selene felt a cold grip squeeze her shoulder and twist her away from the sink. She felt a gasp escape her lips as she laid eyes on the woman with the purple highlights.

The woman's fangs glistened in the dim lights and snarled, though the chomping of her jaws prevented Selene from being able to read her lips. All Selene could do was shake her head and struggle to escape the woman's grip. As Selene grabbed the woman's hand, the woman pushed against her, digging her back into the countertop and shoving her down with both hands. Selene struggled to escape the pin, but the woman had her flattened against the blood-stained steel.

Suddenly, a young man turned a corner and ran to pull the woman off Selene, his pigtail swinging like a pendulum. An eerie chill shivered through Selene's body as the woman finally let go. The man gently corralled her away. The woman scowled at the man and appeared to be shouting down at him.

The man, although initially stepping back from the force of her voice, remained calm and gave her a reassuring smile before placing his hand on her shoulder. As soon as the grin crossed his face, Selene's heart sank, even more so when she read his nametag. "Titus."

Selene shook her head; she had known for a while it was a possibility, but staring right at it, she didn't want to believe it was true. The woman huffed and stomped away, causing Titus to turn his attention back to Selene.

That familiar warm smile she knew so well emerged on Titus' face; the bright reassurance somehow not being dampened by the fangs in his mouth. He raised his hands and signed, "Hey honey, it's been a while."

Selene pushed back the urge to burst into tears, tightly sealing her lips into a grin. "Yeah," she signed back with a nod.

Titus scooped Selene up into a cool embrace with what felt like a chuckle. As she was swept up, Selene was briefly plucked out of her grim reality and brought back to the more peaceful nights where the two of them would cuddle on a park bench and watch the Northern Lights dance against starry skies.

His lips sealed onto her own and Selene felt like a match

was struck inside her chest. She wrapped her arms around his head and let herself melt in his arms. Her heart fluttered like the wings of an owl, and she felt her warmth seep into him.

But Selene's heart quickly sank back down as she felt herself grasping to find some warmth from her dear Titus in return. While she felt the same longing for him as she had before, Titus' touch was still icy cold, and she ached in yearning for any sign of a heartbeat from him. But instead, there was stillness.

After Titus parted from her, Selene noticed they were pressed against the door to the walk-in. Titus frowned and reached a hand out to brush aside a few stray strands of Selene's straw-like hair, tenderly stroking her cheek with his thumb. "What's wrong?" he asked.

Selene accidentally let a small chuckle slip as she watched him stretch his mouth out. Normally, she found it annoying when people stretched their words, thinking it would make things easier for her. However, there was something adorable about Titus' earnest attempts to try to make communication simpler. One aspect that, until that moment, she hadn't known how much she missed.

"I just missed you so much," Selene said tearfully. "I thought I'd never see you again."

Panic was painted across Titus' face as he frantically tried to wipe her tears and pulled her into a tight hug. He gently rocked Selene back and forth. She felt his icy breath stroke the top of her ear and his hand gingerly pat her back.

Selene nuzzled her face into Titus' shoulder, letting her boiling tears soak into his work shirt. After an eternity that still felt too short, Selene peeled away, and Titus wiped away his tears.

"Honestly, I was worried about you, too. A lot of the first-wave vamps skipped the whole turning process and just drained people dry." His eyes dropped to the ground. "Including my folks.

I was just lucky the guy was too tired to rip me to shreds too."

"I'm so sorry." Selene rested her free hand on his chest.

Titus shook his head and shrugged. "It's been months. I've had time to process it."

Selene removed her hand and replied, "The hurt doesn't ever really leave though."

Titus nodded before his eyes suddenly widened in realization. "What about *your* parents?"

Selene sighed and shook her head. "I have no idea. They just never came back from their grocery run the day everything turned upside-down." She pieced her words together carefully, unsure if calling the invasion a bad thing would upset Titus. Luckily, his face didn't give any sign he saw something was off.

"Dang. Well, I hope that wherever they are, they're doing alright," he said.

Selene nodded in agreement, feeling the wave of dread she had felt that day crash into her all over again.

"How do you think they'd react about what happened to us?"

A shock jolted through Selene's system, freezing her in place. It took a few seconds of her staring dumbly at her boyfriend to realize what he meant by saying what he had.

"You mean… our condition?" Her signing was stiff and uneasy. She felt her bones yank back to keep her hands from shaking.

Titus chuckled and scratched the back of his neck. "Yeah, I mean, if they weren't turned already then it'd be a bit of a shock, huh?"

"I guess so," Selene hesitantly replied.

*There's no way… He can't possibly think that I'm one of them too, right?*

Titus shrugged. "Well, they were pretty cool about me before all of this happened so maybe they'll be open about this, too." Titus then jerked his head to the side and called out, "I'll be right there, Mikayla!" He turned back to Selene with a blissful grin. "Before I get to work, I was wondering, there'll be a rave happening later tonight. Would you want to come?"

Selene hesitated, the thought of fanged monstrosities gnashing their teeth to rip open her veins sending a paralyzing chill through her body. Titus seemed to sniff out her hesitation and gave her a reassuring gaze.

"It could be fun," he coaxed. "And you could get to know some more people. That way you won't feel as alone in all of this."

Selene pondered for a moment. Of course, she would've been more than happy to spend time with Titus again, but would it be worth a swim together if the pool was filled with sharks?

*Then again, I could get some more info on how these guys work. And if Titus thinks I'm one of them, maybe some other people could be fooled, too?*

With a heavily beating heart, Selene gave a nod, causing Titus to jump with elation. Before he could start the excited babble she knew he would spew, Selene added, "I just need to fill up these bottles. My plumbing's busted pretty badly, and I could use some extra water."

Titus gave a thumbs-up before signing back. "Of course. I mean, blood's good and all, but I'm not sure how well it does for fires. And take it from me, bathing in blood is not as cool as it sounds. You have to waste a lot of it, and you just end up way too sticky afterward."

Selene nodded, trying not to imprint the image of her blood-covered, naked boyfriend in her mind.

"I'll also tell the rest of the staff not to bug you," Titus reassured. He then turned back toward the swinging doors leading into the bar and gave Selene an enthusiastic wave.

Selene waved back, breathing a sigh of relief once she was

sure she was finally alone.

*You're really tight roping across a razor's edge, Selene.*

After filling her bottles without any further interruptions, Selene tepidly walked out the backdoor and her heart sank, realizing just what she had signed up for.

*A one-way trip to the lion's den.*

Later that night, Selene paced around nervously inside her house, building thick layers of sweat under her parka. Her silver mirror was strapped onto her pant leg and hidden underneath her coat and dress shirt. Her eyes darted up to the clock hanging on the kitchen wall. Four o'clock, about ten minutes or so past the end of Titus' shift. She thought about running back into the basement and pretending she wasn't home. After all, she had never told him that she was still living in the same house.

But what would he think if she cancelled all of a sudden? Even he would start to suspect something was wrong, probably wonder why she would say no to a party now when before the invasion, she would've never even thought about passing up a good time on the late-night scene. She couldn't even use the excuse of not hearing him knock on the door. Titus knew Selene was the type to hover by the door and glue herself to the peephole to wait for him and make sure he was on time.

Selene stopped in her tracks, pressed her hand against the icy kitchen island, and watched as a thin cloud of cold mist puffed out of her mouth.

*No use hesitating now,* she thought, *Just rip off the Band-Aid.*

Selene leaned against the door and gazed through the peephole. Five minutes passed before Titus strolled across the street and stopped on her front porch with a soft, eager smile.

Selene sighed and opened the door with her best grin and stuffed her hands in her pockets to keep her boyfriend from seeing them shake.

Titus began to lean forward, a charming smile eased itself onto his face and he began to close his eyes. Suddenly he stopped and gazed at his girlfriend with concern. "Hey, honey, are you okay?"

Selene nodded but her lips were forced into a pained grin and Titus' eyes squinted with skepticism. Selene took her hands out of her pockets and reluctantly signed, "Just a bit nervous, I guess."

Titus twisted his lips in contemplation before replying, "I guess that's alright. But don't worry, you'll be fine." He gave Selene a reassuring smile and squeezed her shoulder.

Selene couldn't help but grin at Titus' unending optimism. Before she could start walking off the porch, Titus raised a finger and stopped her in her tracks. "Just try to stay close," he warned. "It's pretty easy to get lost in a crowd like this."

Selene gave a thumbs up and linked her arm with her cheery lover. She tried to find warmth and comfort huddling next to the man she loved, especially since it seemed his new condition hadn't turned him into a cruel monster, and yet her heart still ached as she kept searching for the warmth on his cheek that no longer existed.

Instead, his cheek was as cold and solid as stone. She might as well have taped an icepack to the side of her face and tried to find warmth there. Selene's eyes became downcast and couldn't bear to turn back up to meet her love. She could feel Titus turning his head and knew he was struggling to find something to say. Yet what would she say to him if he asked?

Eventually, the pair found themselves standing before a set of doors with flashing red lights pulsating through the cracks. Titus peeled the doors open and greeting him and Selene on the other side was a closely crowded bundle of pale figures covered in wild body paint.

Red spotlights danced around the crowd and streaked across the walls. At the back of the room was a large DJ booth, where the mix master danced under a canopy of dim purple light. Looking at the hoard, Selene could already feel her insides beginning to bubble and the joints in her legs locking up.

As Titus gently ushered her into the building, Selene felt vibrations jolting through the ground in time with the dancing lights. She kept her arm closely intertwined with his and stumbled as she tried to keep up with him. With each bloodsucker the pair shoved past on the dance floor, Selene felt more eyes burrowing into her skull. She was thankful for every second that passed without someone realizing she didn't belong in the crowd.

A few of the longest seconds of her life later, Selene found herself next to Titus in a small gap on the floor. She watched as Titus began to dance happily in tune with the vibrations pulsing through the ground. Selene tried to follow his movements but only succeeded in awkwardly flailing her arms and stumbling about like she had two left feet. Despite the chill of anxiety making her want to shrink into a ball, Titus continued to smile at her.

"Nice," Titus seemed to say. That word lifted Selene's spirits, though it didn't stop her eyes from darting all over the place to study the faces of the other dancing ghouls. Luckily for her, none of the other ravers seemed to be focusing on the two of them. Still, Selene couldn't scratch that itching urge to grab her silver shiv and make a run for it. And yet, Titus' pull kept her in place, kept her anxiety from boiling over.

Titus took her hands and gave a serene smile. "I should thank you, you know," Titus signed warmly.

Selene looked at him with confusedly furrowed eyebrows. "Thank me? For what?" she asked.

Selene watched Titus chuckle before he replied, "For helping me be more ready for the nightlife. If you weren't such a night owl, it probably would've been a lot harder for me to get used to this."

Before Selene could digest the bittersweet bubble expanding in her stomach, Titus twirled her around and twisted her into his embrace. As he rested his chin on her shoulder, Selene couldn't help but ache for his warm breath to graze the side of her face. She suddenly got spun back around to face a wide-eyed Titus.

"Hey, would you want to rest up with me once the Midnight Sun rolls around?"

Selene stood dumbfounded, trying to process what Titus had asked.

Reading the confusion on his girlfriend's face, Titus added, "Assuming you didn't already lock in any plans, of course. Though I think it'd help the time pass faster if we had each other."

Of course, Selene was familiar with the Midnight Sun phenomena. Her parents had brought protective window filters for when it rolled by. A sun that shone past midnight would be a nightmare for her condition, but she and her parents had figured locking themselves in the house for an extra bit would be nothing compared to the extra hours Selene got outside for the rest of the year. And now she was being offered a chance to be sheltered from the sun by the most wonderful man she knew. Selene smiled at the thought of being stuck in Titus' arms for hours, just spending all day alone with just the two of them. But then she looked up and saw fangs peeking out from Titus' hopeful smile.

Before she could ruminate further, Titus' smile suddenly dropped, and he turned around. The rest of the vampiric dancefloor followed suit and the vibrations in the floor halted. Selene stood on the tips of her toes to peek over the gobsmacked crowd.

With an arm twisted behind her back and her body bent over the booth by the DJ, a woman struggled to break free from the mix master's grip. Her jaw was strained open as she kicked about. Selene assumed she was screaming, judging by how the DJ shut his eyes and reared his head back.

From the corner of her eye, she saw Titus mouth worriedly, "A human?"

Selene fought the compulsion to run to the front and yank the DJ off the defenceless woman. But then what would they do against a club full of bloodthirsty vampires? Just as the DJ's fangs sprouted from under his lips, the woman grimly chuckled to herself as she pulled a remote out of her pocket and strained to pull her head up to face the crowd.

Selene saw the woman say a few words, though she struggled to read her lips. She wasn't given much time to ponder what the woman said either, as Selene was quickly yanked away toward the door by Titus.

His cheerful demeanour was replaced with a frenzied panic. The two were swarmed by panicked partygoers as they rushed to spill out the door. Selene looked up and quickly signed, "What's happening?"

Titus didn't respond and instead covered the both of them with his jacket, giving Selene the lion's share of the cover. The stench of burning sulphur corroded the insides of her nostrils and thick smoke clouded her vision. She felt droplets pound against the jacket and her shoes quickly became soaked. When she looked down, Selene saw the floors were covered in puddles, and bits of sickly pale skin floated past her feet.

*Sprinklers rigged with holy water,* Selene quickly surmised. *That button must have triggered it.*

She felt herself begin to collapse into the snow outside before Titus caught her and held her back up. Her legs were violently shaking, with only Titus' grip on her arms keeping her from crumbling into a pile.

Titus looked over Selene and began to fuss over her clothing and figure. She could make out in his panic, "Are you hurt? … wrong? …any… hit you?"

Titus was quickly shoved out of the way by a gaunt man carrying a thick black bag embroidered with a red cross. He and Titus frantically exchanged words, too quickly for Selene to make out, before the man placed his bag on the ground and sat Selene down in a snowbank. He ripped her boot off her leg and peeled up her pant leg. Her pink skin was like a red wine stain on a white tablecloth, and she saw the remaining colour in Titus' face fade. The other man looked up at Selene with a dark gaze and growled, "No burns."

Selene looked up and saw Titus mouth in shock, "Selene?"

Before anyone else could respond, Selene reached for her other pant leg and ripped out her shiv. She jammed the stranger in the neck, barely catching the screech he roared and the ashy blood that spouted from the wound. Selene bolted away from the scene with her shiv still poised in hand and her vision became a dark, icy blur.

She leaped over fences and nearly twisted her ankle in more ditches than she had time to count. Still, Selene ran. She didn't stop running, even as her lungs burned, and she felt bile rise from her chest to her throat. She only stopped running when she found herself back at her house and slammed and locked the door behind her. Selene barely gave herself time to catch her breath, instead taking the garbage bag full of water bottles and rushing to stuff everything she could inside the bag.

It would only be a matter of time before the vampires busted down the walls and clawed over each other to get to her. Her mind was a frenzied blur as she rushed through her house and banged her bag against the walls.

Nearly toppling into the backyard when she busted out the backdoor, Selene made a break for the woodlands, past hundreds of trees and dozens of used rabbit traps with empty snares. With the polar winds nipping at her face and her feet soaked with snow water, Selene finally allowed herself to catch her breath as she leaned against a tree.

When she looked up, she saw across from her a dirt road crowded with roaming vampires. She saw, gripped in the hands of many mob members, chains, garrotes, ropes, and even flails she'd only seen in medieval films or museums. In the cloud of darkness, Selene spotted one spark of light wandering through the mass. Turning to face her was Titus, completely unarmed, his eyes as wide as a rabbit's.

They stared at each other for what felt like hours, and Selene felt like a dagger was twisting inside her heart. Titus then turned to the crowd and cupped his hands around his mouth. The mob turned to face him before he pointed to the other side of the road. The swarm rushed into the opposite woodlands, leaving Titus alone in the middle of the road.

Selene gave a small smile and signed, "Thank you."

Titus returned with a nod. His eyes looked bright, and though he smiled, Selene could see he was holding back tears. His cheeks turned red, and his hands shook as he tried to sign. Despite his quivering, Selene could see what Titus was saying loud and clear and her heart skipped several beats.

"I love you. Goodbye." He then ran into the woodlands and became one with the darkness.

With the coast clear, Selene trudged through the snow and weaved through the trees. Her tears stung as they froze on her cheeks. Still, she continued to break away from the town, cutting the last ties to the life she knew.

*I love you. Goodbye.*

Several days passed and Selene's food was reduced to a few scant crumbs. Her bottles were filled only with frosty fog and every inch of her insides ached. Her vision was a pained blur, but she could make out the early peeps of twilight rising into the sky. Eventually, her body gave out and she collapsed into the snow. She tried to will herself to get up, but her body refused to listen. Selene dug her fingers into the snow, tugging at the strands of grass below.

*Get up, you idiot. Why won't you keep going?*

Selene nearly ground her teeth into nubs as she strained to pull herself onto her knees. There, peeking over a canopy of trees and cast against the mountain peaks, she spotted a towering inukshuk. Gazing upon it, she remembered sitting in the library with Titus, going over a few books on Inuit culture. She had flipped a page that showed a picture of a pile of rocks arranged to look like a man with his arms outstretched.

Titus had been more than eager to regale her with many Inuit facts and the inukshuk was no different. "Oh, inukshuks are used as markers to help guide travellers who were lost. Granted, we have stuff like GPS now that doesn't require as much backbreaking work to make, but you can't deny these inukshuks looked a whole lot nicer. And wouldn't you want something nice to guide you home?"

A warmth spread through Selene that gave her one last ounce of strength. She pulled herself up and smiled at the sight. Then she remembered that night in the club when she hadn't been able to make out the words of the woman who had sabotaged the sprinklers.

As Selene marched toward the grand statue overlooking the horizon, the words from the slain woman at the club came back to her more clearly. "You think you wiped us out? That we've accepted becoming cattle, ready to be a part of your slaughter? No, we're still here! We still survive, and we'll keep surviving, no matter what's thrown at us!"

# The Wrath of Lex Caninis

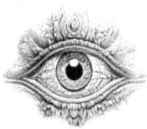

"So, new girl, what do you think happened to them?" Boyd asked. The yellow-clothed triplets leaned toward Marcy in buzzing anticipation.

Feeling herself shrink in the room, Marcy shook her head. "I... I don't know."

The three sighed in disappointment, their drinks sloshing around and nearly spilling out of their cups.

"There's no way you're going survive around here without a smidge of imagination," Oriol grumbled.

Saffron shrugged. "I mean, *you* managed to survive this long, didn't you?" She laughed.

Oriol turned to his sister with a reddened face, "Oh, you fucking—"

"Oriol!" The crinkled voice of a woman sounded from the doorway. The man's face went pale, and a chill fell upon the room. A woman with peppery hair done up in a mass of wiry curls drifted into the room, her black and white floral dress swaying from side to side as she walked in. Her vein-blue shaded lips were tightly pressed together, and her cold grey eyes narrowed on the now shuddering triplets.

"I thought we were clear on the rules of untoward language in this house." Her voice was terse and as sharp as needles.

The triplets lowered their heads in shame. "Yes, Grandma," they said in grim unison.

Marcy's eyes wandered to the old woman's neck and saw a silver locket in the shape of a hand hanging past her dress's doily collar. With another steely gaze from the elderly woman, the triplets hurried out of the room with drinks in hand.

"Later, Mari!" Boyd called before the trio disappeared down the hallway. Marigold gave a small wave before turning to face the elderly woman. The woman grinned, aligning the smile lines on her face into what Marcy assumed were their usual spots.

"Thank you for helping guide our guest back on track, Marigold," the woman said sweetly. "Why don't you go help yourself to something from the kitchen?" Marigold gave a slight bow before walking out of the room and down the hall. The older woman finally turned her attention to Marcy and guided her out of the room.

"And you must be Azura's girlfriend. Your name is… Myrtle, right?"

Marcy shook her head. "Uh, no… it's Marcy."

The old woman whipped her around with a confused expression. "Really? You look more like a Myrtle to me… What are you doing, wandering this place all by yourself?"

Marcy hesitated, her eyes focused on the necklace, seeing now that it was a mutated hand with a rainbow of jewels on its eight fingers. Marcy refocused herself and cleared her throat.

"I got a little lost after using the bathroom," she admitted to the old woman. "Though, I wasn't alone. Marigold helped me to find my bearings."

The woman laughed. "I remember getting lost in here many times when I was a little girl. As did my children. As did little Azura."

The pair entered a room bathed in UV lights and covered from floor to ceiling in plants. Sitting on a stone floral bench was Azura and a woman in either her late teens or early twenties, wearing a long, black ponytail, a pair of black glasses, and a light green sundress. Her smile managed to light up the room, even with the UV lights. Resting in her lap was a clay flowerpot containing a bunch of violet flowers.

The older woman raised a hand and waved. "Hey Azura, look who I found!"

The two girls looked up with a start, and Azura was quick to jump to her feet. She grabbed Marcy to her, nearly breaking her neck. "Grandma, you're a lifesaver!" Azura squealed.

The girl in green softly giggled, "Well, aren't you excited, Zu?"

Azura chuckled, letting go of Marcy and catching herself before she could stumble into the flowerpots behind the group. Azura turned around and gestured toward Marcy. "Laurel, this is my girlfriend, Marcy. Marcy, this is my cousin Laurel."

"Hi." Laurel raised a timid hand and waved.

The old woman cheerfully shook Marcy and Azura's shoulders. "Well, I'm glad we got that sorted. Now, I'll leave you three to yourselves until supper." She began to stroll out of the room before she called, "It was a pleasure to meet you, Myrtle!"

"Um, actually it's…"

Azura shook her head. "Don't worry about Grandma. She's never been that great with names." She carefully coerced Marcy to the stone bench and sat her down. Laurel giggled, the sound like the coo of a dove, before sitting next to the couple.

"Yeah, she used to mess up by boyfriend's name all the time before we tied the knot." Laurel slowly spun her plant around in her lap, gazing lovingly at the flowers in bloom.

Her name echoed in Marcy's head, the tingling of déjà vu tickling her neck. "Wait a minute, didn't Briar name the villain of her story Laurel?"

Laurel's eyes widened, and she squeaked out a gasp. "What? Why?" Her gentle voice became shrill, and her face contorted in shocked offense.

Azura shook her head. "Maybe she's still upset about you growing dandelions out of her shoes?"

Laurel sighed. "That was two years ago, and it was April Fool's. When is that drama queen going to let it go?"

Azura pointed to the plant. "Laurel was just showing me this, uh…" She sighed. "I'm sorry, what was this plant called again?"

"Hyacinths," Laurel replied with a serene smile. "I just bought these a few weeks ago. The new fertilizer's been a real miracle worker." She lifted the pot until it nearly blotted out the lights.

Azura whistled. "I'll say. Those look nice."

Laurel then frowned and sat back down, staring in contemplation at the vibrant bulbs. "I try my best."

As Laurel stared down at the plant, Marcy noticed a large lump in the soil of the pot. She stared at the lump, her eyebrows furrowing as Laurel continued her spiel.

"When you think about it, the environment's been pretty generous with us. Especially when we keep mucking things up for everyone else that lives on the planet."

Marcy held back the urge to sigh and roll her eyes. *Oh no, she's one of those?* But she tried not to make those thoughts physical and instead continued to listen.

A smile reformed on Laurel's face as she dragged her thumb across the dirt. "But I guess there was one benefit to being a worry wart about the state of the planet." The planter set the pot to the side and patted the clay rim. "It helped serve as inspiration for a story. More specifically, a story about what happens when nature finally fights back."

\*\*\*

Balle En Argent was one of the busiest cosmetic companies in the state of Oregon. The corporation had spread its influence across the states, with a building in thirty-two of them.

Even when a third of its buildings were shut down, Balle En Argent continued to increase their profit margins, seemingly maintaining a solid foothold in the makeup industry.

Still, the biggest and most profitable of their factories was in the heart of their home state. A plump two-story building surrounded by an ocean of trees and an iron gate topped with curls of barbed wire. A few miles away from the road that led to the facility was a large lake with beautiful blue water that served as a congregation point for many animals, including deer, rabbits, and badgers. This lake was protected by valleys of dunes and massive oak trees. If only the fauna knew what a blessing the lake provided, how it was a natural shield against the people who cultivated Balle En Argent.

For those unfortunate enough to be trapped inside the building, it was a gigantic house of horrors. But for Chris and Bryan, it was just work.

It was another early workday for the employees who made the tedious commute to work at Balle En Argent's Oregon facility. The one called to wrangle in the workers, Chris Glenn, smeared his steering wheel with freshly applied hand sanitizer, creating a slick mark. He glanced up at his rearview mirror, catching a glimpse of his greying brunette curls, as spick-and-span as he always intended to be. Returning his attention to the road, the man groaned at the sight forming in front of the gate circling the facility. The gates were surrounded by a crowd of irate protestors waving signs in the air and clad in cheap, tie-dye anti-animal testing T-shirts.

"If those hippies put the same effort as they did picketing our shop into getting a real job, we wouldn't have to worry about welfare for the next decade." Chris slowed his car down, stopping a few feet before the rowdy crowd.

The people turned their anger toward him and began to circle his car like a pack of lions surrounding a lone zebra. The people, mostly young adults of course, began to shout obscenities and bang against his car windows.

"Murderer!"

"You torture innocent animals!"

"How does it feel running an animal concentration camp?"

Chris sighed, and, with a roll of his eyes, crushed his hand against the wheel's horn. A few picketers jumped back at the blaring horn, and yet the swarm remained, their anger unrelenting. Chris looked back into the rearview mirror, seeing a row of other cars beginning to line up behind him.

"Great, going to start the shift late. Again," he muttered. He didn't have to bemoan his situation for long as he and the crowd were greeted by a woman in a lab coat, wearing midnight blue heels and her black hair done in a bun, marching up to the other side of the gate.

The woman smirked before unfurling a bulky black hose and spraying a geyser of water at the crowd. The crowd began to scream, and Chris snickered at the sight of their eyes turning red on the retreat. Once the crowd finally dispersed, the woman in the lab coat pushed the gates open and let the convoy into the facility grounds.

Chris pulled into his usual parking spot before stepping outside to meet the woman. "Nice job keeping those hippies out of the joint, Amber," Chris said, coating his hands with hand cleanser.

The woman grinned and gave a casual shrug. "It's no big deal. Just a bit of soapy water can go a long way."

Chris spit out a laugh, barely covering his mouth with his elbow, "You put soap in the water?"

Amber nodded, opening the door to the facility. "They're going to be too busy rinsing out those eyes to bother us for the rest of the day." The pair laughed as they entered the building.

Meanwhile, having just peeled out of the line-up of cars, one of the newest interns for Balle En Argent stepped out of a small blue Pontiac. He was a nebbish-looking young man with shaggy brown hair and thin, grey glasses. He fidgeted his hands around in his pants pockets, fumbling with the various knick-knacks inside. The man looked up and gazed at the building, standing nervously in its shadow. He took a deep breath and followed the other workers through the doors. As soon as he entered the building, he was nearly blown back out by a large puff of cold air.

The odour of bleach felt like it would dissolve his nose hairs in seconds. He could hear the faint shifting of gears from the various devices chugging away in the building's many rooms. The man stepped up to the front desk, manned by a tired older man who looked ready to fall asleep at any moment.

"Name?" the desk man asked, his voice monotone and exhausted.

The younger man pulled out his wallet and slipped out his I.D. "Um…Bryan. Bryan Affleck." He passed the slip of plastic over to the older man. The deskman looked over the I.D. before handing it back to Bryan and pulling out a large, sky-blue container filled with clothes, sanitizer, and various cleaning supplies.

"Locker room for interns is second door from the left."

"Thanks." Bryan nodded, gingerly taking opposing ends of the bin. He went down the sterile, monochrome hallway before opening the designated grey door. Inside the room was a baby blue room lined with towering grey lockers. Sitting in the middle of the room was a navy-blue bench with a mesh-like design. Bryan noticed poking out of the clutter in the bin a slip of paper. He took it out and saw it read, "Locker number 17. Combination: 14-30-17"

Bryan circled around the area, reading the numbers attached to the lockers and stopping at number seventeen. He placed his bin on the bench and got to work on his lock.

Despite the cool air pressing down upon him, Bryan felt himself covered in a blanket of boiling sweat. This was his first day on the job and he knew the best way to survive was to keep his head down.

"Hey, haven't seen you around here before," a voice called.

Bryan turned his head and saw a young woman leaning against the doorway. She had dark hair with a single purple streak near the front, dark olive skin, and a small, melancholic smile.

"Are you new here?" she asked, walking over to the locker neighboring Bryan on the left.

Bryan nodded. "Yeah. Starting an internship."

The girl nodded, twisting at her lock before pulling it open. "Cool. My school thought it'd be a good idea for me to intern here, too." She opened her locker door and pulled out a lab coat, a pair of goggles, a pair of baby blue rubber gloves, and a black ponytail holder. The girl slipped the coat on before pulling her hair back into a ponytail.

"Alejandra, by the way," she said, stretching herself back to tighten her ponytail.

Bryan nodded, pulling open the lock on his own locker. "Bryan." He opened the locker and turned to his bin, picking up the lab coat inside and slipping it on. "So, what's it like working here?"

Alejandra sighed and shook her head. "Maybe you'll like it here, but I'm honestly counting down the days until my internship is over." She stretched out her rubber gloves before yanking them over her hands with a snap. "I'm not going to lie, the sounds that come out of those rooms are pretty rough."

She pulled a cellphone and a pair of red earbuds out of her lab coat pocket. "I've managed to talk my way into using this when they get too intense for me. Chris wasn't for it at first. He wanted me to prove I was dedicated enough without the 'distractions,' a.k.a, pulling out a stupid amount of overtime."

"Chris?" Bryan asked.

The girl giggled. "Don't tell me you took the position without knowing the boss man's name."

Bryan bit his lip and his eyes darted all over the place. "I uh… um…" he stuttered.

Alejandra flapped her hand dismissively. "It's all good. I won't tattle on you," she said, closing the locker and heading for the door. She gave a thumbs-up. "Good luck, dude."

Bryan nodded in return before seeing Alejandra disappear down the hall. He looked into the shadows inside of his locker and sighed. "Yeah, I'm going to need it," he muttered.

Bryan slipped on his gloves before stuffing the bin inside his locker and locking the door. He fiddled around in his pants pockets before buttoning up his lab coat. He took a deep breath and walked up to the door.

"Here we go," he whispered uneasily. Bryan stepped outside and began to meander down the hall. Each step caused Bryan's body to rattle in shivers. He stopped before a grey-blue door labelled, "Chemical Testing #1" and nodded.

"Right, this is my first stop, like the lady on the phone said," Bryan muttered to himself. He raised his hand and knocked on the door's mesh-covered window.

"Come in!" a man inside called.

Bryan grabbed the long silver doorknob and twisted it open. He stepped inside and saw Chris leaning over a white mouse scrambling inside of a tray. However, the rodent's struggle was in vain, for he was being pinned down under the hand of Chris's assistant, Amber. Chris took out a needle filled with a sickly, yellow substance before he noticed Bryan standing in the doorway.

"Ah, you must be the new intern here," Chris said, waving the hand holding the needle. As he waved, a twister of bubbles began to spin around inside the syringe.

Bryan carefully stepped inside the sterile room and let the door close behind him with an ear-bleeding slam. Chris then jammed the syringe under the mouse's eye, causing it to scramble and scream out a flurry of distressed squeaks.

Bryan tried his best not to reel at the crying rodent but found it difficult, looking at Chris's almost overly eager grin.

"For now, you can start by mopping the floors of each of the labs. We like to keep a clean and sanitized establishment here, especially since if not kept under control, this place gets pretty messy," he said nonchalantly. Chris then quickly removed the syringe from the mouse and Amber let go of the rodent. The mouse stumbled around as if it was drunk and nearly tipped out of the tin it was placed in.

Bryan pointed nervously at the mouse. "Is he going to be alright?" he asked timidly.

Amber shrugged while Chris replied, "Well, if he does power through it, we'll know we have the right dosage." He then discarded the syringe in a mustard-yellow biohazard waste bin.

"And if he doesn't?" Bryan asked.

Chris chuckled. "I mean, is anyone really going to complain if there's one last rodent scuttling about in the world?" His grin showed his abnormally pearly-white teeth, almost glowing under the pale white light.

Bryan noticed the white mouse's black eyes become wide with fear. It flailed about until its paws found purchase on the edge of the tin. The mouse whined, staring over at Bryan, and began to shake.

Amber sighed, shoving the mouse back inside of the tin. "Come on; quit squirming around."

Chris eyed Bryan impatiently, tapping at the cast-iron desk. "Well?"

Bryan hesitated before backing up to the door. "Right," he replied uneasily before sliding back into the hall. Sweat pumped out of his pores and his breaths were as shallow as a puddle. His legs begged him to bolt out of the building and never look back. Bryan shut his eyes and dragged himself to the broom closet. He peered inside and grabbed the mop and surprisingly squeaky-clean mop bucket.

*I still have a job to do. Just have to make it through the day.* Bryan steeled himself and ferried the mop and bucket down the hall.

What he saw in those rooms would have him regretting ever stepping inside that building.

The first room held a rabbit sitting on a desk, clad in what looked like a linen jumpsuit. Attached to one of its sides was a petri dish, containing dirt-like sores and what looked like a collection of jellybean-shaped lumps of flesh. The rabbit twisted and moaned on its desk as a pair of workers apathetically jotted down notes on their clipboards.

Bryan walked into another room and witnessed a woman with a facemask cutting open the top of a cat's head with a scalpel. The cat struggled and squirmed under the tight grip of the surgeon's companions. Bryan watched as a thick stream of blood poured down the cat's orange fur and heard its yowls of pain pierce through the room's walls. Before he left the room, one of the surgeon's companions pulled out a peculiar electrical device and prepared to force the pegs of the device into the cat's open wound.

He helped to mop up other rooms where various cats, dogs, rats, birds, and even monkeys were either injected with various strange substances or had their gangrenous sores poked and prodded at by various lab coat-clad men and women without a shred of emotion. By the time he approached the hall's last room, Bryan felt ready to puke out every meal he had had over the week. His heart felt ready to explode and his light head clouded his vision in darkness. He grabbed at the doorknob, feeling the stinging cold steel pierce through his rubber gloves. He looked up and his heart sank into further depths he didn't know he had.

"Euthanasia," the door read. Even before he opened the door, he could hear the shaking and scratching of cages and whimpering of various animals pierce his ears. For a long time, he stood inside the hall, refusing to open the door and letting his intestines twist into sickly knots. Eventually, he twisted the doorknob and began to open the door. He resolved that he would just be in and out and then put away the mop and bucket to get as far away from that room as possible.

Inside the room were rows of steel cages dug into the wall. Inside the cages were various scarred animals filling the room with their desperate cries. Some were left without any of the fur on them; almost all of them were covered in red sores and had even redder eyes. Their paws hung between the cage's bars and their goop-filled eyes were not swollen just enough to trap their tears.

At the back of the room was what looked like a giant steel oven sitting next to a baby blue bench.

His ears caught the whimpering of the beagle before his eyes found her. She sat on the lap of a woman who was sitting on a bench. The beagle hugged the woman's leg, shivering and whimpering. The beagle's eyes were bloodshot, her paws were missing several toes, and half of her right ear was hacked off. The edge of the coat was soaked in dried blood and a sickly substance of yellow and brown.

Bryan looked up and saw the woman had a familiar purple streak in her hair.

She looked up at him with tear-filled eyes and gave a sad smile. "Finally made it to the graveyard, huh?" Alejandra asked, her voice as bumpy as a pothole-filled road.

Bryan sighed, clutching at his mop stick for dear life. "I guess so," he said mournfully. He caught Alejandra occasionally darting her eyes toward the clock above the cages while continuing to pet the terrified beagle. She caught him gazing and gave a mirthless chuckle.

"Just trying to make their last moments as comfortable as possible before it's time," she said, nearly choking on her words. "Figured the best parting gift for them would be a touch of kindness from a human. Though it'd be a nice little change before…" Alejandra sighed, carefully picking the beagle up and letting the puppy rest on her shoulder in a bittersweet hug. The pup whined and burrowed her muzzle into the side of Alejandra's face.

"I know, baby," she whispered. "I'm so sorry. But if Heaven's for real, I'll bet the big guy upstairs is going to spoil you with all the treats you could eat."

The beagle whimpered and began to dig through Alejandra's hair.

The girl shut her eyes and a waterfall of tears cascaded down her face. When she opened her eyes, she looked up at the clock and let out a sob. As soon as Alejandra stood up from her seat, the animals in the case began to roar and rattle in their cages. The rowdiest of them all was a white and grey husky baring her razor-sharp teeth. She slammed her head against the cage door and her eyes were red, not from scars or an obvious after-effect from the experiments like the others, but from pure rage.

Alejandra pulled open the oven door and gently placed the Beagle pup inside. The pup turned around and looked up at Alejandra with wide, innocent eyes and began to whine. Alejandra shut her eyes and gripped the door handle tightly with both hands.

"I'm so sorry," she croaked one last time before closing the oven door. She began to fiddle with the buttons and knobs as the pup's whining became louder and more desperate. Bryan's own eyes began to fill with tears.

"Are you sure one of us can't take her home? You don't have to—"

Alejandra shook her head. "Confidentiality issue," she spat venomously in between sobs. Her hand hovered over a big red button on the stove, reeling her hand back as she heard the Beagle scratch against the door.

"They say it'll be like going to sleep for these guys. It's better to have them go out like this than for them to keep suffering in here," she said, though Bryan was unsure about who she was trying to convince out of the two of them.

Alejandra took a deep breath, shut her eyes, and pressed the red button. The machine roared to life. Bryan could hear the grinding of gears and the hissing of gas being released inside the steel prison. The pup's begging became more panicked, and she began to scratch at the door in a frenzy.

Alejandra continued to sob, though her crying was drowned out by the wails of the other animals sitting on death row. Then, only a few seconds later, the whining stopped, and a large *slam* pounded down from the other side of the door. The cacophony of animal cries dropped as quickly as a pin.

For a while, only the sound of Alejandra's sobs and the ticking of the clock could be heard. Then the machine belted out a loud *buzz* and Alejandra stepped away from the contraption of execution.

Bryan ran to Alejandra and pulled her into an embrace. She sobbed into his shoulder. Her hot tears soaked through his coat and were barely absorbed by his sweatshirt. Her shoulders shook uncontrollably, and her face turned a deep red. "Why did they pick me?"

Bryan held her tightly and rocked slightly back and forth. "I don't know. But the fact that you give them the kindness in their final moments that they missed so much…" Bryan trailed off.

He was about to say it made her the best person for the job since her nurturing words would be their final memory. But still, he had a feeling it wouldn't put Alejandra much at ease.

She reluctantly pulled away from Bryan and wiped her face with her sleeve. She cleared her throat and tried to maintain a cool, casual air, albeit unsuccessfully,

"They'll have someone take care of the body in a few minutes," she stated. Suddenly, the thrashing of a cage caused both humans to jump with a start.

Bryan's eyes fell on the husky, who was now gnawing at the bars of her cage. He pointed toward the cage and asked, "So, what's up with her? She looks unscathed by the experiments."

Alejandra laughed glumly. "Ah yeah, the husky. Came in

about a week ago, just refused to stay down for experimentation from what I've heard. Actually bit a few of the workers pretty badly. Some of them required stitches."

Bryan walked up to the cage and gazed at the scrambling, grey-furred berserker of a canine. "Looks pretty angry."

"I mean, wouldn't *you* be if you were cooped up in a place like this?" Alejandra asked. The husky suddenly stopped clawing at the bars and began to sniff in Bryan's direction. She let out a soft whine and her eyes became so wide their whites seemed to disappear.

Bryan began to raise his hand when Alejandra bolted to him and pulled his arm back.

"Hey, careful," she gingerly chided. "Don't want to end up losing a finger on the first day, do you?"

Bryan sighed. "No, I guess not."

Alejandra jerked her head toward the door. "Come on, you don't belong in a room like this. Besides, you've probably got other work to do."

Bryan nodded, taking his mop and bucket and slowly opening the door.

"Hey!"

Bryan turned his head and saw Alejandra slump onto the bench. She wiped away another tear before continuing,

"Thanks. Not a lot of people here care to be a shoulder to cry on."

Bryan gave a small smile and nodded. "Anytime. I mean, your job doesn't look easy."

Alejandra shook her head. "Whoever said I'd get used to it after a while is either a liar or a heartless dick," she muttered.

With that, Bryan turned back to the hall and with a heavy heart, closed the door behind him.

After two more hours passed, the clock struck twelve and

triggered a blaring *buzz* to sound out through the building.

Meanwhile, Chris was back in his office, filing through bland papers, some bills, and some angry letters from protesting hippies. He happily dropped the papers onto his desk as the droning *buzz* reached his room.

"Sweet. Time for lunch." He launched out of his chair and took out a large paper bag from under his desk before strutting out the door and through the hallway. In the middle of his stride, the lights suddenly went out, plunging his surroundings into shadow.

He sighed. "Goddamn. Are we going to have to call another electrician?" Just as he muttered this, the lights turned back on and nearly blinded him in a pale light.

He snickered. "Okay, guess not." He continued on his way without another care. The mess hall was a wide room with rows of cream-coloured folding tables and deep green plastic chairs. The fluorescent lights were a warmer amber, a much-needed relief from the eye-bleeding white lights in the labs. Of course, many other workers called this room the breakroom, but this title seemed much too casual for Chris's liking.

They were providing a vital service for Balle En Argent. This establishment was above such humdrum terms as a breakroom. Chris sat at the head of the table closest to the kitchen, as usual, and pulled a roast beef sandwich from his bag. As he unwrapped his saran wrap, the new intern took a seat just two chairs away from him.

Chris put on his best sales pitch smile. "Ah, hello Mr. Affleck. How's your first day on the job treating you?"

The meek intern shuffled around in his seat and took out a plastic container filled with a mix of blueberries, raspberries, and blackberries. "Pretty good, I guess," Mr. Affleck timidly replied.

Chris raised an eyebrow. "You guess?" he chuckled, leaning closer to the intern. "What's that supposed to mean?"

Mr. Affleck shrugged uneasily and tried to lean away from his boss. "It's just that…well, some of these tests seem a little extreme," the scrawny young man stammered. "Are they all really necessary?"

Chris rolled his eyes with a laugh, "Of course. Those tests are the best way we can ensure that our products are safe for consumption," he said, jovially patting the intern on the forearm. He stopped patting Mr. Affleck's arm and stared into the cowering intern's eyes.

"Why? You want to take up their job as the professional guinea pig?" Chris threw his head back and laughed. It wasn't unusual for the new hires to be soft-hearted, but it would only be a matter of time before they hardened up and came to terms with what needed to be done to get the job done.

"No, not really." Mr. Affleck said with a frantic headshake. He looked to open his mouth to keep speaking, but no more words came out.

Chris shook his head and chuckled, "Yeah, none of us do. Some of them get pretty nasty and if we did those tests on people, we'd have more lawsuits than there are cities in Texas."

The intern nodded, though he didn't laugh along with his boss. Of course, Chris knew that not everyone got his sense of humour and that was alright. He didn't care as long as they did their jobs.

Just as Chris returned to unwrapping his sandwich, an ear-piercing siren blasted through the mess hall. The head honcho of the building dropped his sandwich and stood up out of his seat. The rest of the workers looked around in a confused panic. Murmurs of worry filled the room.

*Goddamn. They couldn't wait until after we ate?* Chris ran

down the hall and into the security office. The room was a meagre space, a tin-sized room with computer monitors crowding the walls. Sitting below the flickering monitors with a small mouse and keyboard was Evan Tudik, the dirty blonde security guard who had been with the company for three years. The guard had his hand on a switch labelled, "Alert."

"Tudik, what's going on here?" Chris asked, his face twisted with aggravation, "and couldn't it wait until after lunch?"

"Sorry, boss, the monitors went out along with the rest of the power. They were completely fried, took a while before I could get them back online, but when they came back up..."

Evan pointed up to one of the higher monitors, the one showing the euthanasia room. The cages were completely empty, and one of them looked like it had been pried open. The rest of the cages were simply unlocked.

"What the hell?" Chris muttered.

Evan shrugged. "No clue. Didn't hear any commotion. In fact, almost missed the sight on the monitor until I saw one of the cages all chewed up."

Chris gritted his teeth and dug his nails into the desk. There was only one person who had both access to the room during break hours and the nerve to pull such a stunt.

"Alejandra."

Chris stormed out of the room and stomped back over to the mess hall. After blasting through the doors, he screamed, "Alejandra Solis! My office, now!" He jabbed his finger toward the door and glared at the displaced crowd.

The small intern with the purple streak in her hair wasn't hard to spot in a crowd. She quickly stood up from her seat and shuffled over to Chris. He pulled her out of the room by the wrist, prompting a short cry before she was dragged down the hall.

"You couldn't get yourself into more trouble if you tried,"

the irate boss growled.

Alejandra looked up at him with a mix of annoyance and bewilderment. "What are you talking about?" she snapped.

"Oh, don't you play dumb with me."

"Play dumb? I just did what you asked me to do."

"Yeah, and it looks like the camera saw the results of you doing a little extra credit."

"What? Are you high?" Alejandra stopped in her tracks and yanked her hand out of Chris' grip. She waved her hand in the air and rubbed her wrist. "And stop pulling me around," she barked. "I'm not some kid. I can walk by myself just fine!"

Chris felt his blood boil over and his face heat up to a fiery red. "Oh, yeah? Maybe you'll fess up when you see what you've done face-to-face!" he screamed. He continued to stomp down the hall with a fuming Alejandra trailing behind him. That anger would soon be replaced with guttural fear.

Turning a corner, Chris stopped dead in his tracks at the sight of a dark crimson puddle of liquid seeping into the hall. He heard Alejandra's steps scuttle to a stop a few inches behind him.

"What the hell?" she whispered.

Chris crept a few steps forward, keeping his breaths short to avoid making unnecessary sounds. He was halfway to the puddle before he realized he was walking alone. He turned his head to Alejandra, who was peeking her head out from the corner, her body shaking and her jaw agape.

Chris snarled and violently waved his hand to beckon her forward. "What are you doing? Get over here."

"Uh uh, no way. I've watched enough horror movies to know where this is going. I don't get paid enough for this." Alejandra shook her head and wagged her finger. She then ran around the corner and disappeared.

Chris sighed. While he admired her sense of self-preservation, he lamented the fact that no one would act as a witness in case something happened to him. He stopped before the puddle and saw it was leaking from underneath a door. His eyes followed the trail to the door and his heart sank.

The door read, "Security."

Chris gulped, failing to steady his rapidly beating heart. His face twisted as he felt his foot squelch against the slimy crimson puddle before he squeezed his hand around the doorknob. He quickly twisted the knob and shoved the door open. Chris's heart stopped as soon as he opened the door before quickly dropping further down into his stomach.

Evan's body was slouched over the security desk with boiling blood pouring out of his mouth. His body had hundreds of needles stabbed into his boil and puss-covered body. His stomach was torn open, intestines and a bubbly, amber substance pouring out of the gaping wound.

The monitors were destroyed, and glass shards covered the desk and floor like a gruesome mosaic. The monitor surveying the euthanasia room had the console's keyboard shoved through the glass.

Chris stood in stupefied silence, barely able to keep the contents of his stomach from crawling back up his throat. Not helping to make his efforts easier was the stench of blood and rotten meat. Chris snapped himself out of his stupor and reached for the red alert switch. He flipped the switch and let the alarms roar. His breaths became shallow, and his hands began to shake. Despite the panic that was coursing through his body, he tried to slow his mind down so he could construct a plan.

*Okay, I need to get to my office and call the police. Then I need to barricade the door and hunker down until help arrives.*

He nodded to himself; a solid enough plan that should help protect his skin from whoever had torn Tuvik up like a

Christmas turkey. Chris ran out of the room, only to slip on the puddle of blood as soon as he entered the hallway. Some breath was knocked out of him as his body bounced off the beige laminate. His brain bounced around in his skull as he struggled to pick himself up, the sticky red substance coating his palms and soaking into his suit and slacks. Chris shambled down the hall with a weary head and a new metallic-scented cologne soaking in his clothes.

Chris turned into the hall with the labs, the stench of blood and meat became stronger. Pouring out of the lab were heaps of mangled bodies clad in bloodstained lab coats and covered in various guts and internal organs. The floors were coated with a layer of dark crimson liquid and the doors with windows had a thin film of the same substance. Chris covered his face with his sleeve to block out the stench of fresh viscera.

He eventually reached the end of the hall and turned his head to the path leading to his office. Staggering down the corridor was Amber, her hair in a knotted mess and her lab coat torn to shreds. She was fresh out of breath, and she was clutching at her arm, now pumping a river of blood. Amber looked up at Chris, showing her mascara had turned into a pair of inky waterfalls.

"Sir?"

"Amber, what the hell is going on here?"

Amber shook her head, and her body began to tremble. A few chokes left her lips and she collapsed onto her knees.

"It's… it was horrible! That thing tore everyone apart. Oh God, it's still here!"

"What? What tore everyone apart? What's still here?"

Chris would soon find an answer to his questions in the form of a hulking shadow lumbering at the end of Amber's hall. The shadow's owner revealed itself under the flickering fluorescent light. The towering beast was covered in grey fur with streaks of black surrounding its eyes and streaking across its snout. Another streak trailed down from the top of its head, down its back, and stopped at the end of its bristled tail. The goliath canine's eyes were a furious crimson that broke through the shadow cast across its venomous glare. The creature dragged its prolonged talons across the white brick wall, creating a shrill shriek that cut through the air like a knife through butter.

Amber and Chris emptied their lungs with a floor-rumbling scream before scrambling to bolt away from the beast. The monster let out a thundering roar in return and slunk onto all fours. It began to gallop, quickly catching up to the coworkers sliding on the pools of gore.

Amber's heels betrayed her, twisting around in the puddle and throwing her to the ground. Chris skidded to a stop and turned back to Amber. He reached his hand out toward her as she slipped around in the scarlet substance,

"Amber, give me your hand! We got to go!" Just before Amber could take her superior's hand, the beast grabbed her by the ankle and dragged her away, leaving a scarlet streak in her path.

Chris began to book it back down the hall, turning away as the beast threw Amber into the air. He turned the corner to the hall leading to his office. Amber's screams bounced down the hall, stopping Chris in his tracks. He ran back to the corner and watched helplessly as the muscular wolf creature slammed Amber's lower back into its knee.

A thick crunch cracked like a whip, choking Amber's screams into struggling gurgles. The wolf threw Amber into the ground face first. Her arms began to shake, and her hair turned into thick clumps after amalgamating with the puddles of ichor.

Small whimpers escaped the woman's lips as she struggled to pull her hands forward and push herself up the hall. The lower half of her body was unmoving, devoid of all signs of life. Amber sobbed, scraping for every few inches of movement she could scavenge.

The beast loomed over her like a shadow, glowering at her with ravenous eyes and drool drizzling from its jaws.

"C-C-Chris…h-help me!" Amber croaked. She reached her hand out, her arm shaking under the weight of her cries.

The beast snarled and raised a giant paw over her prone and vulnerable body. It quickly dropped its foot down on Amber, splitting her body in two and sending the halves flying into the walls.

Chris turned away and pressed his back against the wall. He felt a sour bile build in his throat and he was enveloped in a frosty embrace. He swallowed the developing vitriol and shambled further down the hall. His light head made him feel like he was moving underwater.

Bodies lined the walls, but not all of them had all their limbs accounted for. Chris saw different human parts scattered across the ground like discarded candy wrappers, though some were so mangled he couldn't tell what they used to be anymore.

Slumped onto the ground by Chris' office door was the body of a young woman. Her sockets were filled with shredded viscera where her eyes should have been, her ears were torn apart, and a crimson necklace dripping with blood was drawn across her neck.

When Chris got a closer look, he could barely make out a purple streak in the cadaver's hair from the congealed crimson. "Just didn't make it in time," he sighed, shaking his head despondently.

But Chris couldn't afford to mourn his intern for long. He had to have help come in and storm the place to bring the monster down. Police, SWAT, FBI, exterminator, basically any force that had the heavy firepower needed to put down the wolf-thing. He slammed the door open and collapsed into his office.

Little did Chris know that hiding behind his desk was another intern, albeit one that had managed to survive the creature's rampage. Bryan sprung out from behind his boss' desk, armed with a stapler, and swung it around like a bowie knife.

"Get back!" The intern shouted before he processed who had broken into his hiding spot. When Chris stood up, Bryan stopped swinging and gingerly placed the stapler back onto the desk. "Oh, it's you." Bryan breathed a sigh of relief.

Chris looked at the anxious intern incredulously. The boss marched up to the desk and slammed his hands against it. "Affleck, what are you doing in here?" Chris asked.

Bryan's eyes darted back and forth, and he began stealing greedy puffs of metallic-scented air. "I, uh… The alarms went off and everyone started running around in a panic." Bryan stumbled over his words, his mouth appearing to move faster than his mind. "I had no idea what was happening, then this giant hairy beast thing busted into the break room and started tearing people apart like they were made of tissue or something."

Chris clamped his hands on Bryan's shoulders and the boss lightly shook the intern. "Slow down, boy. You got to pull yourself together if we're going to walk out in one piece."

The boss reached out and yanked his phone off the receiver and began to dial the police. However, when he placed the phone up to his ear, Chris' heart sank. The other end was completely silent, without even a dial tone showing evidence of any life on the other side.

"What the hell?" Chris muttered, slamming the phone back down. He looked down at the ground and saw the cords attached to the phone were torn to shreds, looking like a cat chewed them up. Chris collapsed onto his knees and futilely tried to tie the cords back together. He looked back up at Bryan, who seemed to be doing his best impression of a deer in the headlights.

"Were they like this when you hunkered down in here?" Chris asked.

Bryan shook his head. "I didn't really pay attention to the phone."

Chris pushed himself onto his feet and narrowed his eyes. "You mean you curled yourself under my desk, but you didn't even bother to check if the phones were working? Maybe to, oh, I don't know, call the cops so they can sort this shit out before more bodies start crowding the halls?" Chris felt his veins push against the skin of his neck as his voice bellowed through the office.

Bryan waved his hands in the air desperately. "Mr. Glenn, keep it down. The monster might hear you."

"Does it really matter at this point? Without any way to contact any help, we're fucked!" Chris roared in frustration and slammed a fist into the wall. "Was it really that hard a job to do a once-over at the place you wanted to hole up in?" the boss growled.

Bryan grabbed clumps of his shaggy chestnut hair and shook his head. "I don't know. Maybe Alejandra tried the phone, but the monster found her before she could do anything."

A petrifying bolt of ice struck Chris' heart. He slowly turned his head toward Bryan and let his fist slide down the wall.

"What?" he whispered.

Bryan's eyes wiggled around nervously, and his fingers began to twitch. "Maybe the beast sabotaged the phone lines before we got here," Bryan whimpered.

Chris wagged his finger in the intern's face. "No, no, no. Before, you said Alejandra may have tried the phone."

"Um…sir—"

"I never even mentioned Solis. But the funny thing is, I did find her earlier. Outside of my office, with her eyes raked out." Chris lunged and grabbed Bryan's shirt.

Bryan was slammed into a bookshelf, watching various books fly off the shelf and flop onto the floor. Bryan shook his head and his heart felt like it was going to explode. "I mean, I did see her body before coming in. I didn't know what to do so I just left it as is," he cried, struggling to wiggle out of his increasingly mad boss' grip.

Chris bared his snarling teeth and chuckled darkly, "Oh, no. You had something to do with it, didn't you?"

"No!"

"Oh, I think you did."

"Why would I want to hurt Alejandra? She was nothing but kind to me."

"You probably left her to die to save your own skin. I think that's what happened. Figured if you left her to the beast then it would be too busy tearing her to bits to even notice your scrawny ass."

As Chris ranted and raved, he continuously slammed Bryan against the shelf, causing the intern's vision to bounce around like an out-of-control basketball. He wasn't given time to formulate a sentence since any words crawling to his mouth were almost immediately knocked out.

By the time Bryan felt most of Chris' strength leave his arms, the boss had nearly knocked all the wind out of the young intern. Bryan's breaths were unsteady and struggled to crawl up his throat. His heavy head was thrown to the side in his effort to turn to the red-faced, raging man pinning him to the wall. Though it felt like walls were closing in on the inside of his throat, Bryan still managed to fish a few words out.

"I didn't kill her, and I didn't leave her for dead." Bryan knew his weak protests would do nothing to change the mind of his boss, but at the very least, he could buy himself some time. A large shadow crept down the hall and tickled the edge of the office door.

"But... I know who's behind this whole thing."

"Excuse me?" Chris growled. His eyes were alight with the fire of a vicious beast, so consumed by anger that he didn't hear the twisting of his office's doorknob.

Icy sweat coated Bryan's face and drenched the back of his neck. He nodded at Chris and tried to force a smile, though his nerves were so shot the muscles in his face couldn't muster the strength to do so.

"My sister."

Suddenly, the office door exploded into a cloud of dust and splinters. Chris turned his head toward the door and screamed, dropping Bryan after getting smacked by the explosion's shockwave.

For many, the behemoth standing in the doorway covered in viscera and ichor would be seen as a monster without pity or remorse and an appetite for the flesh of the innocent.

But to Bryan, she was just baby sister Scout. And she had arrived just in time to, once again, help her big brother out of a jam.

"Wh-what?" Chris barely had enough time to process the information before Scout scooped him up in one of her enormous claws.

She then slammed the older man into the ground and pressed her legs into his arms and the back of his knees. Scout dug her claws into Chris' spine, causing him to let out a bloodcurdling scream that shook the room. Scout let out one last roar of triumph before yanking her elbows back. The skin on Chris' back was split in two, dragging parts of his ribcage and some various internal parts away with them in a storm of flesh and bone.

Hoarse breaths barely escaped Chris as he lay on the ground helplessly. The pits of blood and flesh bubbled and ballooned in time with his laboured puffs of life, his new fleshy wings kissing the ground with each exhale.

Scout looked over to Bryan and gave him a gentle nod. Bryan gave her a sheepish thumbs up, his body still not used to the smell of freshly drawn blood or exposed organs.

After his sister skulked out of the office, Bryan stepped over Chris and kneeled at the doorway. Chris' face was twisted into an expression of permanent horror, doomed to suffer for the last few minutes of his life. Bryan's nerves were still shaking like a maraca, but he still wanted to have the last word with his now former boss.

"Consider this my three weeks' notice," Bryan said, his voice still feeling ripe and delicate.

He gingerly stepped out of the office, unable to look at Alejandra's body. Despite her being a greasy cog in a grizzly system, Bryan wished he could have warned her about the plan. But he hadn't and so there she lay. He was at least grateful that Scout had been quick with her. Bryan slipped his lab coat from his body and gently laid it over Alejandra's body.

Police surrounded the building, their lights almost making the night sky look like day. But both the perpetrators and the lab animals once trapped in that building were long gone.

Over at the lake, the animals rolled around in the grass and splashed around in the shallow end of the water. The sight brought a smile to Bryan's face. He could see the sense of wonder and innocence return to the eyes of the many dogs, cats, mice, and primates that frolicked in their newfound freedom. He felt Scout nuzzle her head into his hand. He looked down and began to pet his sister's husky form.

"Created a lot of noise over there. Probably the biggest blow the company's suffered yet."

Scout wagged her tail and gave a happy bark in reply. Bryan reached into his pocket and pulled out a pen and a slip of paper.

An extensive list of Balle En Argent locations, with a third of the list already crossed out. He clicked the pen and read down the list. He stopped at "Bend, Oregon," the only location on the list that was circled. With a grin, Bryan crossed the name off the list. He huddled closer to Scout and let her peek at the list.

"So, where am I going to apply for my next internship?

# The Artist's Greatest Foe

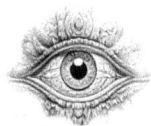

Laurel carefully placed her pot of flowers by a window, settling it on the beige, stone sill. The green-thumbed woman patted the rim of the pot and turned to face the couple.

Azura let a whistle fly through the cavern formed between her lips. "You're really giving me some tough competition there."

Laurel raised a dismissive hand. "Nonsense, I'm sure your story will be just as good."

Marcy raised an eyebrow. "Wait, *your* story?"

Azura nodded. "Yeah, I'm supposed to tell the next story over dinner. Every time we have a get-together like this, someone needs to tell the whole family a story, and I got the lucky draw, I guess." Azura chuckled nervously and brushed a strand of hair behind her ear.

Marcy's first instinct was to sweep Azura into a quick embrace and give her a peck on the lips. "I'm sure you'll do great," she said soothingly.

Azura's cheeks turned beet red, and she chuckled to herself. "Clearly, you overestimate my storytelling skills."

Laurel laughed. "Nah, I'm sure Marcy's right. You'll do great." Laurel then began to guide her cousin to the doorway. "Come on, let's go help get dinner ready."

Once the pair turned their back, Marcy yanked out her phone and began to text Aiden. "Follow the old lady with the black-and-white, flowered dress. May have the key to a treasure room."

The pot of hyacinths danced in the corner of Marcy's eyes. As she waited for a reply from her brother, she began to dig her finger around in the flowerpot's soil. Her riffling through the coarse, warm dirt was stopped when her fingers pressed against a cold lump. Marcy brought the pot fully into her vision and tried to wrap her fingers around the newly discovered mystery chunk. She felt the particles of soil burrow their way into the cracks under her fingernails. Poking out of the soil, she could see parts of her fingers starting to turn black.

When she fished out the lump, it took a bit for her to register what it looked like. At first, it seemed like an oval stone, maybe a rock Laurel had let slip from a garden. But then Marcy began to study her find more deeply, discovering wrinkles and cracks that lined the middle and bottom of the lump. Covering the top half of the oval was a dull, bluish-pink plate with a yellow crescent lining the top. Marcy's stomach turned when she flipped the object over and saw the sickly yellow bone poking out of the layer of dirt.

With a disgusted yelp, Marcy tossed the thing away and yanked out her phone. She had to warn Aiden, but the first message she was greeted with was, *K. In the house now.*

Marcy's heart sank. Her brother was now a resident of the nuthouse.

She looked to the doorway and saw beyond it an empty hallway. With no plan in her mind other than to run, Marcy dashed through the stretches of red and tried to book it for an exit. She didn't care how many secret passageways she had to traverse, she had to go.

"Marcy?" Azura's voice halted her run, turning her bones to ice. Marcy turned her head and found herself staring at a banquet over a long antique table that seemed larger than her house. Everyone Marcy had met, along with a few strange faces, stared at her with a mix of confusion and concern. And there sat Azura, with a jewelled goblet in hand, at the right side of the table.

A man with raven hair and a neatly pruned moustache broke the long silence. "Maybe your little friend here got herself lost again."

The table erupted in laughter, prompting Marcy to awkwardly join them. The man gestured to an empty gold chair next to him with violet cushions, three seats away from the old woman in the floral dress who sat at the head.

"Why don't you take a seat?" he asked. "Azura was about to start telling her story."

Marcy felt all eyes become glued to her. Their gazes followed her as she shuffled her way into the room. She looked down and picked out the dirt under her nails. She tried to take comfort in the belief that everyone was settled at the table and thus less likely to catch Aiden in the act. So, Marcy took her seat and turned to her girlfriend.

With the smell of turkey leg and red wine aloft in the air, Azura smiled down at the man. "Thanks, Dad." She cleared her throat. "So, as I was about to say, I'd like to dedicate this tale to the greatest woman I've ever had the pleasure of meeting." Azura tipped her glass over to Marcy, letting her see the deep red liquid in the ornate cup.

"I feel like for the first time, I can really be myself without having to worry about looking like an idiot. Marcy, you're my best friend, and I hope one day you can be that to everyone else in this family, too."

Marcy gave a small smile, but she looked down at her plate of turkey leg, carrots, and mashed potatoes to hide the sad glimmer in her eye.

Azura, seemingly oblivious to her girlfriend's inner turmoil, put the glass down and rubbed her hands together.

"So, I'll start it off like this…"

\*\*\*

Carola stared into the blinding glare of her tablet, her hand holding a plastic white pen over the glass, poised and waiting to paint a virtual picture across the screen.

*Come on, draw something.* She tried to push a thought through, but her mind was completely blank. Her lips scrunched up and her jaws tightened so firmly she thought she was going to push out her front teeth.

A vague sketch of a griffin began to formulate in her head. But before her pen could make contact with the tablet, she halted her arm and sighed.

*Oh wow, how original. No one's ever seen a griffin drawing before. Probably wouldn't be able to nail all those details anyway. I mean, the feathers, the claws, the face…*

Carola let out a frustrated cry and began to scribble a storm of virtual black ink onto the glass slab. She then pushed her tablet onto the kitchen table and dropped her head onto her arms. She rolled her head over a little, catching a glimpse of a diploma hanging on the wall.

Thousands of dollars had been spent on an art degree and yet she couldn't even put out a half-decent sketch to save her life. If she didn't know better, she'd have thought her place on the honour roll was just a fluke.

Carola lifted her head back up and went back to her tablet. She then saved her work in the drawing app and placed the doodle into the file filled with untitled scribble-fests. She pushed herself out of her chair and looked around the apartment.

The kitchen led directly into the living room, the walls were decorated with replicas of classic paintings and posters of Harry Potter and Star Wars characters.

"No wonder I can't come up with something new," Carola sighed. "Just borrowing from someone else." She groaned, stuffing her face into one of the sofa's pillows.

What kind of self-respecting executive would look at someone's portfolio and be happy just seeing a bunch of works derivative of someone else's? Carola sat up on the couch and took her phone out of her pocket. She went to the email app and began to sort through the replies to her job applications. Her thumb swiped through the emails and guided them to the trash.

"Rejected, rejected, rejected, we'll keep your portfolio on file, keep your application on file, don't call us, we'll call you." Carola's voice was dry and monotonous, but she could feel tears begin to build up. It was an annoyingly regular occurrence. She wasn't sure where she had gotten her stress crying habits from, definitely not her mother.

She had downright screamed Carola out of the house when she learned her honour roll-earning daughter was "throwing away her life" to go to art school. Carola's thumb froze and she stared blankly into her phone's screen.

What if her mother was right? What if she really did just throw a bunch of money away for a career that was never going to get anywhere? It took someone very special to get far in the world of art. It had been like that since the Renaissance. What made Carola think that she had that spark in her?

Her phone rang, pulling her out of her swampy thoughts before they could drown her. Carola breathed a sigh of relief. At the top of her screen was a comforting name: *Kamryn*. A small smile cracked through Carola's weary face as she accepted the call and brought her phone to her ear.

"Hi, hon."

"Hey baby, how's it going?" Even through the digital filter, it didn't block out the boundless energy in Kamryn's voice.

Carola stood up off the couch. "Not much, just having another existential crisis is all." She tried to laugh, but her chuckles sounded wooden. Kamryn was no dummy and Carola knew it, so it was no surprise that Kamryn was quick to rebuke that false laughter.

"Have you been getting enough sleep?" Kamryn asked.

Carola shrugged, despite knowing Kamryn couldn't see her. "Enough. I mean, I've still been able to get up for work and stuff. But I mean, trying to create pieces for my portfolio is like trying to push over a brick wall." Carola began to walk past the kitchen and into her cluttered mess of a room. Her floor was cluttered with clothes, and her desk was covered in coloured pencils, pens, and paintbrushes still sealed in their plastic packaging.

"That's not really answering my question, hon," Kamryn said. "Maybe you should take a break, give your brain a little rest. It's going to turn into mush if you keep pushing yourself too hard."

Carola groaned and rubbed her temples. "I barely have anything worthwhile in my portfolio as is. If anything, I haven't been doing enough, but I have no idea what's making me so slow with all of this."

She hadn't expected a casual conversation with her partner to make her cry and yet the tears began to flow. Carola wiped her face, staining her sleeve with her tears. Kamryn hesitated, and Carola could hear her partner tap against a desk.

"Um… I don't know. Maybe a change of environment could serve as a refresher for your brain. Some new sights and sounds could help you get those creative juices flowing again."

Carola slowly leaned back and lay in her bed. "I don't know. What if I really am just in over my head? Starting to wonder if I made the wrong choice in degree."

"Aw, come on! I've seen you draw. You're amazing!" Kamryn exclaimed. "All you need is the right inspiration. And when you find it, it'll just all click into place. Then you'll be calling me and being like, 'Wow, that was easy. God, you were right Kam, you wonderful genius, you!'"

Carola began to chuckle. "Right, of course." She sat back up and leaned against the bed's headrest. She heard Kamryn give a small laugh from the other end.

"Anyway, I'll let you get back to it. Sorry to keep you distracted."

"Hey, not my fault you're such a cute little distraction." Carola giggled.

"True, it's all mine. So cute it's a curse. Someone should execute me now and put me out of my misery!" Kamryn exclaimed with overly dramatic sorrow.

"Uh-huh. Sure." Carola shook her head. Even at her lowest moments Kamryn had a way of keeping her spirits up and making sure she didn't topple over the edge.

"Anyway, talk to you later, okay?"

"Alright, sounds good."

"Love you, Kam."

"Love you, too. Bye-bye."

"Bye!"

With that final farewell, Carola hung up the phone. She slunk back down in her bed and began to ponder Kamryn's proposal. It would be the best time for her to go out, no work on the weekends, and she still had enough money for gas and maybe a few snacks for the road. Maybe this would be the refresher she needed. Before she could delve further into these plans, a small *creak* emitted from down the hall.

Carola briefly glanced up and leaned over the bed to get a better view of the outside hallway. After waiting several seconds for another sound to follow, she sighed and laid back down in her bed.

"Kam's right. I really do need to get some more sleep." Carola then rolled over and stuffed a pillow over the top of her head. She thought her nerves were just out creating more boogeymen for her to run from. Her apartment was old; it creaked and made a bunch of weird noises, and she knew it. She felt like a paranoid moron for almost letting her mind make a mountain out of such a mundane molehill.

Little did she know, the creator of that creak had slunk into her room under the cover of the shadows. It would watch her throughout the night, would witness all her tossing and turning and every time she felt the need to get out of bed to walk around. And she would be none the wiser. That was because it didn't want to make itself known. Not yet. That was something for tomorrow.

By the next afternoon, Carola was rolling down the old country road, watching bits of gravel fly by her car windows. Her knuckles were white as she tightened her grip on the steering wheel, her heart jumping at every burst of dust that blew against her windshield. Thoughts began ping-ponging around in her head, banging against the sides of her skull.

*What if this doesn't work? Then I'll not only keep having an empty portfolio, but I'll be out a decent amount of gas money.*

She shook her head. *Come on, don't knock Kam's suggestion*

*before you even get to the damn place. What the hell is wrong with you?*

Suddenly, the road in front of her began to end and she gasped before slamming her foot on the brake before she could roll into a ditch. Her heart banged against her ribcage and her hands began to shake. Carola leaned her head into the headrest and took a deep, unsteady breath. She banged a fist against the steering wheel, accidentally blasting the horn and making herself jump, though not enough to lift her foot off the brake.

"Right, let's just focus on getting to the place first, then start wrestling with your self-pity BS," Carola whispered to herself before switching the car into reverse and backing away from the ditch. She whipped the car around and continued down the road.

Carola kept driving until she arrived at a lone log cabin with red paint peeling off the roof. Both a pale blue wooden bench and a stone well sat in the yard. She reached into the back of the car and pulled out a weathered duffel bag, hearing the clanking of paint supplies and gadgets bang against each other inside.

Carola took a breath and rested her hand against the car door handle. Her insides bubbled and boiled like water over a stovetop and her bones suddenly locked up.

*What are you panicking about now?*

She squeezed the handle until her entire hand turned white before taking another heavy breath. Shoving the door open, she leapt out of the car, slamming the door behind her before she could give herself a chance to continue chickening out.

The sharp, sour scent of lake water was the first thing to greet her despite the cabin being several yards away. She tightened her grasp on the strap of the duffel bag and forced herself forward.

Goosebumps sprouted over her body, but for what reason Carola had no idea. Just before passing the well, a low choking sound began to gurgle behind her. Carola froze in her tracks and turned back to face the well. She carefully crept toward the stone structure as the pained bubbling persisted. Carola gingerly placed her hand on top of the well's wall and listened as a low splash appeared to continuously slap against the bottom of the well.

She shook her head. "Well, now I know where I'm *not* going to be drinking from," she said before taking off back to the cabin door.

Inside was a cozy living room with an old, faded red couch sitting in front of a log fireplace and surrounded by furniture made of wood and antlers. Carola dropped her duffel bag onto the couch and unzipped it, pulling out a seemingly endless supply of paints, thinner, easels, paintbrushes, and pencils, along with her tablet and pen. She carefully arranged the supplies on the table, putting them into very specific groups and keeping them from rolling off and crashing into the ground.

Carola turned her head and saw the kitchen area right next to her with a vintage countertop covered in peeling linoleum and a small fridge covered in hunter and wildlife-inspired magnets next to a heavy wooden door. It wasn't until she noticed the fridge that she acknowledged the rumbling in her stomach. Looking back down at her scattered supplies and clutching tightly at a bundle of paintbrushes, Carola sighed. As far as she was concerned, she had procrastinated on her work long enough that she didn't have time to waste on deciding what to eat.

But the rumbling in her stomach rang louder than the shouts from the critics in her head.

So, she dropped the bundle back onto the table and made her way to the fridge. Prying the door open, she was greeted by a mostly empty white chamber with a blinding light. The only contents in the fridge were a tall carton of milk, a half-empty pack of hotdogs, a trio of apples, and a brand-new bottle of ketchup.

"Way to stock up the fridge, Kam," Carola sighed before grabbing one of the apples. Just as she slammed the fridge door shut, the ground began to rumble slightly. She turned her head and stared at the thick door before her. She walked up to it and wrapped her fingers around the door's edge.

*Must be the pantry or something,* she thought. She tightened her grip and gave a sharp pull. She heard the sound of magnets detaching from one another as the heavy slab of wood swung open, nearly escaping her grip and slamming against the wall next to her.

A cold breeze wafted past her, and she saw behind the door was a void of darkness cast against a raincloud of dust bunnies. Carola looked down to see a set of rickety wood stairs descending into the umbra. A low growl rumbled from behind the curtain of darkness and the stairs began to creak. Carola peered into the shadows and shook her head before slamming the door closed.

"Nope."

She had watched enough horror movies to know going into strange basements was a horrible idea. So, Carola walked away and began to rearrange her supplies so that they didn't just look like a storm of clutter making a disaster zone out of the table. Once everything was set in its place, she sank back down into her chair and began to stare into the blank canvas in front of her. Not a sound made its way into the room as Carola held a pencil over the canvas. Every minute that ticked by without progress was like someone had struck her in the head with a brick.

Her eyes began to wander, searching for even a sliver of inspiration so she could quit stalling and start painting. A fridge? Too boring. The ketchup bottle in the fridge? Oh please, she was no Andy Warhol, and she knew it. The coffee table? Who would be impressed with a picture of that? Her eyes then fell upon the couch and then the window.

She was brought back to the outside when she had first arrived, what felt like hours ago. When she had come across the well. It must have been old, hadn't been touched in decades. Then an image began to flourish inside of her head: a sofa with the well blossoming out of the cushions. Carola turned back to the canvas and hesitated before the pencil could make contact.

*Seems a bit out there.* She shut her eyes and sighed; *I've been hesitating long enough. May as well start anyway.* Carola's pencil began to dance across the white weave, the curves and lines slowly forming into a rough outline. As Carola continued, a smile formed on her face, and she began to doodle faster and more easily.

*Well, some people have a thing for abstract and surrealist art. Maybe this will work out after all.*

After the doodle was sketched, she reached for a paintbrush and dipped it into the small vats of paint. She could easily see the colours bloom before the brush even kissed the canvas. As her hand danced over the canvas, a sense of euphoria filled every inch of her body and Carola even heard a slight giggle leave her lips. However, as she started to add the shading to her work, a sickening feeling began to splash around in her stomach. Her hand stopped and she began to stare at the outline of the couch and the well.

The lines split apart and morphed into inky blotches against the muddled purple and blue that now reminded Carola of melted cotton candy. The lines in the couch became broken and bent, seeping into the crooked well with melted colours leaking out of the outline. She could hear the critics then. *What a ridiculous piece. A five-year-old could draw better than that. Was the artist high on something when she came up with the idea for this painting?*

Carola cried out in frustration and flung her paintbrush back onto the table before resting her aching head in her stained hands. She peeked through her fingers and laid her eyes on the clear bottle of paint thinner. She slammed her hands against the table before grabbing the bottle. Her hand shook as she squeezed the bottle tightly and stared down at her wreck of a painting. She sighed and unscrewed the cap on the thinner.

"Sayonara, you ugly thing," she muttered. But before she could squeeze the clear liquid out to dissolve the hideous painting, Carola felt the same rumbling from before quake under her feet. Her face crinkled as she was greeted by an odour, not too dissimilar to sour milk, and a thick warm air suctioned itself all over her body.

Paint thinner still in hand, she pushed herself out of her chair and began to look around the cabin. Her search stopped short when she laid her eyes on the wooden door by the fridge. Leaking from the underside of the door was a puddle of lumpy black liquid as thick as cake mix, with small bubbles popping along the surface. The sludge continued to expand further out of the door and across the floor of the kitchen.

Carola clenched her jaw and kept her breaths hollow and stiff so she wouldn't gag on the stench. She pulled her phone out of her bag and quickly made her way to her contacts to call Kamryn. After all, Carola was just a guest in this part of the lake while Kam knew it as well as the back of their hand. Before Carola could make the call, a bubbling tendril launched out of the puddle and yanked the phone out of her hand. The phone was swallowed by the building puddle until it completely disappeared under the inky gunk.

"Oh, shit! That's not right," Carola cried. The puddle stretched and built, black guck spitting in all directions as it became taller, and limbs broke through the gunk and splashed against the floor. The limbs twisted and shrivelled until they became thin as twigs and the ends became razor sharp. Another column of slime erupted from the top, taking the form of a woman's upper half with the arms flailing maniacally.

Carola shook her head and bolted for the door. *Hell, no. I'm not sticking around here.*

She furiously jiggled the doorknob and tried to yank the door open, her heart feeling like it was pumping in her ears. The hand on the doorknob became warm and wet as she continued to try and shake the door free. When she looked down, Carola saw the doorknob had disappeared into a stream of golden liquid that dripped down the door and coated her hand. She stepped back and watched as the door melted into the ground, leaving in its place a further extension of the cabin's log wall. Carola frantically wiped her gold hand on her jeans and backed away. The pile of gold twisted and turned into an overstretching archway and two front legs that stumbled forward.

"Holy hell. Holy hell. Holy hell. This isn't happening… This isn't happening." Carola looked around as the two gunky creatures shambled closer to her. Her eyes trailed up the staircase just as her vision began to blur in her panic. She shook her head.

*Running upstairs seems like such a stupid idea.* She turned her head back to the door. *But I don't exactly have a lot of smart options right now. Maybe I'll luck out and get a soft landing jumping out of a window.*

Carola began to bolt up the stairs before she felt herself trip in the middle of the steps. She banged her chin against the step above her and felt a cold, thick liquid envelope her feet. When she turned to look behind her, she saw that her feet had sunken into the stairs. Carola yelped as she struggled to pull herself back onto her feet. In her panic, she slammed her hand onto the tube of paint thinner, causing an explosion of clear liquid to shoot down the stairs.

The shine in the stairs disappeared as the thinner trickled over them and Carola's feet were shoved out of the puddle. As the last few drops from the thinner eruption collapsed onto the ground floor, the creatures hissed and scampered behind the pantry door. While their thunderous steps shook the cabin like it was in the middle of an earthquake, Carola leaned against the railing and heaved, resting her cheek against the cool brassy metal banister.

After finally catching her breath, Carola pressed her back against the handrail and cast her gaze down at the partially squeezed tube of thinner. She gingerly picked it up, turning it around in her hand and feeling the cold droplets dance down her fingers and seep into the lines of her palm. A familiar scent filled the air as the creaking of the cabin settled in, a rubbery aroma with a sharpness that burned Carola's nostrils. An odour she had previously inhaled over a harmless white canvas.

"Paint? You're made of paint?" Carola's sweat-soaked eye brows furrowed as she continued to stare at the tube of thinner like it was a mixed-up Rubix cube. Her eyes followed the trail of thinner down the stairs before wandering over to the table she had been working at, now a chaotic mess of supplies and paints mixed together in a streak-filled puddle.

She rushed to the table and began to fish through the messy pool of supplies with her free hand. She reeled out an empty paint tray, her thickest paintbrush, and a spare tube of thinner. Carola turned her head toward the door and took a deep breath. It wasn't until she heard the low growling from behind the door that she noticed how violently her hands were shaking and how her insides had become a caustic acid boiling inside her stomach.

"What the hell am I doing?" Carola whimpered, stuffing

the spare tube into her back pants pocket. She forced herself forward, her fifty-tonne feet dragging across the floor as her hand reached out toward the door. Before she could yank the door open, she jerked her hand back and froze.

"This is the part where the monster jumps out through the doorway to try and get me, isn't it?" Carola sucked in a greedy puff of air before grabbing the edge of the door and yanking it open, though not before shuffling to the side to better use the door as a shield. A shrill screech flew up the steps and blasted into the kitchen. Peeking from behind the door, she watched the gristly clump spread itself across the counter and release a mass of tendrils to grab at the sink's faucet.

The faucet bent like a pipe cleaner before melting into molten steel and disappearing into the puddle. A pair of wings sprouted from the pile followed by a sharp beak. As the mass twisted and turned, Carola quietly squeezed the tube of thinner into the tray's concave chambers. She then jabbed her brush into the thinner before charging out toward the mass. She stabbed the mass through the beak with the brush, causing it to unleash a scream that shook the cabin walls. The black mass twisted around before tearing itself apart and exploding into thin air, leaving the faint smell of paint behind.

Carola looked down at her thinner-coated paintbrush in awe. "Just that little bit did it, huh?" She turned her head back to the wide-open doorway. A cool breeze hugged itself around her, bringing a waft of old paint's odour with it. Carola squeezed her paintbrush until her fingers began to burn against the grains of wood.

"I can do this, I can do this." Carola continued to whisper her mantra as she sauntered toward the door. She continued to whisper to herself as she heard the wooden steps creak and bend under her feet. She persisted with her mantra as the light of the kitchen became dimmer behind her and the warmth of the upper levels of the cabin seeped out of her skin.

A deep orange light snapped itself to life right as Carola settled her feet on the cold cement of the basement floor. Facing her from the other side of the room was an old black lantern bolted to the wall, her sole source of light. She cautiously continued forward and pointed her paintbrush into the darkness like it was the world's flimsiest and least fireproof gun.

Her hesitant stride was halted as she felt something thick snap under her foot, the thunderous crack echoing throughout the basement. The veins of her neck became cold and stiff as stone as the remnants of hope she had left dissolved into nothing. She looked down and almost gagged at the sight before her feet. A half-melted skeleton, with bones covered in noxious, mustard-coloured mould lay on the ground, the skull stuck with a perpetual expression of screaming agony. Locked tightly in its far-reaching hand was an old fountain pen with the ink having long shrivelled at the tip and dried.

*Well, isn't this an uplifting sight, Ms. Grace-Of-An-Ox?* Not too long after the thoughts slipped through her mind, Carola heard a heavy sloshing slap against the cold basement walls. Peeling away from the shadows was the creature in gold, stumbling forward with its two legs and its arch bending and expanding in time with a low moan. As the creature staggered forward, Carola struggled to hold her paintbrush in her shaking hands.

She frantically dipped her brush into the thinner-filled chamber of her tray, nearly piercing the brush through the plastic. The creature lunged forward with a screeching roar, its legs outstretched like a pouncing lion. Carola rolled out of the way, crashing into a wall just as the golden creature crashed into the spot she had been standing in.

Without any hesitation, Carola charged forward and

stabbed the paintbrush into the creature's back. Boiling amber steam spouted out of the wound, exuding the stench of moulding plastic into the cold, wet room. The creature roared, futilely bucking back and driving its feet into the floor with a feverous panic. Spasms continued to roll through the creature until it melted into a bubbling puddle.

Carola grabbed onto the wall to keep herself from stumbling in her efforts to catch her breath. The moment would prove brief as the walls began to rumble under the force of a woman's furious screams. Before Carola could regain her bearings, she felt her paintbrush be yanked out of her hand and saw it go flying back into the shadows. Emerging from the darkness was a woman made of black gunk, creeping toward Carola with her spindly spider legs. She held out her hand and Carola watched as her paintbrush melted into it, leaving a puff of steam in its wake.

Carola jolted her head back and forth between the creature and her now empty hand. She looked behind her and saw the stairs leading back up into the cabin. She turned back to the creature and shook her head.

"Uh-uh." Carola bolted for the stairs and began to scamper upward. However, her fleeing was stopped by a burning sensation suddenly spreading across her back. She let out a scream and accidentally flung her paint tray back. A loud hiss sounded from behind her, followed by the shrill screams of the spider woman. While the arachnid woman reeled back and clutched at her smouldering head, Carola tumbled down the stairs, twisting her ankle on the steps on the way down.

Though her ankle screamed and swelled inside of her sweat-soaked sock, Carola was more focused on the sight in front of her. The steam was fading from the spider woman's face and her flailing began to slow. Though the world seemed to be moving in slow motion, Carola knew she had a matter of seconds to do something before the creature would return its attention to her.

Her eyes cast down to the rotting skeleton, its bone dissolving under the drops of black goop the creature likely flung about after being struck by the paint tray. But shining in the dimming light was the gleam of the pen held in the skeleton's hand. Carola dove for the skeleton and tore the pen out of its grip, sending the finger bones flying into the air. She then reached into her back pocket and pulled out the spare bottle of thinner. She squirted a messy glob of thinner onto the tip of the pen just as the spider woman dropped her hands from her faceless head. Just as the creature turned its head toward Carola, she let out a cry and jabbed the pen into one of the creature's twig-like legs.

The spider cried out in a mix of rage and pain, staring down at its leg as the pen disappeared into a boiling, silver mass that spread up the leg. The creature stumbled back, hobbling on its remaining legs as the silvery substance reached its abdomen. As the shining ooze spread, the creature began to crumble away like old plaster before collapsing into a damp corner. Reaching out for one final time, the creature became frozen stiff and collapsed into a pile of dust.

Carola collected her breath and pulled herself back onto the steps. "Sayonara, you ugly thing," she coughed out, her voice shakier than she wanted it to be. Carola stretched her lips into a grimace as her ankle flared up into a searing pain that crept up her leg. She tightly grabbed the railing, supporting herself with her other foot.

"Yup, I'm definitely going to need some ice on this," she muttered. When she reached the top of the stairs and limped back into the kitchen, Carola yanked open the freezer door and pulled out a tray of ice cubes. She reached into a drawer under the countertop and pulled out a small plastic bag before pouring the ice cubes inside. With the frosty bag, Carola hobbled over to the table and looked down at the pile of supplies.

She caught a glint of her tablet and the pen attached to the side buried underneath. Carola put down the old-fashioned pen and fished her tablet and digital pen out of the mess. She then looked up and saw the door leading to the outside was back in its place.

A serene smile formed on her face. *Maybe I'll get my inspiration after a little break.* Carola hopped over to the door and stepped outside, greeted by the warmth of the twilight sun. She staggered over the lawn and sat on the bench facing the gravel street. Carola then turned her body around to rest her foot on the seat, letting her face the old well.

She reclined and let out a sigh as she heard the bones in her back crack and felt her shoulder blades dig into the old wood. Carola turned on her tablet and restfully navigated her way to the drawing app. She briefly looked up from her tablet and smiled at the old well.

However, after she pressed her finger onto the file filled with untitled drawings, Carola's blood grew cold. She tried to chuckle to herself.

*Come on, after what you just saw, you should have nothing to worry about,* Carola tried to reassure herself. Until she figured out why her nerves suddenly spiked. The first of the file's thumbnails was the drawing of the griffin she had discarded the day before she set out for the cabin. She opened the file and carefully inspected the curves and lines.

Her eyes halted at the beak, and she was suddenly met with a flash of the puddle with the beak bubbling on the countertop. Carola sat up and began to scroll through the other files. Down in the middle was an unfinished sketch of a bridge, the Golden Gate Bridge, if she remembered correctly. The legs were only half-finished and the colour she had used to draw the lines was a deep yellow. No, not yellow. Gold. Carola gasped and zoomed out of the picture. She scrolled to the bottom of the screen and gazed at the final picture, the first drawing she had ever given up on. Only this file, unlike the other untitled sketches, was given a name.

*Arachne.*

Carola's hands began to shake, nearly dropping her tablet onto the grass. Her eyes peeked up, and she saw the bricks in the well begin to buckle and bubble. Shining black tentacles emerged from the hole in the well, slapping the brick walls with a loud moan. While continuing to stare at the creature emerging from the well, Carola took her pen in her hand and pressed the tip against the Arachne file.

The tentacles stopped their creeping approach though the black goop expanded and shrunk back like tar-filled lungs. Carola's eyes darted back and forth from the picture to the anticipating creature hanging inside the well.

Her inspiration was at long last found.

# The Fury Of God

Azura looked over at the crowd with tepid anticipation. A stretch of awkward silence before she finally said, "Well, um… that's the end. I guess." Azura nervously giggled.

Recognizing it as another tactic Azura would use to try and fill the empty air, Marcy opened her mouth to speak but the man sitting next to her beat her to the punch.

"Excellent story, dear." He flashed a reassuring grin and gently squeezed Azura's arm. Azura smiled down at the man before sitting back down. The man enthusiastically clapped for the young woman, and soon he was joined by the rest of the banquet, Marcy awkwardly included. After the applause died down, she looked down at her plate and began to eat her carrots.

*Wow, made up a whole story, thanks to me,* she thought. *She must be prepared for the long haul, huh?*

The sweet smell of carrots was mixing with the bile swimming in her stomach as well as orange juice and freshly brushed teeth. After eating a few carrots, she changed her attention to the turkey leg. She took her fork and knife and began to slice down the bone. Her eyes widened when she saw blood squeeze out from the developing cut. Marcy looked up and saw the man in the seat next to her about to cut into his own turkey. Marcy nervously raised her hand. "Um… I think my leg's a little under…" she stammered.

The man turned to face Marcy and glanced at her plate. "Really?" he asked.

Marcy peeled the meat from the bone, blood spilling out from the black veins into a puddle in the middle of the plate. The man's eyes widened. "Oh, not a fan of extra rare meat, I see?" he chuckled. The man raised a hand and shouted, "Leigh!"

Immediately after, the butler who had greeted Marcy and Azura at the door emerged from the hallway and marched over to the man.

"Master Inigo?" The butler gracefully folded his hands in front of him in anticipation.

The man lifted Marcy's plate from the table and deftly handed it to Leigh. "Our guest would like to request her meat to be more well-done. Thank you very much."

Inigo's voice was light and graceful, his sophisticated tone reminding Marcy of either Zorro or Count Dracula. Leigh gave a quick nod before marching out of the dining room with Marcy's blood-filled plate in hand. Inigo placed his hand back down, laying it gently over the napkin that had once cradled his cutlery.

"So, Marcy, I guess Azura decided to leave my introduction for last," he chuckled.

Azura sighed. "It wasn't *my* fault. Our ancestors should've built a smaller house."

Inigo laughed and patted Azura on the head. "I'll keep that in mind when I finish building my time machine."

Azura rolled her eyes. "Forgot to warn you, my dad thinks he's a comedian."

Inigo smirked. "I think, therefore I am." He laughed as he saw the eyebrows rising higher up Marcy's face.

"Yes, my name really is Inigo. Azura's grandpa was a big fan of *The Princess Bride*, so much he spread that love to my birth certificate." Inigo laughed again, jovially shaking Marcy's shoulder and almost throwing her out of her chair.

Marcy returned an awkward laugh. "Yeah, uh… I remember my sixth-grade math teacher showing it to the class a few times."

"Lots of memorable lines, right? It's one of those movies that never gets old." Inigo thrust his arm out and whirled it around like a makeshift rapier. "Too bad I wasn't as much a natural at fencing as my namesake." Inigo then grabbed his goblet and took a sip of the red liquid inside. A metallic whiff weaved itself in the air as Inigo drank and lingered when he put his cup back down.

"You know, Marcy, you're the second date that Azura has brought to meet the family." Inigo swirled the drink in his cup. "Other people here seem to think of you as a decent sort, which gives me hope that you'll work out better than the last one who came here."

Azura stopped smiling and squirmed uneasily in her seat. The uneasy look was a familiar one for Marcy, one she often saw when Azura was asked about her exes.

"I never asked for details about that stuff," Marcy said, hoping to put Azura at ease.

Inigo nodded. "I get it. Talking about past heartbreak can be uncomfortable. Opening old wounds, reliving those feelings of betrayal." He sliced into his turkey leg and, unfazed, let streams of blood drip off the knife and onto his plate. Inigo gazed up at Marcy, smiling as he apparently relished her nausea at the ichor.

"Betrayal, in my opinion, is the worst pain a human can

inflict on another. You earn their trust, have them believe they will always be there to catch you, but instead…" Inigo lifted bits of meat up with his fork before letting it drop back onto his plate. "You let them fall. But as my Papa always said, burn too many bridges and you'll find yourself at war against the world. And in those circumstances, well…" He gave a dark chuckle. "Look no further than what happened in Joansburg."

\*\*\*

The town of Joansburg used to be such a nice neighbourhood. A town of nice Christian values with nice Christian neighbours who obeyed and feared the word of God. The people went to church every Sunday, and Mass would get so full sometimes, people would need to bring in their own chairs in order to find room to sit. Everyone toed the line and stuck with the status quo. There was no need to rock the boat, after all. For Grace Johnson and her husband, Isaac, this was how it always had been, and, in their mind, how it should have continued to be.

And it was, until the new neighbours moved in.

The Valientes drove into Joansburg, trailing the U-Haul truck in a pure black Sierra. The car would have blended into the night if it weren't for the other houses' Christmas lights bouncing off the hood.

Grace slowly peeled back the thin beige curtains and watched the black car ease itself into the driveway. Stepping out of the driver's side was a lax woman with wild maple hair done in a storm of unkempt curls. Following her from the passenger's side of the car was a sober-looking man with capacious black hair that looked like it had just been struck by lightning. One of the back doors opened to let out a teen girl with pitch-black hair done up in a perm and wearing a neon crop top, large hoop earrings, and a bright pink mini skirt.

"Aw, come on, Mom! Are you seriously spying on the neighbours like a creeper?" Grace turned and saw her daughter standing in the hallway with her new Walkman in hand. Kimberly ran her hand through her blonde hair and tightened her light blue scrunchie in the same motion.

Grace nervously eyed the window and shrugged. "I just want to know who's next to us, that's all," the mousy older woman said.

Kimberly rolled her eyes and threw her head back with a groan. "This is so embarrassing." She began to walk away before Grace scurried over to the hall and grabbed Kimberly's shoulder.

"Kimmie?"

"Ugh, what now?"

Grace looked down at her child's Walkman and pointed to the spinning CD inside the device.

"What are you listening to?"

"Nothing," Kimberly grumbled and she tried to storm back down the hall. However, Grace was quicker and ripped the headphones off her daughter's head. "Hey!" Kimberly shouted as she tried to claw the headphones away from her mother.

But it was too late, Grace already had snatched the headphones and immediately recognized the song blaring in her ear. She stopped the Walkman and began to march toward a towering cupboard.

Kimberly ran behind Grace and tried to swipe the Walkman back. "What are you doing?"

"I already told you not to bring this filth into this house." Grace hissed as she pulled a grey lockbox out of the cupboard. She dropped the Walkman into the box and slammed the lid closed.

"It's not filth!" Kimberly protested, nearly getting her fingers caught in the closet door when her mother shut it.

"That woman flaunts her body shamelessly all over television for children to see," Grace lectured. "I will not be having you follow in her footsteps."

Kimberly stuttered, her mouth gaping open and closed like a fish. "Listening to a little music isn't going to just suddenly turn me into a stripper or harlot or whatever the church is calling her now."

Grace immediately whipped around and smacked Kimberly across the face. "You watch the way you speak about our Lord's house and his servants, little lady."

Kimberly's pale face turned red and she rubbed at her tender cheek. Still, her fire remained untamed. "Okay, well if she's such an evil woman then why would she perform at Live Aid?" the teen asked. "That concert was all about helping people in Ethiopia."

Grace sighed, deciding this juvenile argument didn't warrant anymore of her time. She turned her back to her daughter and looked over to the window. "Go to your room and cool off," she demanded.

She heard Kimberly sigh and stomp up the stairs. From the top of the stairs, Grace saw little Joshua creep out of his room and give Kimberly a smirk.

"Someone got busted," he laughed.

"Shut up," Kimberly hissed before slamming her bedroom door behind her. Joshua snickered before slinking back into his own room.

Grace shook her head and rubbed her throbbing temples. The world was a dangerous and unholy place full of luxurious temptation and now her own daughter was starting to slip away from the Lord. Still, what kind of good Christian wouldn't rise to the challenge of protecting their kin from the Devil's vices?

Grace heard the door slowly swing open and saw her beloved husband walk inside. Isaac's sandy hair was combed back and kept in place thanks to a generous amount of hair gel applied in the morning. His soft blue eyes were surrounded by dark rings and his black briefcase dragged tiredly across the wood floor.

"Hey, honey," Isaac said wearily. "Long day today?"

Grace pointed her thumb toward the window she had been using for observation earlier. "The new neighbours just moved in."

Isaac dropped his briefcase by the sofa and wandered over to the window. He peeked behind the curtain and gave an unimpressed nod. "Oh yeah, I heard they have a daughter around Kimberly's age." Isaac lifted his head away from the window. "What about them?"

Grace shrugged and began to rub her arms. "I'm not sure. The parents seem to be dressed more like the hoodlums that hang around to smoke crack behind the theatre."

Isaac gave a bemused smirk. "Maybe they want to look cool for their daughter," he chuckled.

"And what kind of example would that be setting?" Grace hissed.

Isaac shook his head and gently scooped up Grace's hands. "Hey, hey, if they really are a carton of bad eggs then Our Father will take care of them and try to guide them back to the light," Isaac calmly assured. He carefully wrapped Grace into a soft embrace and began to softly rub her back. Despite being lost in her beloved husband's embrace, Grace could still feel goosebumps sprout across her skin. Something about the family next door had her on edge. They stood out like a polar bear in the desert and anyone who would break the neighbourhood's status quo could only spell chaos.

Days went by without much incident, though Grace did notice a few new oddities as she and her family went about their normal routine. For one, every time she and her family went to church, she saw there was no sign of the new neighbours.

Another peculiarity that stuck out to the God-fearing woman was that Kimberly's hair started becoming wilder and curlier, not like the straight, simple hair she normally kept tamed under a headband. Her daughter seemed unbothered when other members of the church's congregation gave her strange looks, but Grace felt like the articulately painted ceiling of the parish was pressing down on the back of her neck. She wondered, could the parishioners believe she was letting Kimberly slip away from the righteous path?

Then Saturday rolled around. It was just another quiet day in the Johnson household with little Joshua sitting in front of the television watching some cartoons and munching on a packet of fruit snacks. Grace sat on the sofa with the Bible resting on her lap and an eye on the television.

The church warned that people of evil would try to influence their children with violence and sex on television, so she had to remain vigilant. Even though Joshua seemed loyal to the church and could recite the passage in the Bible depicting the Last Supper by heart, one could never be too careful.

Grace's eyes wandered to the clock hanging over the television. Her husband would be driving back home by that point, and yet there was still no sign of Kimberly. Grace began to nervously tap her fingers against the pages of her Bible. Kimberly had said she was going over to grab a bite to eat with some friends and she would be back in two hours. And yet three hours later, she still wasn't home. Grace tightened her lips together. First came the change of hair and now her daughter was running late.

*It sure is mighty convenient these changes have only started when…*

Grace's worried pondering was halted when the front door slammed open and crashed into the wall. Isaac's face was red with anger. The skin around his eyes and mouth were pinched together in furious wrinkles and his knuckles were white from the tight grip they held on Kimberly's wrist.

When Grace laid her eyes on Kimberly, the mother's jaw dropped, and her Bible collapsed in a heap on the floor.

Joshua's eyes widened and he jumped to his feet. "Whoa! What happened to you?"

Kimberly was covered in black clothing that hugged her body and exposed her belly button. Dark blue eyeshadow was drawn around her eyes, her lips caked in black lipstick and her cheeks covered with bright red blush.

Kimberly paid no attention to her awestruck little brother and instead focused on trying to pry Isaac's fingers away from her wrist. "Let go of me!" Kimberly wrestled out of her father's grip and prepared to stomp back up to her room. But Grace quickly intercepted her daughter and roughly grabbed her shoulders.

"Why do you have this junk all over you?" The mother then grabbed the hem of Kimberly's shirt. "And dressing up like a...stripper?"

Kimberly reeled back from her mother's hand as it swiped at her shirt. She looked down at her outfit with doe-like eyes. "They're just clothes. I'm not trying to bring in any boys."

"Well, what idea is going to pop into a boy's head when they look at you?"

Kimberly shook her head. "Does it really matter as long as I feel good in them?"

Grace scoffed while Isaac crossed his arms impetuously. "So, if you feel good streaking around town in nothing but your birthday suit then it's all good?"

Kimberly cried out in frustration and tried to turn back to the staircase. "You guys are impossible!"

But Grace refused to let Kimberly out of her grip and instead turned to her husband. "Where did you find her?"

"Over by the new neighbours' place. She was just about to leave their driveway." Isaac jabbed a thumb to the side, right in the direction of the new neighbours' house.

Grace sighed before dragging Kimberly to the door by the wrist. Kimberly struggled to wiggle out of her mother's grasp while Grace turned to Isaac. "Hon, keep an eye on Joshua. I'm going to have a word with the neighbours."

Isaac nodded quickly before Grace yanked open the door and dragged Kimberly behind her. The cool autumn wind that whistled through the night did nothing to deter the furious woman as she dragged her daughter over to the neighbours' house. As she approached, Grace noticed the windows were lit up with an amber glow and shadows danced against the glass planes. She banged on the black door while Kimberly continued to struggle.

She finally managed to pry Grace's hand off her thin, red wrist. "Mom, come on! This is ridiculous!"

"Be quiet. You're already in enough trouble as it is." Grace hissed. She heard the shambling of footsteps thunder towards the door before it was pulled open. Standing at the entrance of the house was the patriarch of the Valientes, clad in a loose, periwinkle sweater and black sweatpants. He gave Grace and Kimberly a warm smile and leaned against the doorframe.

"Ah, you must be Kim's mother. How can we help you fine ladies?"

Grace narrowed her eyes, though she did attempt to form a small smile to hide the boiling anger building within. "Yes, Mr. Valiente. My husband caught my daughter leaving your house in this strange clothing," she said softly.

Mr. Valiente nodded and maintained his casual veneer. "Oh yeah, Kim comes to visit from time to time after school. She noticed some of my daughter's clothes and asked if she could borrow them."

Grace's eyes widened and a wave of disgust washed over her. She could hardly believe any parent in their right mind would allow their daughter to walk around in such revealing clothing. She tilted her head and tried to peek inside the house.

"Yes, um...well, we don't allow those clothes in our house," Grace said, barely hiding the curtness in her voice. "Does your daughter still have the clothes my daughter came in with?"

Mr. Valiente, seemingly unfazed by the vitriol directed at him, gave Grace another nod and stepped to the side. "Oh yeah, of course. Come on in and I'll go get her."

Grace buried the need to reel back from the man and his surroundings before warily stepping inside and discarding her shoes on the yellow-tan welcome mat, covering up the black crescent moon sewn onto it. The living room looked less like a room for family to gather around the television and more like a rowdy teenage boy's bedroom. The sofa was made of dull black leather, the lights were deep orange, and the walls were covered with posters of Metallica, Def Leppard, Iron Maiden, and AC/DC. The shelf resting underneath the television was filled the VHS tapes of horror movies and recordings of concerts playing the Devil's music. Kimberly was unfazed by the peculiar decor and flopped onto the couch. Grace was slower to approach the couch, trying her best not to stare at the posters of the deviant musicians as she sat down. Mr. Valiente was across from mother and daughter in the kitchen, taking out a silver kettle.

"Can I help either of you to some tea?" he called. Kimberly's eyes lit up and she opened her mouth to reply.

"We'll pass." Grace raised a hand and quickly silenced her daughter.

Mr. Valiente's eyes became fixed on Kimberly as she closed her mouth and looked down at the carpet. He appeared to ponder for a moment before plugging the kettle in and taking out a black mug from the cupboard.

"Alright, suit yourself," he said before dropping a tea bag inside the mug. The man then walked over to the staircase and cupped his hands around his mouth. "Penelope! Kim and her mom are here. Bring down Kim's clothes with you, alright?"

"Coming!" a cheerful voice called back.

Mr. Valiente grinned and took a seat on the other side of Kimberly. He leaned forward to better look at Grace, who was struggling to keep her lunch from crawling up her throat. However, it was when he sat down that Grace finally noticed the necklace around his neck. Tied on a thin black strand of knotted rope was a silver star surrounded by a thin ring. Her eyes widened and her back suddenly straightened itself out.

"Excuse me, but what is that around your neck?"

Mr. Valiente looked down at his chest before letting a small chuckle. He carefully lifted his pendant from his chest and held it in the air. "Oh, it's my pentagram," he replied. "A gift from my wife after I was accepted into my coven."

Grace's face darkened, her simmering anger cooling into ice-cold disgust. She had known there was something off about them, and now she knew what.

"You're a family of witches?" she growled, her eyes turning into daggers pointing at the man she now saw as the Devil's spawn.

Undeterred, Mr. Valiente shook his head and laughed. "I mean if you want to call us that, sure. Though my wife and I prefer the term Wiccan."

"What's the difference?"

"Well, I'm assuming that when you hear the word 'witch' you think of cackling hags who worship Satan." Mr. Valiente then cautiously eyed Kimberly. "I *am* allowed to say 'Satan' in front of your mom, right? It's not like a curse word for you ladies, is it?"

Kimberly shrugged. "I mean, one of the questions the priest asks during mass is if we reject Satan. So, I mean, if he gets to say it then I'm assuming it's cool for us, too," she replied.

Grace snapped her head to face Kimberly and glared. "Not to invoke him. Doing that brings nothing but trouble and maybe a few sparse moments of deviancy disguised as bliss."

Mr. Valiente nodded with an amused grin.

The sight rose the fire building in Grace to temperatures higher than the water in the whistling kettle. She dug her fingers into the arm of the couch and her knuckles became a mix of white and rosy red.

"You think indulging in the Devil's whims is funny?" she asked shrilly.

Kimberly reeled back, looking like she was trying to sink herself into the couch.

Mr. Valiente shook his head and held his hands up in the air. "No, no, it's just that—"

Before he could finish, a teen girl with jet-black hair jumped off the bottom stair and onto the floor. She flashed Mr. Valiente a grin and began to walk to the living room. In her hand was Kimberly's pale, pastel clothes, folded into a bundle. The girl was wearing capri jean pants and a red sweater with a low-cut collar. Around her neck was a necklace with a leaf tied to the wiry black string by the stem. Her face lit up when she saw Kimberly, bouncing onto the couch on the opposite side of Grace.

"Hey, what's up, Kim?" the girl asked before dropping the bundle of clothes onto Kimberly's lap.

A small smile crawled onto Kimberly's face. "Not much. Just came by to get my clothes back a bit earlier than I thought I would," she said in a low, timid voice.

The girl tilted her head and carefully eyed Grace. She then extended her arm out to shake, showing her arm was painted with a dark brown floral pattern that reminded Grace of a doily.

"I'm Penelope," the girl said, her smile quivering under the cold, awkward air forming above the couch.

Grace stared at Penelope's hand, her eyes trailing up the girl's arm and onto her face. "Your parents let you draw on yourself?" Grace asked.

Penelope sighed and dropped her arm onto her lap. "It's henna. And yeah, my folks know about it, and as long as I don't have a reaction to it, then it's fine." Penelope wore a blithe smirk as she leaned into the sofa with her arms defiantly crossed.

Her smug demeanour burrowed under Grace's skin and ground against her bones like a cheese grater. She snapped her head back to face Penelope's father. "You allow your daughter to draw all over herself?"

Mr. Valiente was pushed back slightly from the force of Grace's voice. He quickly regained his composure and gave a casual shrug. "Why not? We did our research and found it to be harmless enough. Not to mention washable," he replied before turning his head toward the kitchen. The kettle's whistling was ready to pierce Grace's eardrums and a tower of steam blasted out of the spout of the kettle.

"Oh, I should probably get to pouring before the steam blows off the roof," he chuckled before hopping out of the armchair and heading toward the kitchen. Grace's fingers curled inward until her hands were formed into tiny fists.

"As I'm sure you find having her around witchcraft to be harmless enough," she growled.

Penelope then raised a hand. "Actually, it's just my folks that do magick rituals. I just do the occasional tribute to Athena and Persephone," she said.

Kimberly curled further into a ball next to her friend. "I'm not sure she's going to see that as much better," Kimberly whispered.

Grace's rage cooled into numb disgust and she mustered the will to roll her eyes. She watched as Mr. Valiente poured hot water into the mug. "And you can't even get your daughter to follow your example?" Grace hissed. "You leave her to just wander and be swayed by every charlatan claiming to know everything."

Mr. Valiente slammed the kettle onto the countertop and exploded into a fit of laughter. Penelope also began to snicker, covering her mouth to try and hide her mocking smile. Grace pushed herself onto her feet and stomped over to the kitchen. She slammed her hands in front of the madly cackling man, who had since turned red.

"What's so funny this time?" Grace roared.

Mr. Valiente hiccupped a few more laughs before calming himself down and lifting his head from the counter. He rested his forehead in his hand and rubbed his temples. "I'm sorry, I didn't mean to laugh like an idiot." He took a breath and his smile faded. "The way my wife and I see it, we'll try to raise our daughter right from wrong but what she wants to call the forces affecting the world should be on her to decide. If we try to force our religion onto her and she doesn't gel with it, then all that's going to do is build resentment towards our faith."

"Then why spare the rod and spoil the child? Teach her how the hierarchy in the household works. Then she won't even think to question you."

"Maybe not, but it'll just inspire her to be sneakier. How can she trust her parents if she worries speaking out is going to result in her getting beaten?"

Grace crossed her arms and glared. "You must have had much too lenient parents."

Mr. Valiente shook his head and his previous joking nature dropped instantly. "Not at all. Neither were my wife's, for that matter," he half-whispered morosely. "They used to beat us black and blue for the smallest things. We actually met sneaking out at night back when we were in high school." The man gave a depressed chuckle before carrying the mug of tea back to the living room.

Penelope observed her father with pitiful eyes that looked ready to water up. Kimberly uncurled from her ball and held her hands out. Mr. Valiente gently handed the steaming mug of tea to Kimberly while Penelope gingerly patted her father's wrist.

"That's why Leah and I decided we wouldn't let any children of ours think they need to be afraid of us." His voice was soft and delicate, like a pussywillow bud.

Grace could easily see he was trying to sway her, make her second-guess her devotion to her faith and the morals she lived by. But she was a stone wall in a buffeting storm, unmoveable. Her glare hardened and she dug her nails into her inner arms. "And I'm guessing you're planting those same seeds in my daughter's head." Her voice slowly became louder as her fury rose. "That it's alright for her to disobey her parents and dance with the Devil!" As she raised her arm to swing a fist down on the man, the door burst open, and the matron of the house burst inside and pushed Grace's arm back.

"Don't you dare lay a hand on my husband!" the newly arrived woman shouted. Her long white coat whipped around as she wrestled Grace's arm down from the air and dug her nails into the Christian woman's wrist.

Grace pulled her arm back, causing the other woman to drag her nails down her arm and leave fresh white lines of scraped skin along it. Grace squeezed her burning wrist and glared at the scowling woman with a black suitcase discarded to her side.

"You just tried to assault me!" Grace shouted. "I will have you and your heathen family run out of town."

The woman remained unshaken, and she pointed her black-nailed finger toward the still-open door. Her eyes were a dark flame burning into Grace's soul. "Get out of my house," the woman snarled.

Both teenagers stood up from the sofa as a heavy silence was cast down on the room. Penelope gingerly held Kimberly's hand as Kimberly's shoulders began to shake and her eyes began to water. Grace stood silent for the longest seconds of her life before finally shuffling her feet toward the door. She stopped at the doorway and turned her head to the living room. "Kimberly Marie Johnson. We're leaving," she growled.

Kimberly placed the mug down on the coffee table and began to shamble away from Penelope and Mr. Valiente. With a closed hand to her chest, the teen girl looked back at the neighbourly family with wide doe eyes, hesitating at the halfway point between them and her mother.

Mrs. Valiente's anger melted, and she gave a comforting nod to Kimberly. "It's okay," the woman whispered. "Go with your mother."

Kimberly hesitated again before letting out a deep breath and following her irate mother out of the house. The short walk back home was deathly silent, but the silence that followed the pair when they went back into their own home drilled harder into the back of Grace's head.

Kimberly shuffled up the stairs to her room while Grace slumped down in her armchair and pinched the bridge of her nose. Alone in the empty living room, Grace let the frustrated tears roll down her boiling-hot cheeks.

*Please, God, my daughter is simply misguided. Please don't let the Devil take her,* the woman prayed, placing her hands together and touching her forehead with the tips of her fingers. The thought of her daughter suffering the flames of Hell, at the mercy of the horrid Devil who tempted her… Grace peered out the window and gazed at the Valiente home, watching as the lights in the windows went out one-by-one. Her hands began to shake.

*Of course, the prince of lies would use puppets to lure Kimberly away from the path of righteousness.* She walked over to the window and burrowed her fingers into the grains of the windowsill. Her mind became polluted with images of fires licking against the house and consuming the den of deception. Her heart felt like it was being melted in a vat of bile while her hands began to shake. She looked toward the staircase with tears welling in her eyes. She shut her eyes and let the tears trickle down her cheeks.

"Heavenly Father, forgive me," she whispered. "Please give me the strength to protect my family from temptation."

Hours after the dark of night fell over the neighbourhood, Grace slipped out of her bed and crept down the stairs. She slithered her way to the kitchen and rifled through the drawers by the cupboards. Pulling out a matchbook, she gazed at the white and blue cross printed on the cardboard and tried to ignore the thumping of her heart against her chest as she slipped outside and down to the garage. She opened the door and quickly absconded from the place with a red can of gasoline.

She wobbled over to the Valientes' house, praying that no one would hear the sloshing of liquid from inside the gas can. The autumn wind blew through her tangled knots of hair and nipped at her ears and fingers. She stopped at the base of the house and tipped over the gas can, shuffling around the house until the can was emptied. The sharp, sweet smell of gasoline pierced Grace's nostrils as she prayed she didn't splash any on her clothes.

She returned to the front of the house and took a few shaky steps back. Grace ripped the matchbook out of her pocket and opened it up. Staring back at her was a row of matches, and her heart leapt into her throat. Her hands shook as she ripped a matchstick out of the cardboard and placed it inside the book's folds. She hesitated, her bones locking in place before she could strike the matchstick.

*Is this really the best thing I can do to get that family away from mine?* Grace's breaths became cold and her whole body began to shake. She shut her eyes as she struck the match, the dark orange light flickering from in front of her eyelids. She reopened her eyes, and the stench of gasoline began to waft into the cold night air.

*I've wandered too far now. I can't go back.* She threw the match at the house and yanked the gas can from the ground. She turned on her heels to run back to her place as the flames roared around the neighbour's home, an inferno that licked at the grey-green sidings.

Grace chucked the can into the garage and slammed the door shut before sneaking back inside her house. She sniffed her hands, her heart skipping as she smelt the same stench of gasoline that surrounded the neighbour's abode. Puffs of breath lasted a mere second in between each gulp of air as she frantically fled to the bathroom and ran her hands under a stream of lukewarm water. She furiously scrubbed at her hands with a bar of soap until it was only half its original size.

By the time Grace was finished scrubbing, the scent of gasoline was blanketed by the scent of lavender, and her heartbeat had slowed down back to its normal pace. She stayed in the bathroom for a couple more minutes before walking back to her room and slipping back into bed.

Grace still struggled to close her eyes and go to sleep; the picture of the house being surrounded by suffocating flames was still fresh in her mind and keeping her wide awake.

Several minutes later, the roaring of sirens filled the room, followed by the thundering honking of a truck's horn.

Isaac stirred under the covers and began to shake Grace's shoulders. "Grace. Grace, honey, get up!" he whispered desperately. "There are sirens lighting up the whole block."

Grace rubbed her face and sat up on the bed. She turned her head toward the window and saw the white blinds covering a bright red glow flashing on and off.

"They sound awfully close," she mumbled, not having to fake the exhaustion in her voice.

"Yeah, I think you're right." Isaac nodded. "Let's get the kids up and out of here!" He ran out of the room, and his rushed footsteps thundered throughout the house. Grace shambled out of the house and floated down the stairs as if she was in a trance. The entire downstairs area was enveloped in a deep, flickering orange glow with an intense red smoulder emitting from the window facing the neighbours. Grace froze in place as the light from the flames embraced her. She held her arms close to her chest and dug her fingers into her silvery robe.

*They should have enough time to get out. Then they can leave town and stop corrupting Kimberly.*

The rest of her family ran down the stairs still clad in their pajamas with heavy eyelids that soon became wide when they saw the bright lights invading their home.

Joshua pushed past Isaac and Kimberly and pointed toward the window with mouth agape. "Whoa! Is something on fire?" His small voice could barely be heard above the cacophony of blaring sirens.

The family ran to the window and yanked back the curtains. The Valiente house was a husk of its former splendour, made into flaming charcoal remnants, a crown of soot and inferno.

A convoy of firetrucks and ambulances lined the streets while an army of firefighters struggled to extinguish the flames with their hoses. Great white streams of water pounded against the flames, but the inferno remained relentless. The EMTs stood by the sidelines with stretchers at the ready with baited breaths, waiting for the flames to finally part long enough to rescue the family.

However, Grace could see there were no signs of life left in the fire. She had thought that her conscious would be clear so she wouldn't suffer the pain of guilt. That changed when she laid eyes on Kimberly. The teen's eyes went wide, and she ran toward the door and her cheeks were covered in runny lines of black ink. She bolted outside, leaving the door wide open as she escaped.

"Kimberly! Kimberly, don't go over there!" Isaac shouted before running after his daughter. Grace looked down at the awestruck Joshua who gazed out the window, the shadows of the flames dancing across his exhausted face. She kneeled and gently placed her hands on her son's shoulders. "Joshua, sweetie, stay in here. Mom and Dad are going to make sure Kimberly doesn't get herself hurt, okay?"

With a couple of nods from Joshua, Grace stepped out of the house and closed the door behind her. Further down the sidewalk, Isaac was holding Kimberly in his arms. The girl was thrashing her arms in an attempt to break away from her father's embrace.

Even above the sirens, Grace could hear Kimberly howl in agony and the girl's legs began to violently quake. When Grace arrived at the pair's side, Kimberly collapsed onto her knees, nearly dragging her father down to the ground with her, and Grace could see in the deep orange glow her daughter's face contorted with grief. She kneeled next to her daughter and draped an arm over her shoulders.

Grace had thought she had done what was best for her child, but in that moment, her baby's anguish struck at her heart and forced tears to pour down her own eyes. Grace let Kimberly sob into her shoulder. The three of them didn't leave until the fire was extinguished, the smoke began to dance into the starry sky, and the three body bags were loaded into the back of the ambulance.

Three weeks passed by, and Grace thanked God that the police were unable to connect her or her family to the fire that took the lives of the Valientes. And yet, Kimberly was still in mourning, and she was quieter around her mother than ever. It was as if the fire stole not only the Valientes' lives but Kimberly's voice as well.

A cold air had filled the home ever since that day, a frozen air that never went away. All those weeks, Kimberly only came out of her room to go to school or eat dinner with the rest of the family. That was until one day, when even that little bit of interactivity with the family stopped.

Grace had taken a pan of steaming, golden chicken tater bake out of the oven and let the crispy, cheesy aroma fill the room. She placed the pan onto the oven and fanned the steam away with her recently discarded oven mitt. She cupped her mouth with her other hand. "Dinner's ready!"

"Tater pot pie! Tater pot pie!" Joshua shouted as he excitedly ran down the stairs with Isaac following shortly after. The boys slid into their chairs around the table while Grace took out a quartet of light blue bowls.

As she set the bowls on the table, Grace noticed an empty chair across from her and sighed. She turned her head in the direction of the stairs. "Kimberly! Supper!" Her shout became terser and her nails dug into the checkered tablecloth.

"Poor girl, she must have taken the loss of that family real hard." Isaac rested his forehead into his hand and massaged the folds of his face. Joshua began picking at his meal with his fork and looked over to his mother.

"If they really were witches, does that mean they're in Hell?" the boy asked. "Is that why Kim is still so sad about them?"

"Joshua!" Isaac hissed, quickly silencing his son. Joshua looked down at the ground glumly and kept idly picking at his food.

Grace sighed and threw back her head before pushing away from the table. "I'll go get her," she muttered. Grace stomped up the stairs and stopped before Kimberly's door. Taped on the door was a paper with "KEEP OUT" written in large, bold, and black marker. Grace tried to jiggle the doorknob to push open the door, but it halted, pushed back against by a large, heavy object. Grace continued to try and push the door open but was only met with the heavy slam of whatever Kimberly had used as a barricade. Grace furiously banged on the door, getting no response from her daughter.

"Kimberly, get out here and eat your dinner with the rest of your family!" Grace shouted. Still, there was no response from the teenager. Grace growled to herself and began to slam against the door with her shoulder. Her blood began to boil, and Grace could feel her face turning a fiery red.

"Kimberly Marie Johnson, if you don't come out here this instant, you'll not only go without dinner, but you're also going to be grounded for a month! We have all had enough of you feeling sorry for yourself and locking yourself up in your room all day!"

Before Grace could spit out any more fiery words of venom, a cry sent chills up her spine and immediately extinguished her fire.

"Mommy! Daddy! Help—" Little Joshua's cries were suddenly cut off and Isaac's footsteps thundered from the room below. Grace let go of the doorknob and rushed back down the stairs to follow her husband. She frantically trailed behind Isaac before they stopped at the bathroom door. Harsh gurgling sounds belted out from the other side of the door before being buried under the sounds of Isaac throwing himself into the door.

"We're coming, Joshua!" Isaac shouted before turning to Grace in a panic. "Get the screwdriver! We need to bust this door open."

Grace nodded, her adrenaline pushing her body down the hall and back into the kitchen. She frantically yanked out all the drawers she could open, nearly ripping them out of the counter. She tossed out all the contents of the drawers in her frenzied search for something to help her husband break the door open.

After what felt like an eternity, Grace pulled out a neon green screwdriver that gave a slight glow and bolted back down the hall to the bathroom. The gurgling continued, but weaker and scratchier, yet Isaac was undaunted and kept trying to break down the door with his slight body.

Grace shoved the screwdriver forward. "I got the screwdriver!" As Isaac ripped the screwdriver out of his wife's hands, Grace grabbed both sides of her head and felt tears spout out of her eyes. "Get our baby out of there!"

Isaac twirled the screwdriver's tip in the doorknob's keyhole and beads of sweat began to form on his face like misshapen rhinestones. He ground his teeth in frustration when the screwdriver continued to fail to find purchase. He slapped the door and cursed under his breath while Grace could only watch helplessly and nearly yank her hair out of her head. Her heart threatening to break through her ribcage and the sound of her son's pained gurgles was an unbearable agony that made Grace want to crawl out of her own skin and run away.

The silence that came after was even more painful. When the gurgling stopped, Isaac froze and stared petrified at the door. The only sounds that could be heard were the faint sobs that escaped Grace's mouth. That was, until the locks suddenly clicked and Isaac slammed the door open.

In the middle of the bathroom floor was Joshua, his skin a deep blue and purple, veiny lines covering his neck. An unholy mixture of blood and spittle dripped out of his mouth and formed a foamy pile by his unmoving head. Grace let out a shrill shriek and shoved Isaac to the side, scampering to kneel by Joshua's side.

"Oh, no. No no no no. Baby?" Grace's voice was hoarse and wooden. The words barely muscled their way out of her throat. She cradled poor little Joshua's figure in her arms and hugged his ice-cold body closely to hers. She was swept back to the day she had held Joshua for the first time in the delivery room. A lull of silence had followed after the babe was pulled out of her and cried his eyes out. His hands, so small, had been reaching out to her, and he had barely cried as he rested in her arms. The moment she had laid eyes on him, Grace had promised God that she would protect him with her life, just as she had when she had first held Kimberly in her arms. But she was quickly brought back to reality. It was not the lively baby but a cold, lifeless boy in her embrace. Grace let out a howl and rocked her baby back and forth. She buried her face into his cold shoulder and let his shirt soak up her tears. In her head, she begged God to forgive her for breaking her vow.

"Oh, my poor baby. Mommy's sorry. Mommy's so sorry!" she wept. "Isaac, what do we do?" She turned her head, only to be faced with an empty doorway. Grace scooped Joshua's body into her shaking arms and dragged herself out of the bathroom. She looked around the hall with tears making her vision as blurry as a scratched-up mirror.

"Isaac?" she called, her voice hoarse and scratchy. The room was filled with a heavy silence that pressed against the back of her neck. Her breaths were hollow, and it felt like a cold hand was squeezing her heart as she moved through the hall and back toward the kitchen. Just after passing the staircase, a loud *bang* echoed from the top of the stairs. Grace jumped with a shriek and turned around. Isaac tumbled down the stairs like a ragdoll. He collapsed onto the ground with his neck bent back like a roll of raw dough. Low croaks escaped from his throat and his hands twitched slightly with each creaking breath. All the strength in Grace's legs left her and she collapsed onto the ground next to Isaac's mangled body. She sank down further until her forehead rested against Isaac's. She felt his head shake and his quiet croaks become quicker and more panicked. Grace lowered Joshua's body so he could rest next to his father. Her eyes then cast onto the staircase and one name cried out inside her head.

"Kimberly!" Grace stepped over Joshua and Isacc's bodies and ran in a mad panic up the stairs. Her hands slipped from the railing as she tried to grip it on the way up but still, she kept running. Her mad dash was only halted right before Kimberly's bedroom door, when she was yanked back and pulled into the air by her neck. Sharp, icy talons dug into her skin, feeling like rows of tiny holes were being burned into her neck. Streams of warm liquid trickled down her neck and soaked into her shirt. Grace could faintly hear the hissing of snakes behind her before she was thrown into the wall in front of her. A sharp ringing pierced her ears and her vision began to darken. She struggled to crawl onto all fours and pull herself toward Kimberly's door. A shrill cry shook the room, threatening to bring her crashing back onto the ground. Facing her from the other side of the hallway was a gangly, naked woman, glaring at Grace with all the fires of Hell.

Her hair was composed of maroon snakes hissing and waving wildly and large, black wings stretched out from the woman's shoulder blades and across the room. The woman's claws dug into the floor before she pounced at Grace like a crazed animal.

She felt herself slammed against walls, the floor, and the ceiling, her body covered in agonizing burns, and she heard several thick cracks with each impact her body made. Her world was a maddening blur of blood, black feathers, and the dimmed colours of her darkened house.

Finally, when her entire body cried for a reprieve, the winged creature threw Grace into the ground like a javelin. Grace's vision began to spin, though she could make out rubble from the ceiling piled onto the ground and walls filled with cracks and holes. Her neck was stiff and heavy so she couldn't move it to stare at the ceiling. She tried to cry out for her daughter, but only disgusting gurgles came out of her mouth, and a warm liquid pooled over her lips and created a puddle below her chin. The winged woman stood up and roared at the petrified Grace before flying out a downstairs window in a blur.

Grace tried to crawl to Kimberly's door, but all her muscles wept and her joints were locked in place. Each breath felt like her ribs were poking into her lungs and her heart felt ready to punch itself out of her chest. She felt a low rumble from under her limping body, followed by a thunderous crack that reverberated around her with the force of a hammer swinging into the side of her head.

Suddenly, the floor underneath her collapsed into rubble and she was sent tumbling helplessly through the air. After being pelted with pebbles and choking on chalky clouds of dust on the way down, Grace slammed into the ground and had all remaining air knocked out of her body.

For what felt like days, Grace felt herself floating helplessly in a sea of black. Her limbs were as rigid as rusty pipes, so she couldn't even dog paddle her way out of the dark. Her lungs felt like they were full of dust, and yet they were still open just enough to force the oxygen into her system. She wondered when the pitch-coloured curtains would part and make way for the light of her Holy Father and invite her into His kingdom to be reunited with her family.

Alas, it was not yet her time.

Grace returned to the world of the living with a body screaming in bloody anguish. She found herself trapped in a field of stony debris under a night sky filled with stars covered in clouds of pale dust. Her neck was squeezed so tightly she could barely force the oxygen up her throat, and the pressure on the sides kept her from swivelling her head around. However, she was able to move her eyes far enough to see a bloody, mangled hand sticking out from the rock field.

She could only assume it was her hand, since there wasn't another soul in sight, even though she couldn't even feel a breeze kiss the palm. She opened her mouth to cry out, but the back of her throat felt like it had been sprayed with a high-pressure hose filled with gasoline. She tried to kick her legs to gain some traction, but her body was squeezed tightly against the jagged edges of the remains of her home, and she only succeeded in puncturing her stomach and hips.

Amid her struggle, Grace heard the scuffing of feet against stone not too far from her. These footsteps were later accompanied by a shadowy silhouette creeping behind the cloud of smoke. Grace's eyes widened and she opened her mouth to call for help. Even though a shriek had pulled itself out of her throat instead of any words, the shadow still turned in her direction and made its way forward.

The heaviness in her heart was further lifted when familiar colours and shapes revealed themselves as part of the shadow. None other than the colours that made up Kimberly, covered in soot and scratches but still alive.

A relieved smile formed on Grace's face the closer her daughter's approach got. Kimberly stopped before her mother's head and she reached her hand down to one of the rocks. But then, Kimberly stopped and pulled her hand back.

Grace's heart felt like it was torn apart as the stench of smoke and rubble made their presence known once again.

Kimberly's eyes were revealed to be full of venom in a glare that had enough hatred to boil all the world's oceans. The teen girl shook her head. "You know, one time, when I visited Penelope and her folks, they told me about a rule that the Wicca follow. They call it the three-fold law. The basic idea is that any energy you bring into the world, good or bad, will eventually be returned to you three times over."

As Grace felt her breaths become shallower and her lungs become cluttered with more dust, Kimberly turned her head and surveyed the site. She let out a joyless chuckle and scoffed. "Maybe the so-called witches had a good point. Who knew?" Kimberly then turned her back to her mother and trudged away, back into the darkness.

Tears poured down Grace's face as soundless sobs were choked out of her throat and all her strength was soaked into the rubble. Minutes turned to hours and night began to creep into day. The whole time, Grace remained trapped and could only pray for God to take her where He believed she deserved to go. Then, just as she heard sirens wail, her prayers were answered.

# The Lonely Tale of The China Doll Girl

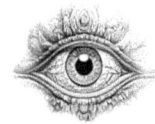

As Inigo told his tale, Marcy felt his gaze planted on her face. Studying her, waiting for a crack to form in her mask. Once he finished his story, Inigo sliced off a sliver of turkey and slowly began to chew after placing it in his mouth.

Other than the clattering of cutlery from the other diners, Marcy could feel the silence pressing against the back of her skull. She cleared her throat. "So, where did you hear of that story?" Marcy asked, trying to hide the unease in her voice.

Inigo shrugged. "It was an old tale passed around the neighbourhood when I was a kid. Kind of grew into an urban legend as time went on." He gave a mischievous grin before eating another bit of meat. "But you know what they say: some legends are born of fact."

Marcy nodded uneasily. "Yeah, I guess so."

Azura craned her head to peer at Marcy and sighed. "Dad,

are you trying to give Marcy the stare-down?"

Inigo laughed. "I have no idea what you're talking about." Just as Inigo turned away, Marcy felt her phone buzz in her pocket.

She reached for her pocket when she was frozen in place by Azura's glare. "Marcy, please don't take out your phone at dinner," she hissed.

Inigo gave an apologetic shrug. "One of the rules at home is no phones at the table." Marcy's beating heart sank at the thought of Aiden wandering into a member of the family and the whole plan blowing up then and there. And yet, Inigo's spiel of betrayal and her imagination giving form to the furies tied Marcy's brain into knots. Her heart ached as she relived each encounter with Marcy's family members, how they had opened their home to her after being closed off from everyone else in town.

*But we're too far into this now to turn back, even if I could convince Aiden,* Marcy thought, her mind a storm of aching melancholy and sickening guilt. She looked around the banquet table. Everyone else had almost finished eating and their plates contained only a few crumbs of food. At any moment, someone could get out of their chair, wander the house, and accidentally bump into her brother. Marcy gulped a ball of air. She quickly stood up from her seat. The screeching of the chair garnered the attention she had aimed for. Everyone's heads turned up from their plate and gazed at her.

"Um…I'd like to tell a story!" Marcy announced. Her voice quaked and gave a peek into the state of her nerves.

Azura's eyes widened with surprise. "Wait, for real?"

Inigo raised a fascinated eyebrow. "Well, this should be interesting. Do go on."

Marcy took a breath. Beads of sweat trickled down her face and her heart banged furiously inside her chest.

*Here we go. Let's hope they don't catch on that I'm pulling this out of my ass.*

With all eyes on her, Marcy began to scramble together her tale.

\*\*\*

The sunset sky was moulded and mutated into a slimy storm of pinks and oranges. Shadows stalked the small concrete minefield that was the small town of Revelstone. The great mountain peaks spiking out of the ground, while usually being a symbol of wonder and mystique, now cast a great shadow on the town as it hid the sun away from the people. As Dinah made her way down the streets with her hefty black bag slung over her shoulder, her heart skipped a few steps. Despite the streets being empty, she still felt eyes staring down upon the back of her head. Dinah clutched her strap as she stopped in her tracks. She turned her head to look behind her, only to be greeted by an empty sidewalk under the sunset. As Dinah turned back to look forward, she heaved her chest up and let out a gallon of air through her nose.

*You're just being a little paranoid,* she tried to tell herself. Dinah hesitantly continued marching down the sidewalk, her destination still set in her mind. A slight breeze blew across her face as the hairs on her arms spiked up and her eyes darted from place to place. Each slight noise behind her almost made Dinah jump out of her skin, but still, she kept marching. At the top of a slope that caused a sharp dip in the road, Dinah found herself staring down at her destination. The wooden roof had moulted into a murky green, with only chips of brown paint remaining of its previous splendour. The top half of the house's walls were a smooth beige while the bottom half was made of a grey and rusted brown cobblestone. The top half of the house had a row of three windows with dark brown hatches barely holding onto the window frames, while the bottom half had a single wooden door with a rounded top surrounded by a stone archway.

Dinah heard a low buzz and wind chimes play from her phone inside her front jeans pocket. When she took it out, she saw her mom's phone number light up her screen. She slid the button with the phone in the middle to the right of her screen and placed her phone to her ear.

"Hey Mom, what's up?"

"Hey, Dinah, just want to know how much longer you are going to be out. It's going to be dark soon and I'd rather not have a heart attack wondering where you've been."

Dinah sighed, throwing her head back. "I'll just be out for a few more minutes. Just need to get a few more shots of the old house."

"The one on Edmond Road? Do you have any idea what went on in there?"

Dinah held back a laugh. Of course, she had heard the legend. How a girl had been held hostage inside of the house until she and her family had disappeared. The story had been told for years before her parents moved to town and maybe even longer than the town itself.

"Relax, I'm just taking some pictures of the outside. It's not like I'm going inside to pay the China Doll Girl a visit."

"Just be careful. Don't wander out of town and call me if you need a ride home."

Dinah rolled her eyes. "Okay, okay." Just as she went to pull her phone away from her ear, her eyes widened as a thought suddenly came to her head. "Oh hey, how's the job search going?" The line was silent for a few seconds before Dinah heard her mother sigh.

"About as well as it can be, I guess. Look, don't worry about me. Just get your own work done and I'll try to figure this thing out, okay?" Dinah nodded absently as she began to carefully walk down the slope of the sidewalk.

"Okay. Sounds good."

"Alright, stay safe, okay? Love you."

Dinah smiled. "Love you, too. See you later." Dinah waited until her mom had ended the call before she slipped her phone back into her pocket. A pit formed in her stomach as her mind became a collage of pictures of her mom leaning over her paper-covered desk, her head seemingly glued to her hand, trying to live off a diet of coffee and painkillers. Dinah shook her head. One day she'd make it big when she turned her photography hobby into a career, get her and her mom out of the hole and maybe make enough to take her no-good dad to court.

But for now, she had to focus on the present. And the present required a few more pictures for her school assignment. The assignment called for pictures of town landmarks and what better landmark than the town's own local haunted house? Dinah unzipped her bag and took out a stocky camera. She peered into the camera's viewfinder and pinched her fingers around the lens. The house first appeared to be reflected in a foggy mirror, Dinah bit her lip as she turned the lens around and the picture of the house became sharper. Just before she could take her first shot, Dinah suddenly felt a hand roughly grab her shoulder.

"You know voyeurism is a crime, right?"

Dinah saw before her an all-too-familiar trio of girls she had hoped she'd only have to suffer on school grounds. Of course, no such luck as she found herself face-to-face with the Barbie Doll trio. All three had their hair styled into curly ponytails, were decorated with gold and silver jewelry and their nails glistened with magenta nail polish. The leader of the pack had a smirk that made Dinah's neck hairs stand on end, her nose was pointed toward the sky as if everything had a stench to it and her high heels clicked incessantly against the sidewalk.

"Um… I, uh…" As Dinah stumbled over her words, the trio guffawed and cackled.

"Hey, don't think too hard about what you're going to say. You might hurt yourself," the blonde leader laughed.

The girl to her right pointed a finger toward the house, her gaudy bangles jingled and clacked together. "I mean, no one's been in that house for years, Abby. So, I'm not sure Dinah can be convicted of—"

The blonde rolled her eyes, "It's called a joke. Relax, Jazz." The brunette to Abby's left loudly chomped on her gum before beginning to blow a dirty pink bubble. "Heard that when the police came to investigate, all that was left of the family was a bunch of furniture and a mask."

Dinah turned to her. "A mask?"

The girl nodded before Abby cut in. "Yeah. It was pretty ornate, not much of a shock since the dad was said to make them for a living." Abby gently pushed Dinah forward, closer to the house. "How he made so much on just masks before the internet, I have no clue. Might have mooched off of his wife or something." Abby's nails dug burrows into Dinah's shoulders, forcing her to keep stumbling forward.

Jazz looked at her two cohorts nervously, beads of sweat bubbled out of her pores. "Are we really doing this?" she asked. Abby scowled at the raven-haired girl, cowing her back into silence. Abby then brought back her sickly-sweet smile and leaned close to Dinah's ear.

"You know, if you really want to get some good shots of the house…" Abby hissed.

Dinah jerked her shoulders around, but with each movement, Abby dug her nails in deeper. "Stop, let me go!" Dinah shouted.

"You can always ask the ghosts what the best places are." Abby laughed. Suddenly, she shoved Dinah forward. In a blur, the brunette sprinted for the door and whipped it open. As the musty odour of the house's mould and the cold shadows embraced her, Dinah was pushed onto the ground by the door. Her palms scraped across the old wood floor and her bags were scattered across the ground. From the other side of the door, Dinah could hear the Barbie Doll pack cackling before their shadows zoomed past the scratched-up windows. Dinah scrambled to her feet, nearly slipping over her bag as she rushed to the door.

"No! Please! You can't do this!" Dinah cried. She slammed her fists against the door, feeling the old wood push back against her. She slapped her hands around to find a latch or a doorknob, anything to let herself out. But all she felt was old, splintered wood.

"Got to get out. Got to get out." Dinah turned her body around and threw her shoulder into the door. Her body bounced off the door and she was thrown onto the ground. She pounded her fist into the ground with a frustrated shriek. Dinah then crawled over to the door and began to pound her feet against it.

"Come on! Come on!" she shouted. Dinah kicked the door until the fire in her legs faded to numbness. When she stood up and looked behind her, Dinah saw that her bags and camera were both gone. In a panic, she searched her pockets. Instead of her phone, she was greeted by emptiness and denim. She let out a bemoaned howl and slammed her head into the door. Dinah looked into the shadows of the cobweb-infested house; a cold chill trailed up her spine. She dug her nails into the grain of the door.

"This is just how people die in scary movies," Dinah muttered. Still, the door wouldn't budge, so even if her stuff wasn't missing, she knew she'd need to investigate the house for another way out. So, Dinah marched forward. The floor underneath her creaked with each step. She made her way to the next room, which looked to her like a lounging area. A long couch with faded purple fabric and upholstery that was torn to shreds. A neglected fireplace was gathering a hutch of dust bunnies, and the curtains were ribbons that covered the scratchy windows. A few feet away from the fireplace was a withered foot stool with the same dying upholstery as the sofa. Dinah rushed over to the footstool and gripped the pale gold edges, the engravings digging into her palms. With a shout, Dinah cocked the foot stool behind her head and chucked it toward one of the windows. Rather than the expected shower of glass shards from a broken window she had been expecting, Dinah instead saw the foot stool bounce off the pane and crumple onto the ground.

"No!" Dinah cried. She turned around and pounded her fists against the wall behind her. Tears of boiling frustration trickled down her face as she slid onto the ground.

"Don't cry," a soft voice cooed.

Dinah's neck hairs stood up and the teen jumped to her feet and twirled around. "Who said that?" she called.

"I'm no one important," the voice said melancholically. "What's wrong? Why are you crying?"

Dinah sighed. "What's wrong is I'm stuck in a creepy house with no way out and without my stuff. That camera cost my mom so much money and now it's gone." The teen buried her face in her hand.

"Um… I think I found it. It's up here in my room."

Dinah lifted her face up and eyed the hall leading out of the room skeptically. A spiral staircase in the middle that looked ready to collapse with a sneeze led up into darkness. The railing was nothing more than twigs and the carpet was nearly dissolved. Dinah took a step back.

"Yeah, uh… can you just help me get out of here and then

leave the stuff outside?" Dinah called. A cold breeze blew past her as silence crawled into the room.

"I'm not supposed to leave," the voice whimpered. "I've been so awful to my parents. They said I'm not allowed to leave until I learn my lesson."

Dinah sighed and shook her head. "This is a horrible idea," she muttered. Still, Dinah pressed forward, inching closer to the staircase. As she laid her hand on the railing, she felt the structure buckle and heard it shriek like nails on a chalkboard. She quickly retracted her hand and backed away from the railing.

"Yeah, no. I'm not touching that," Dinah said. The girl took a breath before planting a foot on the first step of the staircase. A low creak moaned from the woodwork and Dinah swore she could feel the wood cave in under her foot. Her face stretched into a grimace before she pushed her other foot up and onto the next step. Much to her relief, the staircase remained intact, so Dinah continued up the stairs. She kept her arms outstretched but refused to touch the untrustworthy railing. As she ascended, shadows began to envelop her, and Dinah found her breaths becoming shorter. Her heart began to race, fearing that one wrong step would send her tumbling several feet down into a heap of mangled flesh and wood.

Suddenly, a light snapped on, illuminating the edge of the top of the staircase. On the next floor was a wall lined with doors that looked like someone had tried to paint over them, a failed attempt at beige and mustard camouflage. In between each door was a floral-styled light with a rusted yellow beaded chain, acting as a switch.

"In here," the voice croaked. Dinah turned her head in the voice's direction. After stepping onto the next floor, she saw at the end of the hall an old brown door. The door was covered in a variety of locks, deadbolts, padlocks, latches, and combination locks. Dinah figured there were enough locks to open a small lock shop. As she got closer, however, Dinah saw that all of the locks were covered in rust and none were actually locking the door. So, Dinah gently pushed the door open to reveal a desolate room with a piece of thin, used cardboard in the center. Greeted by a waft of a sour, rotten stench, Dinah quickly became aware of a blue bucket in the corner with dark stains on the inside and on the rim and handle. Sitting under a window covered with iron bars was a petite, hunched figure squeezing their legs close to their chest. Sitting in front of the figure were Dinah's bag and her camera, left without a scratch. Dinah was frozen in place. It seemed too easy. She still wondered how the figure had managed to nab her belongings in the first place. She gave the shadowy figure an awkward wave.

"Hey, um…are you the one that's been talking to me?" Dinah asked.

The figure shrank back into the floor at the sound of Dinah's voice.

"Yes, yes that was me," the figure stammered.

Dinah gripped the edge of the door as she carefully watched the hunched figure. "Alright. Uh…would you mind passing that stuff over to me?" Dinah asked.

The figure turned her face away and furiously shook her head. "Oh no, I couldn't. I don't want to wreck your things." The figure dipped her head behind her arms and began to shiver.

Dinah watched, puzzled by how jumpy the girl was. Dinah swallowed the urge to gag on the acidic smell of the room as she took a cautious step forward. "Well, you did a good job taking care of them. I don't think just passing them over would hurt," Dinah said reassuringly. Still, the figure shook her head.

"No, I know how it goes," the figure cried. "Doing one thing right doesn't mean I should let it get to my head. I'm always making mistakes. Always. Always." The figure's shoulders began to shake, and Dinah could hear soft sobs hiccupping into the shadows.

Dinah shook her head and tried to smile. "Aw, come on, there's no need to think like that," she said. She heard the figure snort and sniffle.

"But that's what my parents say and they're very smart so if they say so—"

"Then they're not that smart," Dinah interrupted. "They don't sound like parents; they sound like bullies. And you should never let bullies bring you down." The figure sniffed and rubbed her arms against her forehead.

"You're the first person besides my parents that has come to visit me," the figure said, her voice as delicate as a wine glass.

Dinah shrugged. "Admittedly, it's not entirely by choice. I got locked in here by a bunch of jerks."

The figure's shoulder stopped shaking and she dragged her nails up her knees. "Oh, I see," the figure murmured. "Well, I don't blame you. I mean, no one comes to visit someone that looks like me because they want to." The figure then lifted her head off of her knees.

Dinah wasn't sure what she had been expecting when the figure decided to show her face, but she hadn't been expecting to see a tear-stained mask. The mask completely covered the figure's head, not even showing a lock of hair. Instead, it gave the girl plastic brown curls with red bows painted on. The face of the mask was milky white with chubby cheeks that had a dusting of pink for blushes. The lips of the mask were blood red and the holes the mask had for eyes held no light, not even from a sparkle in the figure's true eyes. Dinah gasped and her blood felt like it had been replaced with caustic acid.

"Why are you wearing a mask?" she whispered.

The masked girl bowed her head. "My dad made it. My mom

painted it so I could look pretty. They said they would take it off when I became a more obedient daughter. But I haven't seen or heard from them for so long."

Dinah's heart felt like it was split in two. The thought that parents could do that to their own child made her insides twist and turn. "Guess we got something in common," Dinah said as she picked up her things. "While my mom would never lay a hand on me, I've kind of been hounded by some bullies myself."

The masked girl raised her head. "Really? But you're so nice and so much prettier than me. Why would anyone be mean to you?"

Dinah shrugged. "Some people are just jerks, I guess." She then sat down and took the masked girl's hand. "Maybe if we hung out more, we'd both feel a bit less miserable."

The masked girl looked down at Dinah's hand before staring up at the teen with hopeful eyes. "You mean, you'd really be friends with me?"

Dinah nodded. "Yeah, of course. I'd be glad to be."

The masked girl's back straightened and her sniffling came to a stop. Dinah hoped that behind the mask was a smile in the making. "Wow, I've never had a friend before."

Dinah smiled. "I'm glad I can be your first."

The masked girl stood up, bringing Dinah back to her feet as well.

"I'm Dinah by the way." As she finally introduced herself, she could barely make out in the shadows of the mask's eyeholes a twinkle.

"My name is Cecilia." The masked girl bounced with new-found giddiness. "I can't believe you actually want to be my friend!"

Dinah smiled, though a deep chasm in her gut began to bubble and sweat began to form on her palms.

Cecilia suddenly perked her head up. "Oh, but I can't just let you do all of this without giving you something in return," she exclaimed. Cecilia seemed to ponder to herself before giving a small gasp. "Anything you want, I can get it for you by the end of tomorrow."

Dinah raised an eyebrow. "Really?"

Cecilia nodded. "Of course. I mean it's the least I can do."

Dinah laughed. "Well, for one, I wish my mom could find a good job. It sucks seeing her stressed out so much."

Cecilia bowed her head and nodded. "You really care about your mother. Don't worry, if she's as nice as you then fortune will come her way in no time."

Dinah chuckled. "Yeah, I hope so." She then began to walk out of the room but not before stopping at the doorway to wave goodbye. Cecilia gave a small wave back.

"It'll be nice to not be so lonely anymore," Dinah heard Cecilia say before descending down the stairs. When Dinah arrived back at the entrance, the door was wide open and the warm twilight peeked inside. Dinah didn't give it much thought as she bolted out of the house and pulled out her phone to call her mom.

The next morning, Dinah was still clad in her baby blue pyjamas as she sleepily placed a slice of bread into the toaster. Her heavy eyelids could barely make out her mother excitedly rushing into the room with a black binder in hand.

"Dinah, I have incredible news!" her mother exclaimed. As Dinah rubbed her eyes, her mom came more into focus and the young girl could see her mother wore a glowing smile.

"Yeah, what's up?" the groggy teen asked.

Her mother began frantically flipping through the pages in her binder. "I just got a call back from the Chinese restaurant downtown. They said they were so impressed with my resume that they were going to make me their general manager!" Dinah's Mom looked ready to jump through the roof and her smile ignited the room.

Dinah's fatigue was replaced with a sudden jolt of energy. "Oh my God, Mom. That's amazing!" Dinah cheered. "Are you going to be starting today?"

Dinah's mother nodded. "That's right! I can't believe this. It looks like our luck is finally turning around." The giddy woman reached into the fridge and quickly grabbed a plump, round apple. "They even accommodated my hours so I can still drop you off at school," she added.

Dinah gazed out the window as her mind wandered to her meeting with the masked girl the day before. Could this really be Cecilia's doing?

For weeks afterward, Dinah would visit Cecilia every day after school. For the most part, the two girls would chat about their lives, both their grievances and the moments that they treasured. Even if she couldn't see her face, Dinah would feel Cecilia's spirits rise with each visit and her voice became less shaky as she talked.

However, after leaving the house, Dinah's mind would be stuck on the prospect of another wish. How could she ever top what she did for her mom? Dinah was elated to see her mom no longer looking like death whenever she returned from a job interview. Now, it was almost like her mother was dancing around the house and her smile never waned. There were days when Dinah thought she wouldn't need another favour from her new friend.

Unfortunately, the feeling wouldn't last.

It was an afternoon like any other. Dinah had settled into her routine of walking to Cecilia's house to talk about her day and chat about whatever came to their minds. But as she made her way through the neighbourhood, Dinah couldn't help but feel a crowd of eyes on her. Her steps became more sluggish, and she tried to cover her head with her pale green hoodie. Sadly, the hoodie proved ineffective in camouflaging her.

"Nice day for a stroll, huh?"

Dinah's heart sank at the sound of Abby's mocking hiss. When Dinah whipped around, there stood Abby with her pair of minions standing by her side. Jazz looked at her two companions nervously, twisting and turning her manicured hands. "Guys, are we really going to do this?" she asked anxiously.

The other girl standing by Abby shrugged. "Why not? I mean, we're already here."

Abby rolled her eyeshadow-caked eyes. "Well, at least *you're* willing to have a little fun, Vickie." The head of the pack strutted towards Dinah with her blush handbag swinging around on her wrist. "Anyway, we saw you creeping around the old house." She sharply jabbed a finger into Dinah's shoulder. "Did the China Doll Girl possess you? Or are you really that desperate for friends that you'll hook up with a banshee?"

Vickie guffawed at Abby's quips while Jazz continued to fidget around nervously. Dinah stumbled back as she looked into Abby's venomous eyes. How long had she and her posse been watching Dinah? How much did they know about Cecilia?

Dinah shook her head. "Come on, guys. Just leave me alone," Dinah said. She tried to walk away, but Abby yanked her shoulder back just as she was turning around.

"I mean, it's either that you got all buddy-buddy with a ghost or you're just trespassing for the hell of it" Abby jeered.

"And that's a crime. We can't allow that," Vickie added with a snort.

Jazz began to step away tepidly. "Alright, we had our fun. Can we just go now?"

Abby shot daggers at Jazz, freezing her in place. "Don't go

all holier-than-thou on us now, Jazz. Unless you want to end up taking her place."

For a moment, Dinah hoped that Jazz would finally come to her senses. That she would finally put her foot down and help guide her away from her tormentors. However, instead, Jazz maintained the status quo and cast her gaze toward the ground. "No, not really," the girl muttered.

"Yeah, I didn't think so." Abby leered toward Dinah's bag, the one that held her camera. Before Dinah could make a grab for it, Abby snatched the bag and roughly yanked the strap off Dinah's shoulders, plucking a few strands of her hair out along the way.

"Hey, give that back, you jerk!" Dinah shouted. As she tried to lunge toward Abby, Vickie shoved her shoulder into Dinah's chest, becoming a stone wall as Dinah helplessly flailed her arms in a futile attempt to reclaim her camera.

Abby triumphantly held the camera in the air like a trophy, the lenses casting a flare against the afternoon sun. "Well, if the cops ever caught you sneaking in then this camera could provide them an orgy of evidence against you."

"Don't you fucking dare," Dinah hissed.

Abby shook her head and tsked. "Ooh, wrong answer." With a flick of the wrist, Abby threw the camera onto the sidewalk. The camera exploded like a grenade into a billion pieces of plastic and glass shrapnel.

As it shattered, Dinah could feel her heart shatter with it. Her mom had spent hundreds of dollars to buy her that camera when she had discovered her love for photography. Dinah remembered the tired eyes of her mother as she had given her the camera for her birthday and the proud smile she had worn when Dinah saw it for the first time. Now, that memory was nothing more than a disintegrated mess on the concrete. All feeling in Dinah's body became numb and her ears were stuffed with a sharp ringing noise. Vickie dropped her onto the ground, letting Dinah land harshly on her knees.

"Oh, come on, don't give me that look," Abby ragged. "I was doing you a favour. Maybe now, you'll get a new hobby that doesn't involve being such a voyeur."

The pack then took their leave, with Abby and Vickie laughing their way into the slowly setting sun. Only when they left did Dinah notice the tears boiling on her face. As her breaths struggled to surface from her lungs, she began to pick up the remnants of her camera.

*What did I ever do to deserve this?* she thought. *I never bothered them. I just kept my head down like I did with everyone else.* Soon, her sorrow ignited into a flame that licked at her insides. The blood in her veins screamed and her eyes felt like they were lit on fire. After gathering the pieces of her camera into her bag, her hands *curled into white-hot fists.*

*Well, whatever the reason, they're not going to get away with it. Not this time.*

Dinah stomped down the rest of the way to the old house. Her eyes continued to burn like caustic acid. She busted the door open and tried to wipe her reddening eyes. Cecilia peeked down from the staircase before rushing down the steps.

"Oh my God, Dinah! What happened?" the masked girl exclaimed.

Dinah crossed her arms and looked over to her bag. She waited for Cecilia to reach her side before unzipping her bag and showing her the fragments of her camera.

"Your camera," Cecilia breathed.

"Some jerks thought it'd be funny to smash it up," Dinah growled. She then threw herself onto the steps and burrowed her fists into the wood.

"Do you know them?"

"All too well." Dinah ground her teeth so hard she thought they would turn into bone dust. "They think they can just walk around and treat me like garbage for no real reason." Cecilia sat down next to Dinah and gently grabbed her shoulder.

"I'm so sorry," Cecilia whispered.

Dinah shook her head. "Not your fault. You're not the one that smashed up the most expensive thing my mom ever bought." Dinah sunk her head into her hands, feeling the tears slip in between her fingers. "I just wish that they'd suffer for everything they've done. It's not fair that they can just walk all over everyone and not have someone give them a taste of their own medicine."

As Dinah ranted, Cecilia hesitated, anxiously tapping the railing. "Are you sure that'd be the best thing to do?" the masked girl asked.

Dinah's eyes narrowed and she bolted onto her feet. "Well, walking away from them hasn't done anything," Dinah growled. "And ignoring them just makes them want to bug me even more. So, what do I have left to do, huh?"

Cecilia looked down at the ground. "So, you really just want to take revenge on them?"

Dinah gave a firm and curt nod. "They need to pay for everything they've done." She began to walk away before a thought rushed to her head. Before she could stop herself, Dinah added, "And I want to watch them suffer."

She heard Cecilia gasp. Dinah herself felt surprised at how easy it was for her to say that. But there was no use taking it back. After years of frustration boiling over, it was finally out. Dinah turned her head and saw Cecilia slink back into the shadows of the staircase.

"Okay, if it's what you really want then it'll be done," she said in a shaky voice. Just as Dinah turned back around to open the door, Cecilia added, "I just hope you're really ready to see your wish in action."

Dinah turned to face her friend one more time before she left, but Cecilia had already vanished and the only sign of life remaining in the house was the creaking of the old wood.

During the walk back home, Dinah was left with a sickly feeling twisting and turning in her stomach. Her footsteps felt as heavy as concrete, and her body was covered in chills. The sensations lingered even as she returned home and threw her bed's covers over her. She tossed and turned throughout the night and barely got a wink of rest, even as she tried to tell herself to go to sleep. All the while, Cecilia's last words bounced around in her head like a tennis ball.

Throughout the next day at school, Dinah kept her head down and refused to meet anyone's eye. Everywhere she went, she could feel a billion eyes burrowing into the back of her head and a cold trail seemed to follow her. By the end of the day, her nerves felt like they were on fire and that her heart was going to burst out of her chest. After running her hand against the railing, she reached the stairs and clung to the stairs' railing for dear life. Deep within, Dinah hoped that Cecilia would ignore her wish this time and that the Barbie Doll pack would finally leave her alone.

But of course, Lady Luck was not on her side.

"Watch it, peeper!" Abby snorted before she shoved Dinah down toward the steps.

Dinah tumbled down, hearing her books flop and flip behind her before she landed in a heap with them on the platform leading to the ground floor's set of stairs. A shrill ringing filled Dinah's ears and her head felt like it was being compressed inside a giant vice grip. She flailed her arms around to try and find a railing to grab a hold of to try and pull herself back up. The ringing eventually quieted down to allow her to hear the mocking laughter of the pack back at the top of the stairs.

As her blurred vision realigned to clear itself, Dinah could barely make out a pale face behind Jazz's shoulder. A shiver seemed to rapidly surge through Jazz's body, and she quickly went to wrap her arms around her body. However, Dinah saw that Jazz's arms now had a glassy sheen to them and her arm's peachy skin had become a pastier white.

Jazz looked down and finally noticed the change. Her jaw dropped and her eyes became as wide as saucers. She tried to wiggle her fingers, but they became as rigid as rusted gears before becoming frozen entirely. "What's happening to me?"

Her two companions halted their laughter and turned to face the commotion. Their malicious joy turned to panic when they turned to see the cause of Jazz's distress.

"Holy crap, what's going on with your hands?" Abby screamed.

"You see this, too?" Vickie whispered, her jaw hanging so low her glob of gum nearly fell out of her mouth. Jazz's arms became more rigid as she stumbled back with tears in her eyes. Her neck became slick and white, and her shoulders seemed to freeze.

"Someone help—" Jazz began to shout. However, her cries of distress were choked out as her face became shining porcelain. Her eyes and lips were turned to paint on the surface of her new ceramic face. Just as her hair began to thin, Jazz toppled over the balcony and flipped around as she fell. Dinah heard the newly formed porcelain figure shatter against the first floor of the school and Jazz's final screams left one last echo before departing from the world of the living. Vickie huddled close to Abby, causing them both to clumsily stumble back in their high heels.

"Leave us alone!" Abby shouted, placing her arm in front of Vickie. What Dinah heard next made her heart sink and all colour drain from her face.

"I can't. I made a promise." Cecilia's voice echoed through the empty school halls. Vickie was suddenly yanked back away from her would-be protector. Dinah rushed up the stairs and turned around the corner to see Vickie struggling to grip the lockers as she was dragged back, kicking and hollering. The second-in-command of the pack watched with horror as her legs and arms became glassy and milk white. As the ceramic substance slowly trailed up her limbs, Vickie slammed into the lockers multiple times, the sound concealing her terrified screams. As she was repeatedly thrown into the metal, Vickie's legs and arms began to crack with each impact. Dinah winced each time she saw the cracks in Vickie's body grow longer and larger. Mercifully, Vickie's torment was put to an end as her body shattered into a million pieces, with only her head left intact on the ground. The face was painted with a perpetually petrified gaze of horror.

"I need to get out of here." Abby's breaths became short and shallow, her movements loose and uncoordinated as she continued to hyperventilate. Dinah watched as Abby rushed down the stairs in a panic, the bully nearly tripping over the steps as she tried to retreat. A cold snap ambushed Dinah as she watched her terrified tormentor reach the bottom of the stairs.

"Cecilia, stop. This is going too far," Dinah cried. But her pleas fell on deaf ears as Abby was lifted into the air like a marionette. Abby watched with widened eyes as the milky porcelain substance stretched up her arms and legs. As the substance reached the tips of her forearms and knees, her arms were stretched out and her legs were yanked into the splits. Abby screeched, shutting her eyes as her arms began to twist.

"No! Please, stop! It hurts! Mom! Someone, anyone!" Abby shrieked as her arms twisted and her legs were torn apart from each other. With a final, chilling howl, Abby's body was torn apart and her limbs were slowly lowered back to the ground. The ends of her limbs were smooth and flat, minus a single hole in the middle for each body part.

"Did I do it right, Dinah?" Cecilia was heard whispering. After what seemed like hours of standing as still as a statue and without taking a single breath, Dinah pulled herself together enough to rush down the stairs, past Abby's limbs and the ceramic shrapnel that was once Jazz and bolt out the door.

For several weeks after, Dinah never said a word to anyone. Not her mother, not her teachers, and not Cecilia. She never visited that house again; she made it her mission to find every route in town that would keep her away from that place. At one point, she thought Cecilia could have been a new friend. But all memories Dinah had of the girl were now drowning in the shadow of the memory of that horrible day she had watched her former bullies be slaughtered before her eyes. The thought of seeing the mask Cecilia wore made Dinah want to puke out her insides and her skin became infected with goosebumps. She hoped if she ran far enough away, Cecilia would be nothing more than a ghost of the past, just as she had been before Dinah was thrown into that house.

But after those weeks passed, Dinah was woken up in the middle of the night when an ice-cold hand grabbed at her shoulder. When Dinah pulled herself up, she felt like her heart was stabbed with a dagger as she laid her eyes on Cecilia's masked face. Dinah scrambled back on all fours, slamming the back of her head against her headboard.

"Why don't you visit me anymore?" Cecilia asked, her voice pleading and fresh tears rolling out of her eye holes and down her face.

Dinah clutched at the edges of her blanket and tried to look away from Cecilia. "I'm sorry," Dinah whimpered, "but whenever I think of coming by, I just think of that day when you…" Dinah stopped as her throat was stuffed with sobs and tearful hiccups. Cecilia looked down at the floor and her shoulders slumped.

"Isn't that what you wanted?" Cecilia asked. "To have them suffer the consequences and for you to see for yourself?"

Dinah shook her head, feeling as small as an ant and like Cecilia was holding a magnifying glass over her. "I was mad. I didn't want them to die. It was horrible, sadistic!" Dinah wept, backing herself into the corner of her bed, stuck between the headboard and bedroom wall. She heard heavy puffs of breath from behind Cecilia's mask.

"How was I supposed to know?" Cecilia snapped. "I just wanted to help you. You're my friend and friends do anything for each other, right?"

Dinah froze, trapped between her room's walls and the girl who had killed three people before her. "Y-yeah. We're friends." Dinah's heart raced as she hoped Cecilia would fall for her lie. That the fib would spare her the same fate that had befallen her former oppressors.

Cecilia pondered for a bit before roughly grabbing Dinah's wrist. "There's only one way to be sure," the masked girl wept. "It's horrible being alone." Dinah looked down at her arm and saw it begin to turn milky white, glinting in the darkness. Dinah gasped as her arm became numb, her nerves froze, and she found herself unable to move her arm.

"I can't let myself be alone again," Cecilia whispered.

They said when people passed the old house on Edmond Road, they could see sat in front of one of the front windows, a China doll with dark hair and a toy camera sitting in her lap.

# Welcome To The Family

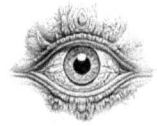

As she wrapped up her improvised fable, Marcy looked around anxiously, goosebumps sprouted from her skin and her mouth dry as sandpaper. Azura was the first to break the silence as she enthusiastically gave a round of applause.

"Great story, Marcy!" she cheered, getting out of her chair and scooping Marcy up into a hug. Others sitting at the table joined in the applause, some with more reluctant awkwardness than others.

Briar gave an impressed grin and tapped the rim of her goblet. "I didn't think of you as the storytelling type," she said. "At least, judging from your reaction when I told you about the family tradition."

Marcy shrugged. "Well, what can I say? You guys gave me a few good ideas. I thought I might as well throw my hat in."

Carmine raised an eyebrow. "Funny how these things work themselves out." He leaned forward and seemed to study Marcy's uneasy reaction. Marigold rolled her eyes and continued to finish her meal. Suddenly, a large crash thundered through the room and shook the contents of the table. The diners still in their seats gasped and frantically began to look around.

Azura let go and went to join her shocked father. "What was that?" Her concerns were one of many that joined the chorus of panic that rose in the dining room.

Finally, the old woman sprung from her seat. "Everyone, calm down!" she shouted, her voice like bark peeling off a tree. "Let's lock down the house until the police arrive."

The triplets threw their seats onto the ground, and each grabbed their knives with white knuckles. "We're on it!" Oriol exclaimed before leading his siblings out of the room in a furious charge. Others got out of their seats and spilled out through the various doorways connecting the room to the rest of the house. Marcy caught Laurel squeezing herself into a corner and pulling out a rhinestone-covered cellphone.

She could've stayed in the room and played innocent victim, but Marcy's stomach twisted into knots, imagining Aiden absconding with ill-gotten gains from her girlfriend's more than generous family.

"Wait, Marcy!" Azura's cries soon blended in with the others as Marcy peeled away like a drag racer. She shoved past other panicked reunion attendees and blasted past the cacophony of madness. Above the heads of Azura's rushing relatives, Marcy noticed a bookshelf swung open like a cupboard door, the books nearly tumbling out of their resting place. She stumbled away from the crowd and entered the shadowy passageway sandwiched between bookshelves.

Marcy's feet clacked against the crumbling concrete steps and a waft of frostbitten, musty air blindsided her nostrils. She brushed past swarms of spiderwebs and scattered corpses of beetles and spiders. Suddenly, her foot gave out from under her, and she tumbled through the cold, empty air. She crashed against the smooth, glassy ground. A loud ringing noise bounced around in her rattled skull and every joint in her body screamed in agony. Marcy let out a bestial cry as she forced herself up and continued stumbling forward.

"Marcy!" a familiar voice called from the shadows. Marcy flailed her arms around, trying to find purchase on a wall or anything else to help keep her failing balance. Out of the darkness, a young man with dark hair and a dishevelled jean jacket fumbled toward Marcy.

When he met Marcy's gaze, his eyes lit up and a relieved smile crossed his face. "Hey, sis. Nice of you to show up."

Marcy sighed with relief upon being reunited with her brother. However, her relief was replaced with panic when she saw what he held in his hand. "Aiden, the whole family's set up a patrol upstairs," she warned. "Go put that thing back before someone sees you!"

Aiden stared at his sister like she had suddenly grown a second head. "Are you kidding me?" he shouted. "We planned this whole thing out and dove into this nuthouse only for you to chicken out right when we got the golden goose?" He shoved past Marcy and wandered aimlessly around the room. "Now, where the hell are the stairs?"

Marcy followed closely behind, her heart beating so fast it nearly blocked out all sound. "Aiden, I'm telling you, we need to put that thing back and get you out of here."

Aiden scoffed, waving his ill-gotten treasure around in exasperation. "Oh, quit your whining already. I'm not ditching this operation just because you became a lovesick puppy."

A pale, decrepit hand pierced the veil of shadows and dug its nails into his shoulder. His eyes widened and Marcy felt the air press down on her and petrify her in place. The owner of the hand stepped forward. Azura's grandmother, who loomed over Aiden with a lecherous grin.

"Strange, I don't remember anyone inviting the likes of you." The old woman's sweet eyes darkened into a pair of almond-shaped shadows. Dark blue veins spread from the corners of her eyes to the rest of her newly pale face. Marcy whipped her head around, hoping she could find where the woman had entered from.

Instead of an exit, Marcy found herself surrounded by each of Azura's relatives as they breached the darkness and showed their misty black eyes. Each member of the family had a wolfish grin and their posture was like a pack of wolves ready to pounce on a helpless deer.

Standing at the head of the hoard was Inigo, who turned Marcy around and clamped her head, so she was forced to face Aiden and the old woman.

"I get being loyal to family, I really do," Inigo hissed, "but did you honestly think trying to steal from the Bender-Vee family was the best idea you could've come up with?"

Sweat poured down Aiden's face, and his chest heaved violently as the rest of his body began to shake.

The old woman caressed his shoulder and leaned down to whisper into his ear, "Poor, poor Aiden. If you had only done your homework, you would've realized one thing before deciding to invade our home…"

Aiden's hand rose up as if it were the limb of a puppet on a string. The treasure shone in the darkness, the golden hand like a will-o-the-wisp that lifted the shadows around the captive young man. Eight jewels, a rainbow of gemstones, sparkled on the ends of each of the hand's eight fingers. In the area between the knuckles and the wrist, an eye was shut closed, but Marcy could see the wrinkles in the eyelid begin to crease and smooth, as if in tune with someone's breathing. The grandmother's eyes darted to Marcy's gaze and her smile revealed rotting teeth with black stains covering the crowns.

"The Hand of Iris won't let itself be possessed by some common thief."

A short gasp left Marcy's lips as the hand's eye sprang open, revealing rotting yellow sclera, dark purple veins, and an iris of clouded green and red.

Cracks filled the room as the hand's fingers bent and curled against the palm. The wrist twisted itself, so Marcy saw the pink and orange lines of the palm pulsate like veins of magma on a volcano.

Aiden grew sickly pale. The film of sweat that stuck to his face made it look like he was a melting wax figure. Before he had a chance to scream, the hand yanked itself out of his grip and thrust itself through his stomach. Stifled whimpers crept out of Aiden's throat, his eyes like that of a child left alone in a shopping mall.

When the old woman let go of his shoulder, Aiden ripped open his jacket and rolled up his cerulean T-shirt. To both siblings' horror, a large lump began to worm its way up from Aiden's stomach to his chest. Aiden screamed as he tried to claw at his chest, a futile attempt to halt the lump's path. The lump turned away from his Adam's apple and began to burrow into the back of his neck. Aiden continued to scream furiously as he scratched at his throat until his fingernails were stained with blood and his neck was covered in a veil of crimson.

The young man collapsed onto his knees and banged his head against the floor. Marcy tried to run toward her brother, but she was held tightly by Inigo and could only struggle helplessly as her brother continued to smash his head.

The banging stopped when Aiden's back was thrown rearwards. His jaw was pried open as the hand rose out of his mouth. The meat connected to his jaws was ripped apart and his teeth shot out like popcorn kernels. The fingers clawed into his nose and the bags under his eyes before they found purchase inside his eyeballs, squishing them into thick mucus of red and yellow. The middle of Aiden's face was peeled apart and a cavern was caved into his head. The hand sunk back into the sinkhole of ichor before popping back out of Aiden's stomach with a bundle of flesh in its grip.

Bile burned the insides of Marcy's throat, and her legs shook with such a force that Inigo's grip was the only thing to keep her on her feet. Boiling tears gushed down her cheeks as the congregation of black-eyed creatures began to close in around her.

"No, please," she pleaded. "Please, don't kill me." A hand rose out of the crowd, stopping the pack's shamble toward Marcy. The rabble parted like the red sea, showing Azura with her hand raised and her eyes as umbral as the rest of her family's. She stepped forward and leaned down to meet her helpless girlfriend's line of sight.

"I mean, if you don't want to end up joining the others like your brother, you can always join the family," Azura suggested sweetly.

Marcy's breaths puffed out in hollow clouds and the beads of sweat became ice-cold droplets. "What do I have to do?"

Azura gave a casual shrug and stroked Marcy's chin with icy black nails. "Tell me another story."

# About The Author

R. Van Brabant was born in 1998 and grew up in Morinville, Alberta. Ever since elementary school, she was keen on writing, to the point where her teachers tried to hide the paper she used to write so many stories. Though she always kept finding more to use. She graduated from Vancouver Film School's game design program. Her younger self would have been shocked to find the first genre she wrote a book in was horror as she used to run out of the room whenever her father and sister would turn on the scary movies. Her debut novel *Rusalka* would be released on November 2022 and her first YA novel *The Meaning Of Mischief Night* was published in February 2024.

More information on R. Van Brabant's books can be found online at https://www.rvanbrabant.com/.

www.ingramcontent.com/pod-product-compliance
Lightning Source LLC
LaVergne TN
LVHW021700060526
838200LV00050B/2435